BLOOD
ANGEL

Also by Bernard Schaffer

An Unsettled Grave

The Thief of All Light

Superbia

Guns of Seneca 6

Grendel Unit

The Girl from Tenerife

Whitechapel: The Final Stand of Sherlock Holmes

BLOOD ANGEL

BERNARD SCHAFFER

KENSINGTON BOOKS

www.kensingtonbooks.com

KENSINGTON BOOKS are published by

Kensington Publishing Corp.
119 West 40th Street
New York, NY 10018

All Kensington titles, imprints, and distributed lines are available at special quantity discounts for bulk purchases for sales promotion, premiums, fund-raising, educational, or institutional use. Special book excerpts or customized printings can also be created to fit specific needs. For details, write or phone the office of the Kensington Special Sales Manager: Attn. Special Sales Department. Kensington Publishing Corp, 119 West 40th Street, New York, NY 10018. Phone: 1-800-221-2647.

Library of Congress Card Catalogue Number: 2019953571

Kensington and the K logo Reg. U.S. Pat. & TM Off.

ISBN-13: 978-1-4967-2762-6
ISBN-10: 1-4967-2762-2
First Kensington Hardcover Edition: June 2020

ISBN-13: 978-1-4967-2763-3 (ebook)
ISBN-10: 1-4967-2763-0 (ebook)

10 9 8 7 6 5 4 3 2 1

Printed in the United States of America

To Michaela Hamilton and Sharon Pelletier,
for everything.

I

NOTHING EVER ENDS AND NOTHING EVER GOES AWAY

1

I am The Master.

Tucker Pennington spoke these words aloud, wanting them to be true. He cradled the black book to his chest and lowered his head against its cover. "I am The Master," he whispered, and turned to the first page. He ran his hand delicately across the three invocations written there.

Blood of the virgin.

A visage perfected.

The purified flesh.

They were written in dark red streaks that stained the page. This ink had dried long ago and left red dust flakes scattered inside the book's seam. Tucker dragged his finger down the page until his skin was covered in red dust, then he stuck it in his mouth. He sucked his finger until his skin pickled. "Blood of the virgin," he said. He ran his finger down the page again and sucked it again. He mixed the dried flakes of blood inside his mouth with his spit and swallowed.

"A visage perfected." And it had been. By acid.

The purified flesh was all that remained.

Tucker looked through his car's windshield at the Hansen Town Square. Most of the shops were closed for the evening. The town square was a small patch of civilization in the midst of the vast woodlands and gravel roads that surrounded it. People came there to stroll the sidewalks lined with coffee shops and artisan boutiques and secondhand record stores.

He was parked along the side of the road on Main Street. He could smell the gasoline on his hands. He'd filled the largest gas can he could find at an Exxon ten miles away. It was sitting in a crate in the station wagon's trunk next to a fire extinguisher and a duffel bag filled with rope and duct tape.

At last, a girl appeared in the distance. Tanned and blond, in cutoff jeans shorts and a tank top. She was exactly what he'd been looking for. He watched her stand in front of the Walgreens, waiting for someone inside. She smoked a cigarette and flicked the ashes into the storm drain.

He put his car in drive and drove toward the Walgreens. She turned at the car's approach and he realized they knew one another. He'd gone to school with Brenda Drake since third grade. She'd been a scrawny, giggling thing in pigtails back then. He still remembered her crooked smile in their class photograph from that year. Now, she was glowing with life.

You'll glow brighter still, he thought. Much brighter.

Tucker parked along the curb next to her and got out. Brenda flicked her cigarette away and ran her fingers through her long hair and said, "Hey, Tucker."

He stepped up onto the sidewalk next to her. "What are you doing out and about?"

"Waiting for my mom," Brenda said. "She gives me so much shit for smoking."

"Do you have another one?" he asked.

"I didn't know you smoked."

"I just like fire."

Brenda laughed and said, "You're so weird." She opened her purse and dug inside, then held the bag at one end and tilted it downward. She shuffled through the makeup and tissues and hair bands piled inside.

Tucker reached back and opened his station wagon's passenger door. No one was watching from the Walgreens. No one was walking down the street. No one was driving past.

"Here you go," Brenda said. She pulled a crumpled cigarette out of the purse and held it out toward him.

Tucker snatched her by the head with both hands. He wrenched her sideways over his hip, sending her body windmilling into the air as he drove her headfirst into the cement. Tucker stood up to catch his breath and see if anyone was looking. Brenda's arms and legs convulsed on the sidewalk.

He scooped her up by the arms and dragged her toward the station wagon's open door. He shoved her through the open door and slammed it shut, then raced around the other side and jumped in.

A woman ran out of the Walgreens, screaming for him to stop. She ran toward the sidewalk, flapping her arms, screaming for help.

Tucker stomped on the gas pedal and sped away.

Brenda slumped against the car window, smearing the glass with lipstick and drool. White foam was spilling out of her mouth. He touched her bare arm and the side of her face as he drove. He eased her back in her seat. He stroked her hair to move it away from her face. Her skin was so pure, so perfect. But not purified. Not yet.

The interior of their county detective car was a mess because of the way Bill Waylon ate on nighttime surveillance details. Empty coffee cups and candy bar wrappers were scattered on the passenger side floor so that every time Jacob Rein moved his feet, he was stepping in trash. Waylon finished the last of his latest extralarge coffee and tossed the cup into the backseat. Drips of coffee clung to Waylon's patchy mustache and he mopped them gingerly with a napkin, like he was afraid the hot liquid might burn away the struggling hairs on his lip.

Waylon was ten years older than Rein. He'd been a detective with the Vieira County District Attorney's Office a few years before Rein hired on. Waylon had the misfortune, as he often said, of being the only person in the office who could tolerate Rein long enough to work with him. For a police officer, having a partner is like being in a marriage. When it's bad, it's bad all around and infects everything. When it's good, the world just goes easier.

But just like marriage, even the good ones, you still have to put up with the other person's shit.

"It's not this guy. He's too old," Waylon said.

They were parked deep in the woods on a hillside overlooking the dilapidated farmhouse that belonged to Walter Krissing. The Krissing family owned that farm for generations. It had once been the main source of corn for that entire region. Now it was nothing more than the broken-down old house and acres of brown, un-tended fields.

Rein raised his binoculars to check the house's windows. Each one was dark and hidden behind blinds.

"No way a guy that old can even get it up anymore," Waylon said.

"These aren't sex crimes, Bill," Rein said. He leaned forward to inspect the windows on the second floor. There was nothing. "Our suspect is a sadist. The pleasure he feels is from the grief he causes. Hearing his victims shriek is what gets him off. "

"Well, he's too weak, then. Whoever our doer is, he's gotta be strong enough to manhandle these kids. Think about it. Some of them are teenagers. Shit, my little one, Katie, threw a tantrum in the store the other day and it was all I could do to hold on to her when she started kicking, and she's only two. So first, this old man has to grab them, then he has to subdue them, then he's got to get them all the way back to his layer," Waylon said, ticking the points off with his fingers.

"Layer?"

"What villains have," Waylon said. "Then, he's got to get them inside and do what he does, even if they fight back. After all that, he's got to get rid of the bodies. You and I know how heavy dead bodies are better than most people. My back hurts all the time from the bodies I've had to drag all over the place. I'm telling you, it's not this guy. Krissing is too old for all that."

"What if he has help?" Rein asked.

"Two sickos working together?"

"Or he's using one of the children. A strong young male, specifically recruited and groomed for that exact purpose. It's probably not hard for him to find children willing to go with him back to his house."

"What kind of kid goes with some creepy old dude in this day and age?" Waylon said. "Kids learn about stranger danger on the first day of school now."

"Kids that want drugs," Rein said. "Or alcohol. Or money. Or maybe just food and shelter, if they're on the streets. Attention, if they come from screwed-up families. There are a million ways to exploit people in need, Bill. All it takes is insight and willpower to do it."

"There's some really sick shit going on inside that head of yours, isn't there?" Waylon said. "A child rapist and murderer using one of his victims to help him with the other victims? Come on, man. This isn't the movies. In real life, it's always something a lot simpler. It's always the uncle or the mom's boyfriend."

"Between 1970 and 1973, twenty-eight boys went missing in Houston," Rein said. "Dean Corll's family owned a candy factory in the area, and he was always handing out free goodies to the kids in the area. They called him the Candy Man." He lowered his binoculars, giving his eyes a rest. The entire house was dark below. The truck in the driveway hadn't moved all night. He checked the dial on the police radio in the center console, making sure it was on, but that it was low enough not to make too much noise.

"Corll had recruited two teenage helpers," Rein continued. "It was their job to lure their friends over to his house so he could rape, torture, and murder them."

"What pieces of shit. How'd they catch him?" Waylon asked.

"One of the accomplices shot him."

"Well, let's hope that happens here," Waylon said.

"I'd rather catch him before he hurts anyone else, instead," Rein said, raising the binoculars to check once more.

"You know what I meant. I gotta piss again," Waylon said. He grabbed the door handle and threw it open before Rein could stop him.

Light flooded the car interior and flared inside the binocular lenses. Rein clenched his eyes shut, blinded. "Bill!" he hissed, trying to keep his voice down.

Waylon left the door open as he hurried to the nearest tree and unzipped his pants. "Hang on," Waylon said.

"Shut the damn door," Rein whispered, rubbing his eyes until he could see again.

"Give me a damn second," Waylon said, bouncing up and down on his heels to shake off and then zippering himself back up. He raced back to the car and slid in. "Sorry about that. It's the coffee."

"When you open the door, the light comes on," Rein said. "When the light comes on, we stand out in the darkness, and the bad guy can see us. Do you understand that?"

"What do you want me to do, piss through the window?"

Rein reached behind the seat and picked up Waylon's discarded coffee cup, "Go in this next time."

Waylon scowled. "I can't piss in a coffee cup sitting down in the car. What if I spill it on myself?"

"It's better than lighting us up and letting everyone know where we are," Rein said.

Waylon looked at the cup, then down at the house below. "How do we know he's home anyway? It's dark as hell in there."

"You know, you're right," Rein said. "Maybe he's not home. Maybe he's out here in the woods somewhere looking for victims. Lucky for him there's two imbeciles sitting in a police car that he saw a mile away because one keeps opening his door!"

"God damn, I'm sorry. I have to piss again," Waylon said, pulling the door handle. "I broke the seal."

"If he kidnaps us, I hope he rapes you first," Rein said. "I really do."

"He probably likes skinny guys who read a lot," Waylon said over his shoulder.

"Not with that 1970's porno mustache you keep trying to grow," Rein said. "You're definitely his first choice."

"You making fun of the Burt Reynolds?" Waylon asked, getting back into the car and shutting the door.

"I thought it was the Tom Selleck," Rein said.

"I switched it back. Burt Reynolds is a classic. Just like me."

A high-pitched tone sounded on the police radio. The radio was turned down so low that both of them had to lean forward to hear it. Every cop in the world is trained to stop everything at the sound of that kind of tone. It's the kind that only sounds when a fellow police officer is in imminent danger, or something really fucked up is about is about to come out over the radio.

They waited. A second later the dispatcher reported, "Female abduction at Main Street and Grove Hollow Road, Hansen Township. All units in the area please respond."

Waylon slammed the car into reverse so hard that Rein had to brace himself against the dashboard.

"Careful on this turn, Bill," Rein said, seeing the steep embankment off the side of the road. "Slow down, shit!" he shouted as the car bounced so hard, he whacked his head on the roof. He yanked his seat belt across his chest, trying to click it as Waylon spun the wheel, sending gravel and dirt flying. "We're no good to anyone if you wreck before we get there," he said, seeing trees whipping past them in the headlights as Waylon jammed the gas pedal to the floor.

"How far?" Waylon shouted, spinning the wheel into the turn to keep the car righted as the road veered to one side.

"Make a right at the next—" Rein called out, slamming into the door handle. He grabbed the leather strap dangling from the ceiling and grabbed on to it with both hands.

"Caller reports her sixteen-year-old daughter was abducted by force," the dispatcher continued. "Suspect is a white male, light brown hair, driving a station wagon. Caller believes it's her daughter's classmate, name unknown, no direction of travel."

Rein raised the radio mic, trying to hold it steady enough to click the button. "County detectives in the area, we're en route," Rein called out. "Any weapons displayed?"

"Nothing at this time," the dispatcher said. "Hard to get any info out of the caller. All she's doing is screaming."

The radio came alive with chatter. Four other police departments were assigned to that radio zone, and each of them only had one cop working. They were all coming. The state police units covering the unincorporated areas outside of those jurisdictions were coming. Even other officers from different zones had switched over and they were coming too.

Waylon sent the car leaping out of the woods onto the main road. It landed so hard, the undercarriage sent sparks flying across the asphalt. Waylon gunned it, racing toward the distant streetlights, miles ahead.

Rein spun in his seat to look through the back window for any signs of activity inside the Krissing house. It was still dark. Rein sat back in his seat and said, "Slow down, Bill."

Bill had the wheel tight in both hands, perched forward in his seat like a diver at the starting block. The speedometer needle was bouncing over the 100-mph red line. "The road's empty!"

"You're racing to the place we know the bad guy isn't," Rein said. "Think about it. Getting us there won't find him."

A police car with blazing lights came ripping up the road behind them, driving so fast, they could see its lights blazing in their rearview mirror before they could hear the siren. It swerved around them, blowing past their car and leaving them rocking in its wake.

Rein watched it vanish ahead of them. "If I'd just committed a crime, I'd park in an alley and wait until all the cops had clustered together at the scene, then roll out nice and slow so I didn't attract any attention."

Waylon slowed down, running his hand through his damp hair. They crawled toward the scene, looking down every side street, searching for any parked station wagons. The traffic signals inside the borough had already been set to blinking yellow all around.

Waylon twisted and turned to check all of the mirrors in his car and look through all of the windows for signs of anything outside that moved.

A cluster of flashing blue and red lights formed several blocks ahead of them. All the cops were racing right to the scene, all of them eager to get the same information and see the same thing. They were pack animals, prone to run in groups, and never needed a better reason than that someone else in the pack was running so they ran too.

Rein picked up his binoculars and peered through the windshield. There were uniformed officers bunched around the distraught woman. They stood there looking at her. They were there because everyone else was, doing what everyone else was doing. A few of the ones toward the back were already smiling and cracking jokes to one another. They were only looking for an away game.

He put down the binoculars. "Just take us in."

They parked behind one of the marked units and draped their gold badges over their necks, letting them dangle where they could be seen. Everyone stopped talking when they saw county detectives walking toward them.

"I never knew county dicks worked past dark," someone called out.

Past the sea of pale blue uniform shirts, Rein saw the sobbing woman being comforted by a young Hansen Township police officer. He was trying to ask her for more information, but he was either too young or too new and doing a bad job of it.

"Who is in charge here? Is there anyone with rank?" Rein asked, and all of the cops there stared back at him silently. "Okay, then, here's the plan. Each of you is going to spread out from this location in a different direction. No lights, no sirens. Go slow and check for any parked vehicles matching the suspect description. If you see any cars on the back roads, stop and ID them and ask them if they saw anything suspicious."

No one moved.

"Hey!" Waylon barked. "Let's go! We've got a missing kid to find here! Time's wasting!"

The cops did what they were told, but took their time doing it. Rein watched them head toward their individual squad cars and drive off. Technically, county detectives didn't have authority over the cops in the local municipalities, but none of them wanted to be accused of not doing their part in a big investigation. There are men who want to be involved, and men who want to appear to be involved, and as Rein watched the group of cops drive off, he could not tell how many of either he had. "Think they'll all just drive back to their stations? It looked like it might be some of their bedtimes."

"As long as they look for a station wagon along the way, I can live with it," Waylon said.

The Hansen officer standing with the woman pulled his notepad and pen out of his pocket. "Ma'am, I need to get some details from you," he said.

She sank down onto the sidewalk and buried her face in her hands.

"Ma'am?" he said. He put his hand on her back. "Do you need an ambulance?"

"What's your name?" Rein called out.

"Dave Kenderdine," the officer said.

"Not you. Her. Ma'am!"

The woman's head snapped up. Her face was streaked with black tears. Ruined eyeliner streamed down her stricken face into her mouth.

"What's your name?"

She started to moan again.

Rein snatched her by the arms and shook her. "Answer me!"

"Hey!" Kenderdine said, trying to wedge himself between Rein and the woman. "I don't think this is—"

Waylon pulled the kid back. "Just hang on, son. It's all right."

"Look at me!" Rein said, pulling the woman close to his face. "Do you want your daughter back?"

"Yes!" she sputtered. "Why, God? Why did this happen?"

"Then stop acting like a child. We need to find her. What's your name?"

She swallowed and wiped her face. "Diane Drake."

Rein glanced up at Kenderdine, waiting for the information to be written down.

Once it was written down, Rein said, "What's your daughter's name?"

"Brenda."

"Same last name?"

The woman muttered it was. She pressed her hands over her face and began to scream. Rein yanked her hands away and snapped his fingers at her. "Look at me, I said. Tell me everything about her. Height, weight, hair, what she's wearing, everything. Spit it out, right now."

"She's sixteen. Oh God, oh my God! Blond hair. Five foot four. I think a hundred and ten pounds. She's in sh-sh-shorts." She moaned and clutched her face again. "I watched him take her and I couldn't do anything!"

Waylon leaned over Kenderdine's shoulder and held the notepad steady to read it. "Detective Waylon to all units," he said into his radio. When they responded, he walked off to read them the rest of the information.

"Tell me about the man," Rein said.

"He was young," she said, rocking violently back and forth. "Her age, I think. Taller. It looked like they knew each other."

"What makes you say that? Have you ever seen him before?"

"No. I was in the store," she said. "And I could see her talking to him. I could see him! They were standing in front of his car. Everything seemed fine. When I came walking out, I saw him dragging her into the car and driving off. What's he doing to my baby girl?"

Rein turned around, still kneeling and pointed at the street corner in front of the Walgreens. "Did it happen right there?" he asked.

When she nodded, Waylon said, "I'm on it." He headed off to check the surrounding buildings for any security cameras or ATM's that might be in the area.

"Tell me about him," Rein said, returning to the woman. "Taller than her, you said. Taller than me?"

"I don't know."

"Skinny, strong, fat? What was he wearing?"

"I-I'm not sure."

"Focus!"

"I don't know!" she screamed. "Stop asking me all these fucking questions and go look for her!"

"What about the car?" Rein said. "It was a station wagon?"

"Right," Diane said, wrapping her arms around herself. "It was white, with brown sides. It had those wood panels."

"All right," Rein said. "Did you see anything else? Did the man have anything in his hands?"

"Like what?" Diane asked.

"A weapon. A gun or a knife or anything?"

"No," Diane said, shaking her head violently. She clutched the sides of her face and moaned for them to go find her.

Rein put his hand on Kenderdine's shoulder. "Stay with her. If she remembers anything else, put it out over the air." He headed for the street corner in front of Walgreens, circling wide around it to take his time moving inward to make sure he didn't miss anything. There was nothing to miss. Garbage along the side of the road. A storm drain. An elevated sidewalk, with hedges running alongside it, and beyond that, the Walgreens.

The employees inside were pressed up against the side windows, trying to see what was happening. If any of them knew anything, they'd have come out already, he thought. Still, they needed to be asked. He'd have to get all the names of the people inside the store, including the customers, even if they said they hadn't seen anything. In this kind of case, a person doesn't always know what they know, not until it's all over. This was the kind of shit any uniformed officer could have done, but instead, their incompetence forced him to abandon his surveillance post to come handle it.

Anger rose within him. At the mother's ridiculous whimpering. At the cops' attitudes when he told them what to do. At Waylon for taking them away from such a perfect vantage point at Krissing's house and likely ruining it for future use. At himself for being out in the night, standing in front of the Hansen Walgreens wasting his time when he needed to be working his real case.

The sound of someone running up the street shouting his name made him turn.

"Rein!" Waylon cried, flapping his arms. "Come on! Let's go! Move!"

Rein started running with him, both of them racing across the street to get back to their car. "What is it?" Rein said, throwing his door open.

"They found the station wagon," Waylon said.

The radio crackled with an incoming transmission. "White station wagon . . . brown . . . side panels." He left the mic open as he exited the police car and ran toward the car. They could hear his keys jingling on his duty belt. Adrenaline had taken the man's voice and breath, until he could hardly draw in enough air to say, "It's clear. I don't see anyone."

Multiple units announced they were en route, a dozen officers coming from all directions. Waylon snatched the microphone and said, "Clear the air except for the car on scene. Stay with that vehicle until we get there."

"Don't touch anything," Rein reminded him.

Waylon put the microphone back to his mouth and added, "And don't touch anything!" He set it down and put both hands on the steering wheel, flooring the gas pedal until the engine whined. The lights of Hansen vanished behind woodland trees as the car skirted over loose gravel, fishtailing at each turn with Waylon gripping the wheel, turning into the skid each time, keeping them upright and going straight.

"You all right?" Waylon asked, spinning the wheel hand over hand.

"What do you mean?" Rein said.

"You went a little hard on that mom back there."

"She was in shock. She needed to be shocked out of it."

"Fair enough," Waylon said. "Just try and remember, she's a victim too. Her daughter just got snatched in front of her eyes."

"Are you questioning my methods, Bill?"

"No, come on."

"Good. Because you asked to work with me, remember? You asked for me, I didn't ask for you."

"Hey, calm down," Waylon said. "What the hell's gotten into you?"

Rein pounded the dashboard with his fist. "Patrol had this under control! There was no need for us to break position on our surveillance! You took off like a bat out of hell without even asking me."

"What in the fuck is your main malfunction, Rein? We just caught the biggest break of our lives with this case and you're acting like somebody pissed in your Cheerios! A surveillance detail? Are you high? We've got a description, a vehicle, and an active lead on the asshole we've been looking for!"

Rein took a deep breath and ran his hands through his hair before he answered. He didn't want to tell Bill Waylon what a goddamn moron he was, but it was hard to speak without clenching his teeth. "One, this victim is too old. Two, our suspect doesn't snatch women off the street, Bill," he grimaced. "He grooms them and lures them."

"You know what? You walk around like you're some high and mighty bullshit, but maybe this one time, just this one time, you're wrong."

"I'm not wrong."

"How can you be so sure!"

"Because we don't have any other fucking reports of abductions, Bill! Jesus, our kids are a lot younger and they just go missing. How in the hell can you be this dense?"

Waylon stomped on the brake, tires spitting gravel into the air. He jammed the car into park and leapt out, slamming the door shut before Rein could unbuckle his seat belt.

The station wagon was parked a hundred feet ahead of them, off the side of the road, hidden in the shadows. Five cop cars surrounded it, but mercifully, Rein saw none of them were using their flashlights. They hovered around the car, quiet, with one hand on their pistols. All around them, the woods were alive with bugs and frogs and things that crept through the brush close enough to smell them, then scurry away.

Rein pressed the back of his hand on the station wagon's hood, feeling it was still warm. It hadn't been there long. "You and you," he whispered, pointing at the two nearest officers, "stay with the car in case he comes back. Everyone else, split up in different directions. Let's find this girl."

"Look for tracks. Stop and listen. Use those hunting skills, boys," Waylon added. "Sneak up and get the drop on him if you can, then raise hell so the rest of us come running."

The group dissolved into the woods. They crouched low, rolling the soles of their boots over the soft earth instead of crashing through them.

"That's one good thing about working in an area filled with redneck cops," Waylon said, watching the men disappear. "They know the woods."

Rein eyed the path leading through the trees beyond the station wagon's passenger side door. "I'm going this way," Rein said, tilting his head.

"Sounds good. I'm coming with you."

"We'll cover more ground if you go a different way."

Waylon raised a handful of thorny branches out of the way so Rein could duck beneath them. "You don't leave your wingman," Waylon said. "Dumbass."

"Fine. Just don't complain about how I do it."

"Let me tell you something," Waylon said. "Being your partner sucks. Most guys come to work and complain to their partner about their relationship with their wives, but guess what? I go home to my wife and complain about my relationship with you. Think about that for a second."

"And yet here you are."

"Because I know if I can put up with your bullshit for long enough, we're probably going to catch the bad guy."

The darkness all around them took shape and form as their eyes adjusted, revealing the outlines of trees with thick foliage that shimmered in the moonlight. Waylon waved for Rein to follow him around a thicket of burrs and long, thin vines covered in vicious little thorns. Rein stopped and lowered to his haunches, sniffing the air. "What is that?" he whispered.

Waylon stopped and sniffed too. "Something dead nearby?"

"No," Rein said, inhaling deeply. "It's gas." He shot to his feet and spun around, searching for the right direction.

"Shit, I smell it too," Waylon said. He pointed east, farther into the woods, "This way, come on."

Brenda Drake came to and opened her eyes at the first splash of gasoline across her shirt. Tucker had not stripped her naked, like he'd first intended. He'd realized if he soaked her clothes, they would burn faster against her skin. He splashed gas on her across the face and hair and soaked her good from her shoes and socks all the way back up her bare legs to her short-shorts and wetted down her tank top until it was see-through. He sprayed until the can was empty, and set it on the ground next to the fire extinguisher.

She struggled against the duct tape binding her wrists to the branch over her head, kicking wildly, but it was useless. The tape covering her mouth muffled everything, but her eyes said enough. They were open so wide he could see white all around the bright blue disks there.

He wondered how long he could let her burn before he had to put her out. It was going to be tricky.

Tucker picked up a towel from his duffel bag and wiped his hands clean, then raised his Bible ceremoniously and opened it to the third and final section. "The purified flesh," he said, reading the words written there.

Brenda thrashed against the tree limb when she saw him raise the lighter in his hand. He flicked the button to ignite it. "I now burn away your impurities and consecrate you."

He bent down to light the trail of wet earth between them. Just as he was about to touch the flame to the gas, two men came crashing through the woods, running right at him.

Jacob Rein cut left, lowering his shoulder like a linebacker and launching into the air, square at Tucker's midsection to knock him to the ground.

Bill Waylon went for the girl. He grabbed her wrists, trying to wrench her free of the tape but couldn't, then ripped at the tape, trying to tear it away but couldn't, and finally just grabbed the entire branch and tried to snap it from the trunk, but all the goddamn thing would do was bend.

Behind him, Tucker and Rein were fighting. Tucker had wrapped both of his arms around the back of Rein's neck, squeezing as hard as he could. Rein was trying to punch his way free, driving his fists into Tucker's ribs, but clutched in such a way he couldn't get his arms back far enough to gain any momentum. To Waylon's horror, he saw the lighter was still in Tucker's hand, and he was trying to get it to light.

Gas saturated the ground all around them. Puddles of it lay at the girl's feet. It was smeared all over Waylon's hands and clothes now too. The fumes surrounding them all would ignite first, consuming them in a ball of fire that would send them running blindly into the darkness as they burned.

Flick. Tucker's thumb rotated the lighter's dial, *flick-flick-flick*, and Waylon gave up trying to free the girl, ignoring her muffled screams to come back. He raced for the first thing he could find, a red fire extinguisher just a few feet from where Tucker and Rein lay flailing.

Flick. A spark.

Waylon yanked the extinguisher's pin free and drove the nozzle between Rein's and Tucker's faces and pulled the trigger.

The chemical foam blasted Rein in the eyes and filled his mouth and nostrils. He retched and reeled back, straining to breathe over the powdery chemical cloud that seized his lungs. His eyes burned as he swiped the foam away with his shirt. Hot, stinging tears spilled out of his eyes as he bent forward and coughed, trying to bring up the foam from inside his chest.

The woods all around were alive with the sound of crashing. Cops ran toward them, shouting, "Over here!"

Rein saw that Waylon had Tucker Pennington pinned to the ground, one knee in the side of the young man's neck, and one in the small of his back, using the leverage to crank Tucker's arm.

Tucker's face was covered in foam, and he'd vomited across his chest, screaming he was blind.

Thick branches all around them shook and cracked as the rest of the uniformed officers rushed in. They shoved Waylon out of the way to get to Tucker. The away game had begun. They piled on top of him and beat him until the woods were filled with his pleas for them to stop.

2

*T*ucker Pennington stared at Bill Waylon through the darkened glass of the window and didn't blink once. Waylon was standing in the hallway outside of the interview room and Tucker could see him clear as day. Real police departments have two-way mirrors, where suspects can do nothing but stare at themselves. Where they had no idea who was watching on the opposite side of the glass. In all the local stations in their county, it was rarely anything more than a cheap tinted sticker slapped on by the local public works department.

For years, non-verbal communication courses had taught criminal investigators all around the world that a suspect was guilty by the way they folded their arms or what direction they looked in when they had to answer a question. It was all snake oil.

Some cops graduated from those courses and tried to testify in court that even though the bad guy never confessed, and even though they had nothing but circumstantial evidence, the suspect looked right when he should have looked left, or yawned before giving an untrue answer, or some other bullshit. This kid Tucker had creepy, dead eyes.

None of those bio-linguistic quacks ever said anything about a dead-eyed kid just staring right the fuck at you, Waylon thought. He didn't think Tucker blinked even once and watched him, waiting to see if it was true.

Tucker's parents sat on either side of him. They'd arrived in a pristine Mercedes S-Class and parked it in the handicapped spot next to the Hansen police station's front door. Thad Pennington sat with both his hands on the interview table, resting his heavy gold watch on the same surface Waylon had seen countless rapists and drug addicts sneeze and bleed on. Grace Pennington was a sniveling wreck. She rubbed her little boy's back incessantly and dabbed at the cuts and bruises on Tucker's face with a balled-up handkerchief. She had a tiny nose that curled upward at the tip, like a ski slope. Through it all, Tucker just stared.

"This kid doesn't blink," Waylon said. "I've been watching him this whole time, and I'm serious. Not once. It's freaking me out."

"He's doing it. You just can't see it." Rein pulled pages out of various police reports and reassembled them. He examined them, then rearranged them again into a new order and examined them again.

"He's trying to Anthony Hopkins us."

"What?"

" *Silence of the Lambs?*"

"Ah, another illuminating reference from the mind of Bill Waylon. I didn't see it."

"Are you kidding me? Anthony Hopkins played Hannibal Lecter in *Silence of the Lambs*. He never blinked once on camera. It's just one of those subtle things you don't notice at first, but just shows how terrifying Lecter really is. The guy's a supergenius, right? He knows everything about wine and foreign languages and opera. He's like James Bond, except he's also a cannibal."

Rein tapped the bottom of the papers against the desk. "That's ridiculous."

"No, man. It's great. And by the way, I've been watching this whole time, and this kid still hasn't blinked, not once. He's definitely trying to Anthony Hopkins us. We'll have to ask him if he listens to opera when he eats people."

"Have you ever met a cannibal, Bill?"

"No, of course not."

Rein closed the case file and slid it into a brown shopping bag from the local supermarket that had been donated when the local police departments couldn't afford actual evidence bags. "They aren't into the opera."

"Oh, bullshit," Waylon said, rolling his eyes. "You never met no cannibal. Wait, did you?"

"Sometime when you're tired of sleeping at night, I'll tell you about The Blue Worm."

"Whatever. You know, I'm surprised these assholes haven't lawyered up yet," Waylon said. "Most rich folks start screaming for one right away."

Rein peered through the window to study Tucker and his parents. "What makes you say they're rich?"

"The dad is Thad Pennington," Waylon said. "As in Pennington Real Estate. Signs all over the place with his face on them. Jesus, you really aren't from around here, are you?" Waylon glanced at his watch. "It's been half an hour. I say we give it another twenty minutes. He can't sit there being a non-blinking hard-ass too much longer, not with Mom falling apart. A few more minutes of basting in there and he'll be ready to talk."

"Disagreed," Rein said, moving past him toward the door.

"Hey, wait a second, partner," Waylon said. "This kid's not ready to talk yet."

"He'll talk to me," Rein said.

Waylon stopped him from opening the door. "Don't you want to game plan this a little first before we rush in there?"

"Why is this one any different? You take notes and I do the talking."

"Hey, I'm serious," Waylon said. "What's the rush?"

"We have to get back to Krissing. I'm not waiting on this little fool any longer than we need to."

Waylon made excuses for his partner in his mind, telling himself the man was one of those people who was so talented that it made him an asshole. One of those artistic, genius pain-in-the-ass types who people had to put up with between masterpieces.

Jacob Rein's police work, Waylon liked to think, was akin to abstract art. The kind critics and college professors creamed their khakis over, but no one else understood. The kind of work important people celebrated, but that normal people had absolutely no clue what to make of. To folks like Waylon, it was all just a bunch of colors splashed around, without form or pattern, too bright and confusing to be assimilated into anything resembling, well, anything. Or everything. He didn't fucking know.

Bill Waylon's police work was more like paint by number. He was aware of it and wasn't ashamed of it either, because after years in law enforcement, he realized almost everybody else in the field was still doing preschool-level finger painting. Hell, that was being generous. Half those idiots were probably eating the goddamn paint.

"It's about time, Officers," Thad Pennington said as Rein opened the door.

Grace Pennington pounded the table with her fist. "I want the names and badge numbers of every single officer who contributed to injuring my son. I also want to know how we go about pressing charges against that Brenda Drake slut for setting my son up! He told us what happened, Detective. It was some kind of sex game. Her idea, by the way, and when the police showed up, she lied. I want to press charges, and I want to press them this instant!"

Rein set the paper evidence bag on the floor and sat down across from Tucker at the table. He stared back at Tucker, both of their eyes locked.

Great, Waylon thought. Now neither one of them is blinking. Hard to tell which of them is crazier.

Waylon cleared his throat and pulled a yellow rights card from his shirt pocket. He laid it flat on the table in front of Rein to read aloud. Rein didn't move. He stayed locked on Tucker and Tucker stayed locked on him.

"Just have to do this little piece of business first," Waylon said. He slid the card back toward himself. Walking the family through the Miranda and Juvenile Rights process was tricky, but integral. You had to inform them several times that they had the right to speak to an attorney, and that they could stop the questioning and confer privately anytime they wanted to.

Saying it all without being cut off was one thing, but the real magic was in getting them to sign it.

Anything you say can and will be used against you. But it's in your best interest to talk to me anyway. Sign here please.

Not an easy sell, Waylon thought. And he wasn't nearly as good at selling it as Jacob was.

Having two excitable, entitled, pissed-off parents in the room didn't help matters at all.

Waylon cleared his throat. "Listen, I realize you have a lot of questions for us, and we have questions for you. But before we can talk to you, I need to read you this."

"Is my son under arrest?" Thad Pennington asked.

"Let me just read this off first," Waylon said.

"Do we need to hire an attorney for him?" Grace asked.

"Now, hang on a second," Waylon said. "We're getting ahead of ourselves here."

"I know a little something about the law, Detectives," Thad said. "You're only required to read someone their rights if they're in custody and being asked guilt-seeking questions, isn't that right?"

Waylon glanced at Rein, waiting for him to jump in. Any day now, you pain in the ass. "Yes, that's correct," Waylon said. "For juveniles there's some extra information as well."

"So if you're reading my son his rights, that means he's under arrest, and that also means you're about to ask him questions to prove he's guilty. Therefore, we should probably get him an attorney," Thad said.

"Well, now, see," Waylon said. This was a tricky part too. As long as they didn't specifically ask for one, it was not a technical invocation of the right to an attorney. The fish was on the line and it was dancing, jerking, but it was still on the line. Waylon knew he had to reel them in slow. "How about you just let me read this. I'll explain what we're doing here, and then we'll make that decision."

Waylon reached to pick up the card and slide it back in his pocket, but instead Rein grabbed it and crumpled it into a ball. His eyes never left Tucker's as he cocked back his hand and pitched the wadded-up paper card across the room.

"We don't need this because I didn't come in here to ask you anything," Rein said. "I came to tell."

Rein lifted Tucker's black Bible out of the evidence bag and laid it on the table between them. Both Thad's and Grace's eyes widened in surprise. It was clear they'd seen it before, most likely being carried around like a precious thing by their son, but had never bothered to look inside of it. Rein patted the book with both hands. "I only had a few moments to look through this, but that's all it took. The Master. Is that you?"

Tucker didn't speak, but his eye and lower jaw twitched each time Rein touched the book.

Rein coughed into his hand and wiped it on the book's cover. Tucker's hands tightened into fists.

"Last year, someone stole a bottle of concentrated sulfuric acid from the science lab at your high school," Rein said. "Six months later, that same acid was thrown into the crowd at the Winter Ball bonfire. Most of it hit a sophomore named Alexis Dole in the face, leaving her disfigured for life." Rein opened the book and read a line from the first page. "'A visage perfected.'"

He looked down at the next entry. "'Blood of a virgin,'" Rein said, taking a minute to examine the red ink used to inscribe the words there. "I don't need to get this page tested to know it's written in blood. Is it yours, I wonder? You look like a virgin to me."

"This is ridiculous, Detective!" Grace Pennington cried out. "That is nothing more than red pen. A child's prank, nothing more. Thad, stop this nonsense immediately."

"If I had to guess, the blood belongs to one of your relatives,"

Rein continued. "Probably younger than you, someone you've been assaulting for a long time."

"That is enough!" Thad Pennington said, slamming his hand down on the table. "You will not sit there and accuse my son of such disgusting things."

"Don't play foolish with me, Thad. You already know who I'm talking about," Rein said. "Who is it? What little girl used to come around all the time, but now refuses to come to the house anymore? Who refuses to be with him? A family member? A neighbor?"

Neither of the parents spoke, unable to do anything but blink stupidly, trying to process what he was saying.

"That's right," Rein said. "You're thinking about who she is right now. Don't bother. I'll find her soon enough."

Rein looked down at the book again. "'The purified flesh.' Obviously, that brings us to Brenda Drake. Poor, poor, Brenda. I won't even need her to testify, Tucker. I saw it all for myself. I was impressed you brought the fire extinguisher along to make sure she survived. The court might see that as an act of mercy, but you and I know different. You were trying to imprison her in a body of melted flesh for the rest of her life. Now, I'm a bit of an expert on sadism lately and I must say, for such a pathetic little shit like you, that's really swinging for the fences."

Grace Pennington gasped, and her husband reached into his pocket, digging for his cell phone. "That's enough, Detective. I'm calling my attorney."

"Call him," Rein said. He closed the book. "Precious little Tuck here is never going to see the light of day outside of custody again anyway."

"Listen," Waylon interrupted, trying to regain control of the situation. "Before you call your attorney and we keep going back and forth like this, we really just want to help your son. Tucker, we want to ask you what happened tonight, because there's two sides to every story."

Waylon got up to walk around the table and pick up the crumpled rights card but was stopped by Tucker Pennington speaking for the first time. "Apostate," he said. It was nothing more than a whisper of the word, directed at Rein.

"What was that?" Rein said, cupping his hand to his ear. "I'm an apostate? With pride, Tuck. With pride."

"My son is still a juvenile," Thad said, holding the phone to his ear as he waited for someone on the other end to pick up. "You cannot intimidate or fool us, Detective. Even if he's arrested, it all goes away when he's eighteen."

"See, that's where you're wrong, Thad," Rein said. "After he turns eighteen, the Commonwealth can enforce what's called a civil commitment. You know what that is, Tuck? Oh, you don't? It's for people deemed to be psychotically dangerous violent predators. We don't need a conviction. We don't need a judge or a jury. We just need a doctor. One doctor says you're too deranged to go free, and we can keep you for the rest of your life in a hospital. Let me tell you what kind of people you'll be with in there, friend. People who make you look like Disney animation. People who make all the sick little things you dream about doing look like Sunday afternoon at the park. I'll visit you there in twenty years, if there's anything left of you after all the shock treatments and lobotomies. Just try not to drool on me."

Grace Pennington cried out at Rein's words like he'd physically struck her with them.

"Hello?" Thad said into his phone. "I'm at the police station with my son. He's been arrested. They're threatening him and terrifying my wife."

Rein dropped the black book into the evidence bag and stood up.

Thad covered the phone's mouthpiece and said, "My attorney says this interview is over and you are not to ask us any further questions until he gets here."

"Tell him to take his time," Rein said and turned for the door. "I never needed to ask him anything anyway."

Waylon made sure one of the uniformed officers was standing by the interview room who could keep an eye on the family. He ran his fingers through his damp hair and took a deep breath, trying to collect himself. His face was so red with anger, it felt hot.

Rein was in the back office, typing. His fingers flew across his computer keyboard's keys, hammering the details down of the juvenile petition that would get Tucker placed in the detention center that night. The paperwork for a juvenile arrest was minimal and the rest could all be filled out in the following days. Rein hurried through the last of it and pressed PRINT.

Rein hovered by the printer, impatient for the pages to emerge. He saw the look on Waylon's face as he came into the room and said, "Before you say anything, I was just offering a cold dose of reality to people who have never had any. That's all."

Waylon's teeth clenched. "You didn't even ask him any questions."

"I didn't need to. We've got charges on him for the Brenda Drake job, even if he doesn't testify." He tapped the printer, waiting for the last page to come out.

"How many times have you told me we need to talk to these people and see what else they give us? There could be other victims. There could be stuff at his house we need to get a search warrant for. You didn't even bother trying to lock him in on the acid case!"

Rein yanked the last page free and carried it over to the desk to sign. "Right now there isn't time for that. We have a larger case to deal with and something a lot worse than that little pissant is out there." He grabbed a pen off his desk and scribbled his name on the line marked AFFIANT. "I need you to call juvenile probation and make sure Tucker is placed tonight. Fax them this and give me a call after you take him to the detention center." Rein slapped the petition into Waylon's hand as he walked past him, heading toward the door.

"Where the hell do you think you're going?" Waylon called out.

"Back to get eyes on Old Man Krissing, which is what we should have been doing this entire time, instead of playing games with

Anton LaVey Junior in there. You stay here and handle the light work while I stay focused on the big cases."

"Who?" Waylon said. He looked down at the juvenile petition paperwork and started to sort it. "At least people understand my cultural references, asshole."

3

*T*he security risk section of the Vieira County Juvenile Detention Center was filled with screams and high-pitched laughter that sounded like the insides of someone's soul being scraped raw.

"This way, Pennington."

The guard was a tall man with mahogany skin that rippled with thick veins and muscle. His arms looked ready to burst the seams of his polo shirt if he bent them.

Tucker Pennington followed him down the hallway, past a series of locked rooms. Each door had a window made of reinforced glass. Groups of children were gathered inside the rooms, but Tucker was led past them too fast to see much. They passed a large gymnasium with children younger than him playing basketball. Another room had a gang of girls cornering another girl, about to fight.

Everyone was dressed in dark maroon, short-sleeve jumpsuits and white slip-on shoes, just like the ones he'd been issued upstairs.

"Here you go," the guard said as they reached the last door on the right-hand side. He grabbed the keycard dangling from his neck and bent forward to hold it up to the door's sensor.

Tucker stuck his head in and peered from the doorway. The walls were lined with shelves holding books that were obviously donated to the detention center and never read.

The only furniture in the room were couches and worn-out

easy chairs with ripped sides and stuffing that showed through the cushions. One corner was filled with bright orange bean bags made of vinyl, in case no one could find a seat. That wasn't going to be a problem, Tucker thought. He saw only one other inmate in the room and a middle-aged, bored-looking monitor sitting in the corner, reading a newspaper.

"Go on in there," the guard said. "Mind yourself and don't cause any problems, and you'll be all right. Don't be nervous."

The door closed behind Tucker and he could hear the lock activate, shutting him in. The monitor was a middle-aged man with long, floppy hair that had turned silver on the sides. It was tucked behind his ears and fanned outward, like duck wings. He licked his thumb and flipped a page on his newspaper, snapping it as he raised the page to read the headlines printed there. His wet thumb was black with ink and smeared the newsprint on the pages he held.

The monitor folded the newspaper forward to look at him and Tucker turned away. He went to the bookshelves and ran his finger across the spines of the books lined up there. The only one he recognized was the Bible.

Tucker was about to pull it out when he jerked at the feeling of someone's hot breath in his ear. It was the other boy. He was tall and lanky and he said, "Are you into Jesus?"

"Mr. Moon," the monitor called out from behind his newspaper. "Calm yourself, please."

Gregory Moon hiked up his elbows and knees like a cartoonish minstrel, dancing when he said, "Nice and quiet, now. Keep it down. Don't disturb the loonies. They get agitated and start squawking and next thing you know they're smearing themselves with their own shit so when the guards come in to grab them, that's what they grab. What's your name?"

"Leave me alone," Tucker said. He sat on one of the bean bags and opened the Bible to read it.

"That's good you're reading that," Moon said, sitting down beside him, pointing at the page. "It's good for your brain. Lots of ideas in there. You ever read it before?"

"Many times," Tucker said.

"My mother always wanted me to love Jesus. Hey. What did you do to get in here?"

"Nothing," Tucker said, turning the other way.

"If you did nothing, you wouldn't be in this room," Moon said. "Maybe another one, but not this room. This is the last room before they put you in with the loonies. So who was it? Your mother? Your sister? It was your mother, wasn't it?"

Tucker tried to get away but Moon followed close behind him. "Just tell me who it was. Give me a few details. That won't hurt. Come on. I'm tired of what I did and I need something new. What did you do? Did you ever have a nurse? My last one was a nurse. Tell me what you did and I'll tell you all about what I did to her. Come on. Tell me."

"Mr. Moon," the monitor called out. "That's enough. Go sit down and leave him alone."

Moon held out his hands in disbelief. "Look, I just want to know if he fucked her before he killed her or after! Is that so much to ask?"

"That is enough!" the monitor shouted, tossing the paper aside. "One more remark like that and you're going into solitary. Do you understand?"

Moon drew a line across his mouth, zippering it shut. He slinked back to the other side of the room, all knees and elbows once more. He pressed the back of his hand to his mouth, muttering against it, like the words would leap out of him at any moment if he did not keep them physically restrained. He watched Tucker the whole time.

Tucker turned one of the beanbag chairs around so he did not have to look at Moon and collapsed down inside it. He was lost in despair and could feel it welling in his chest. He was going to cry. Everything had gone so impossibly wrong after everything was going so impossibly good. He had failed and he had lost everything in the process. He thought that he would most likely kill himself when he realized a woman was sitting in a chair directly across from him.

She had long black hair and bright green eyes that peered at him from behind a pair of cat-eyed glasses. Her lips were bright red and full, and she smiled at him. Hello, Tucker, she said.

She crossed her long, bare legs, visible from the upper reaches of her thigh down to the curve of her foot where she let her high-heeled shoe dangle from her toes. She wore a gleaming white lab coat and a blouse, left open to reveal the clasp of her bra. A long silver stethoscope dangled between her breasts, and she toyed with it with the tips of her carefully painted fingernails. I see you've made a new friend, she said.

"He's not my friend," Tucker said, turning around to see if Moon was still staring at him. The maniac's eyes lit up when he saw Tucker looking, but Tucker spun back around, getting out of view. "He's crazy."

Crazy people can be useful. You should try to get along with him, she said.

Someone screamed from across the hall, a blood-curdling howl from deep within the caverns of the solitary confinement cells. It set off the rest of loonies, making them pound the doors and shriek. It went on and on until he let go of the Bible and put his hands over his ears, pressing them tight. "I hate this place," he whimpered.

The woman leaned forward so no one else could hear her. If you show them that you are afraid, they will use it against you, Tucker.

"Who are you?" He pointed at her stethoscope. "Are you my doctor?"

One of them. The most important one. I'm the one you're going to talk to about all of the things you don't tell anyone else. And I'm going to help you.

"Will you help me get out of this place?" he asked. Hot tears were forming in his eyes and making them sting. "I don't want to be around these people. I want to go home. I really just want to be home, okay?"

If you do everything I tell you, the way I tell you to do it, then you will be. Will you listen to me?

"I'll try," he said. He glanced at the corner of the room where the monitor was sitting. The man's face was still hidden behind the newspaper.

Good, she said. Let's start at the beginning, shall we?

"The beginning of what?"

The beginning of you, of course. When you first realized your true destiny. Tell me about The Master.

"I've lost him," Tucker groaned. The tears were blinding him, making everything swirl and blur, except the woman. "I've lost him and I'll never find him now."

Don't cry, Tucker. You must be strong in this place.

"All right," he said. He wiped his nose on his sleeve and took a deep breath to settle himself down.

There you are. Now start at the beginning, and we can find him together.

"You don't think he's gone?" Tucker asked.

My dear, sweet Tucker. You can never lose what you are.

FIFTEEN YEARS LATER

4

"Do you remember the man who saved us, Nubs?"

The little girl looked down at the menu on the table, avoiding the question, as she always did whenever Carrie Santero brought up that night. Almost two years had passed since they'd stood together in the locked room, Carrie holding the shivering child, ready to sacrifice her own life if it meant Nubs would escape. Two years since Jacob Rein had appeared in the doorway standing over the monster's body, clutching the bloody stump of his right wrist. All he'd wanted to do was see the little girl, to get one good look at her alive and breathing. Carrie remembered the way Jacob smiled then. How his eyes fluttered shut and he fell.

A third menu was laying on the table in front of an empty seat, beside an unused place setting. The waitress appeared. "Will your guest be joining you soon, or would you like to order now?"

"Just give us a few more minutes," Carrie said.

Nubs pushed her menu away. "You already know what I want."

"Chicken and fries." Carrie sighed. "Are you sure you don't want to try anything else? There's an entire menu of other stuff. How about a burger?"

"Nope."

"If I get something you've never had before, will you at least try some of mine?"

"Nope. Just chicken and fries."

"Oh," Carrie said. She turned the menu over to look at the

drink section. "I guess we don't need to get any of these fancy milkshakes, if that's all you want. Just plain water to drink, then?"

"Hold it!" Nubs said. She yanked the menu back and flipped it over, smiling as she scanned the selection of milkshakes.

Carrie draped her arm across the little girl's back and stroked her hair as she read. It was a luxury just to feel Nubs breathe. To sit with her at a restaurant and do normal things and have a normal life. She'd never lost sight of that in the two years since that awful night.

Carrie looked at the restaurant's front door as a couple entered. The man held the door for his wife. They held hands quietly as they waited for the hostess to greet them.

Jacob Rein wasn't coming, Carrie thought. Why was she surprised?

"Aunt Carrie," Nubs said. "I have something to tell you."

"What is it, sweetie?"

"I don't want to be called Nubs anymore."

"You don't?" Carrie asked. "Why not? Is somebody teasing you because of your name?" Carrie felt her face get hot. Did she need to go to the school and have a chat with the principal? Did she maybe need to wait in the parking lot for the fat cow of a mother who raised a fat cow of a child that was picking on Nubs because of her name? If somebody's ass had to get kicked, that was no problem, Carrie thought. Bring it on.

"I just don't like it anymore," Nubs said. "It doesn't sound like a real name. You have a real name. Grannie has a real name. I just don't want to be called Nubs anymore, that's all."

"Honey. Nubs is what your mommy always called you."

"I know. But she's not here," Nubs said with a light shrug.

The waitress reappeared at the table, flashing a wide smile. "Okay, are we ready to order some delicious food? I thought I heard somebody say something about milkshakes!"

Carrie felt tears in her eyes and wiped them away as fast as she could. Nubs said, "I'm getting chicken and fries, and a chocolate milkshake with whipped cream and sprinkles."

"That sounds wonderful! And how about you, Mom?" the waitress asked.

Carrie took a sip of water and cleared her throat. "Just Aunt. Not Mom," she managed to say. She pointed at a salad on the menu, letting the waitress know what to bring.

When they were alone, Nubs leaned against her. "Are you upset with me?"

"No, baby. You're just growing up, that's all." Carrie wiped her cheeks with a napkin. "So what do you want to be called?"

"Natalie. That's my name, right? I figure Mommy wouldn't mind, since that's what she named me."

"Okay," Carrie whispered. She leaned down and kissed the top of her head. "Natalie it is, from now on."

Carrie lifted the little girl out of the backseat and raised her up against her chest, getting Natalie's head nestled against her neck. She kicked the car door shut and hurried up the sidewalk. Penny was already standing on the porch with her hands on her hips, looking down at them. "It's a little late. She has school tomorrow."

"I know, I know," Carrie said, climbing up the steps. "We were having too much fun to come home."

Penny grabbed the door and pulled it open for her. "She tell you it's Natalie now?"

"She certainly did." Carrie stopped inside the entrance and sniffed the air inside the living room. "What's that?"

"What's what?" Penny asked sheepishly.

"That! The cigarette smoke I smell." She glared at Penny, "Tell me you didn't."

"I had one!" Penny said. "First in six months. What's the big deal? I took two drags and threw it out. I realized I don't even like them anymore. There. Now I can be done forever."

"I found Grannie smoking two days ago," Natalie said, eyes still closed. "She's been doing it in the basement since."

"Aha!" Carrie said. "Caught red-handed!"

"Oh no," Penny said, waving her hands in the air as she retreated into the kitchen. "No way. I had to put up with you and Molly gang-ing up on me all those years, I am not going to put up with it from you and the kid now! Forget it!"

Natalie giggled against Carrie's chest and said, "We're gonna team up all the time, right?"

"You bet your butt we are." Carrie held up her hand. "High five, partner?"

Natalie slapped her hand. "High five."

Carrie felt her pocket vibrate and let Natalie down. She saw the words *County Dispatch* on the screen and held it to her ear. "De-tective Santero, can I help you?"

"This is nine-one-one, Operator four-fifteen. Are you available to assist Terrell Township with an investigation?"

"Did you already try the on-call detective? Tonight's not my night," Carrie said.

"We've been trying for a little while, but no one's picking up," the dispatcher said. "I saw your name coming up most often on the computer so I figured you're the one who always answers your phone."

"That will teach me," Carrie said. "What do they have?"

"D.O.A., adult female. Came in as a suicide."

Carrie looked at the time. Natalie was going to bed soon any-way. It wouldn't hurt to pick up a little overtime, she thought. "Sure, I'll respond. Text me the details."

She bent down to give Natalie a hug. "Aunt Carrie's gotta go to work, baby. You get some sleep, okay?"

Natalie said she would. Carrie kissed her and they wrapped their arms around one another again. "Love you so much."

"Love you too," Natalie said.

Penny emerged from the kitchen, holding a full coffee mug in one hand and a to-go cup in the other. "I heard," Penny said.

Carrie took the to-go cup and sniffed it. "There's no liquor in this, right?"

"Not enough for anyone to notice." Penny leaned in and kissed Carrie on the cheek. "You be careful out there, you hear me?"

"I will," Carrie said. "Stop smoking."

"I already did."

"Don't lie to me. I'm the police."

"And I'm practically your mother."

"Good point," Carrie said. "I'll call you in the morning. Good night."

Penny held the screen door open on the porch and called out, "Hey, I mean it. Be careful."

"I'm always careful," Carrie said, tapping the right side of her hip where she kept her gun.

The GPS guided her through the unmarked roads that wound through the dark woods leading toward Terrell Township. Terrell was a small town, even by Vieira County's standards. People who lived in small towns, out in the deep woods, were there for a reason. Usually, not good ones.

The night air was humid and dense. It was mid-October and she was still using her air conditioner. Her windshield fogged and she flicked on her wipers, leaving a wet smear across its glass surface.

Carrie saw a wooden sign for CHUVALO TRAILER PARK—SLABS AVAILABLE ahead and turned at the entrance. At ten o'clock at night, the park was still alive with activity. People sat on folding chairs in front of their trailers drinking beer and tossing the empty cans into trash bags hung from their mailboxes. Some had firepits dug in the ground, surrounded by ornate stone arrangements. Some just had rusted-out metal barrels where the flames licked through the openings along the sides of the barrel like winding fiery tongues.

There were flags strung from the trailers like medieval banners. American flags, Confederate flags, NASCAR flags, Steelers flags, and dozens for Budweiser. One of the trailers had a sign in the front window that read FUCK WITH ME AND YOU FUCK WITH THE WHOLE TRAILER PARK.

Carrie saw two police cars parked at the far end of the lot. They were facing the last trailer in the lot, wedged against the wooden fence surrounding the property.

The trailer's door was open, and Carrie could see one officer standing in front of it, guarding it to keep anyone from going inside. The second officer leaned over the open door of his police car. He was tall and skinny, with a long neck and an Adam's apple that looked like he'd swallowed a cue ball. He reminded Carrie of Ichabod Crane, from the old cartoon.

A crowd of people roamed the street nearby, wanting to see what was going on but not wanting to get too close. They clustered together and gossiped and pointed but none of them said anything directly to the cops.

Carrie parked behind the police cars and radioed the dispatcher that she was on-scene. As she went to get out of her car, Ichabod Crane came around the side and rapped his fingers on her window. "You the detective?"

"That's right," Carrie said. "You called?"

"Great. I need you to back your car up so I can get out of here."

"How about you give me a second to take a look at what we have first?"

"No can do," he said. "I have to get going."

Carrie turned and looked at the people skulking in the shadows. There were a lot more of them than she thought. She pointed past Ichabod at the officer standing at the trailer and said, "Is he staying? I could use someone to watch my back while I'm in there."

Ichabod worked up a batch of tobacco spit and let it fly. He cocked his head and hollered, "Jimmy, you staying?"

"Does she need me to?"

Ichabod looked back at her. "Do you need him to? That'll leave just me to answer calls."

"You understand this is your township, right?" Carrie said. "I'm just here to assist you with the investigation, not just get it dumped in my lap."

Ichabod turned his head and spat again. "Jimmy, stay and give her a hand but keep your ear to the radio in case we get any calls."

"Ten-four," Jimmy said.

"He said he'll stay," Ichabod told her.

"Yes, I heard," Carrie said.

"So, can you move your car?"

Carrie pulled into the vacant lot across from the trailer and watched Ichabod hustle to his car and hop in. The wheels on his police car spun as he jammed it in reverse and cranked the wheel, kicking up dirt and dust. He cranked the wheel the other way and stepped on the gas, gunning it as he raced toward the trailer park exit.

She grabbed her evidence bag from her trunk and lugged it across the street. Jimmy waved at her from the trailer's entrance. He was fresh-faced and chubby. His uniform was too old to belong to him and didn't fit well. Small departments don't get new officers measured for uniforms, she thought. They just handed you down whatever they had in the closet.

"Did he have somewhere to go?" she asked.

"No, he just don't do dead bodies, is all," Jimmy said.

"How can you be a cop and not do dead bodies?"

"I guess he just has me do them instead."

Okay, Carrie thought. "So, what do we have?"

Jimmy pulled a small spiral notepad out of his left shirt pocket and flipped it open. "Manager said this lady was a few days late on her rent. He tried getting hold of her and she wouldn't answer the door. He made entry with the master key. Found her dead."

"How'd she die?"

Jimmy checked his notes. "Manager didn't say."

"What did it look like when you went in?"

Jimmy looked up at her in confusion. "We didn't go in."

Carrie shoved her evidence bag against his chest with a thud. "Here we go. You're carrying this. Write down the time and *Detective Santero, arrived on scene. Entry made.* Got it?"

"We're doing a crime scene log?" Jimmy asked. "I thought this was just a regular suicide."

"Everything's regular right up until it isn't," Carrie said. "Let's go."

"Yes, ma'am," he said. He struggled to maneuver the bag as he checked his watch for the time, then wrote everything down on his notepad.

Carrie pulled out her phone and snapped several photos of the trailer's entrance. She leaned in and grabbed a few close-ups of the front door and lock, documenting that it was undamaged. No forced entry, she thought. Manager's story about making entry checked out. So far, so good.

She leaned her head in and instantly reeled back at the stench of decaying flesh.

The trailer's entrance was filled with trash bags stuffed with clothes, and cardboard boxes marked KITCHEN, BATHROOM, CLOTHES, and more. They were all taped shut.

"How long has she lived here?" Carrie asked.

"Manager didn't say."

Carrie slid on a pair of nitrile gloves and handed a pair to Jimmy, waiting for him to do the same. She raised her cell phone and snapped photographs as she walked inside the trailer, getting pictures of it from one end to the other. She slid her phone inside her jeans pocket and stopped, scanning the room before taking another step.

More trash bags and boxes, stacked along the right side of the trailer. The dining section was a small fixed table and built-in seats along the wall with ripped cushions. Bags and boxes were stacked there as well. On the opposite side of the trailer was the kitchenette. A counter and sink, set between rows of cheap particle-board cabinets.

Every flat surface in the kitchen area was covered in filth. Beer bottles filled with cigarette butts. Paper plates smeared with grease and dried pizza sauce. There were unopened letters from the utility company marked URGENT—PAYMENT DUE scattered on the floor. Carrie stepped over them, making her way toward the back of the trailer where the dead body sat.

The woman was sitting upright in bed with her arms at her sides. Her head was cocked sideways so that she was looking at Carrie. Her eyes were bulging and vacant. Her blond hair was cut jagged, uneven, and short, like she'd cut it herself with a pair of electric clippers.

She was dressed in a soiled pink nightgown, now stained yellow and brown by the release of her body's secretions.

Around the woman's throat was a pair of tan nylon stockings, tied into a knot under her chin. The other end of the stockings was stretched up to the roof and tied around the handle of the skylight.

"What's her name?" Carrie asked. She saw Jimmy look down at his notepad again. "Wait. Let me guess. Manager didn't say."

Carrie bent down to scoop up several bills from the floor. They were all addressed to Brenda Drake, at that address. Carrie sifted through the letters and set them aside.

She moved closer to the body. The stench was horrific. It would only get worse when they moved her. At that moment, all the remaining fluids inside Brenda Drake had settled deep inside of her. When they cut the nylons holding her upright and started jostling her to maneuver her body out of the trailer, all those putrefied fluids were going to slosh around. Things would spill out of her from all kinds of places.

Death investigation is a disgusting business. I must have been an idiot for wanting to do it more often when I was young, she thought.

On the nightstand next to the bed were more bottles filled with cigarettes, and a cell phone and keys. Laying on top of them was an open letter, written by hand.

Who sends handwritten letters anymore? Carrie thought. She picked it up and read.

My Dearest Brenda,
I so look forward to seeing you at our reunion.

I long to look upon your lovely face, to relive everything we had before.
All that we might have yet.

Carrie read the letter's signature, a sprawling thing in elaborate script.

Until Then, I Remain,
The Master

5

*C*arrie walked into the Vieira County District Attorney's Office just as a flood of people came pouring out through the front door. She had to step aside to let them pass. In the center of the crowd, she saw Salvatore Vigoda, the oldest detective in the office, following the rest. "What happened, Sal? Bomb threat?"

"Worse," Sal said. "Black mold. They found it in the vents. They're shutting down this entire section of the courthouse until they can get it cleaned."

Sal had retired as a patrol sergeant and come to work at the county detectives a short time before Carrie was hired. Technically, he was the second-most junior person in the office, just above her. Most of his police experience involved little more than writing tickets and handling car crashes. He knew next to nothing when it came to detailed investigations and complicated prosecutions, but he looked like he'd been on the job since Prohibition. He looked like someone's old Italian grandfather, with thick, black framed glasses and a large, beak-shaped nose. He always wore a fedora. Carrie liked the fedora. It seemed old school.

She found Harv Bender at the back of the line, just as one of the maintenance workers was shutting the doors and locking them. "I heard we had some black mold, Chief," she said.

Bender scowled. "These sons of bitches. I've been a cop for thirty years. Made tons of arrests. Survived a thousand violent encounters. I caught two serial killers! None of it left a scratch. But you watch. I'll die of some black mold bullshit I got infected with just sitting in my goddamn office."

"Right," Carrie said. "Listen, can I run in there real quick? I have to check for previous contacts with my suicide victim in the archives."

"The office is closed, Detective. We're all relocated until further notice. Anything you need in there will have to wait. Anyway, your suicide victim isn't going anywhere, is she?"

Carrie looked back at the office. People bumped into her as they filed past. "No, I guess not," she said.

The courthouse was shut down while environmental contractors came in with sensors and ventilation machines and chemicals to prevent the mold from spreading. All trials and hearings were postponed until further notice.

When the contractors looked, they saw that the air filters leading into the DA's office hadn't been changed in years. Maybe not changed since the original ventilation system was installed when the building was built. Black mold spores had taken root deep inside the air ducts of that entire wing, and the cost to fix it was enough to make the county commissioners angry.

The facilities staff for the courthouse said they weren't even aware there were filters in that area. The facilities staff manager said it wasn't his people's fault, because replacing the filters had never appeared on any of their work orders. It helped that the facility staff manger was related to the chairman of the county commissioners.

Somehow, it then became the DA's office staff's fault that the filters were never changed or checked. The decision was made to temporarily relocate the entire staff, including the district attorney, all of his assistant district attorneys, and the county detectives, to other locations.

Most of them were able to fit into the Children and Youth Services office, located in the basement of the Juvenile Justice building. CYS had a good space, with several bathrooms, a kitchen, and multiple mousetraps set up in every corner to try and clear out the rodents that had infested the building.

Anybody who couldn't fit at CYS was parceled out to various county-owned facilities wherever there were vacant offices. A detective and two ADA's were sent to a back room in the radio repair garage. A detective, an ADA, and an intern were sent to occupy the spare desks at the park rangers' headquarters. Carrie sat at home until her phone rang and Harv Bender told her he'd found a spot for her. "Good news," he said. "You got your own command post. Hope you feel special. I'll text you the address."

"Meaning, you're sticking me in a trailer," she said.

"It's got phones, computers, the whole nine. Plus, there won't be people bugging you out there. Here we can't go five minutes without somebody screaming because they saw a mouse. One ran up a secretary's arm while she was on the phone, and I thought they'd have to tranquilize her."

"Am I out there by myself?" she asked. She didn't mind the thought of that. Her own place to work, uninterrupted.

"Just about."

"What's that mean?"

"You'll be with your buddy Sal," Bender said. "He'll probably sleep the whole time. Just stick a mirror under his nose before you leave each day to make sure he's still breathing."

"Very funny," Carrie said, and hung up the phone.

She copied the address into her phone's GPS but it didn't register. The only thing it could find in the area was Bubba and Zeke's Gun Store. Under the address were photos of two smiling hillbillies with beards, posing with various weapons.

She knew the stretch of road. It was an old two-lane highway that used to connect to the turnpike before they'd built a newer four-lane highway on the other side of town. There wasn't much left on it, from what she recalled. Just hillbillies with big guns now, she thought. Perfect.

She drove to the gun shop. It was a small building with a yellowed sign out front that said GET YOUR GUNS BEFORE THE DEMO-

RATS TAKE THEM! The glass door was covered in bumper stickers. THIS IS MAGA COUNTRY. LOCK HER UP!

The word *Open* blinked in red neon from the store's front. Above it was a sign that read LOCAL MILITIA RESUPPLY STATION.

She opened the door. Rows of handguns in glass display cases ran the length of the store, with racks of long guns mounted on the walls behind them. Posters of women in bikinis holding AK-47's were thumbtacked to the walls above the long guns. The rest of the store was filled with targets and holsters and hunting gear.

Speakers mounted in the corners of the ceiling crackled with a radio talk show. Someone was frantically describing the invasion at the Mexican border and how real Americans were going to have to take up arms to defend it themselves if the liberals in the government wouldn't allow the military to do it.

Bubba, the heavyset one with the black beard, was seated behind the counter looking at a motorcycle magazine. Zeke, the smaller one with a red beard, was inventorying boxes of 9mm ammunition. Both stopped what they were doing when she walked in.

"Uh-oh, it's a lady cop. Look out, Zeke," Bubba said. He turned down the radio. "Did Hillary send you?"

"Not this time," Carrie said. She showed him the address for the trailer on her phone and said, "Do you know where this is?"

Bubba peered at the phone's screen. "That's still down the road a piece, near the Carver Dam sign. 'Bout two more miles."

Carrie thanked him and put her phone away. The top row of guns in the case in front of her were all revolvers. Everything from compact snub-noses to massive long-barreled weapons the diameter of a silver dollar.

"You want to see our lady guns?" Bubba asked.

"What are lady guns?"

"Down here," he said, waving for her to follow him. He showed her a display case of purple and pink weapons. Some of them were laser engraved with the American flag. Others had faces etched into their frames, surrounded by stars and eagles. Bubba pointed to one of the guns with a baby's face etched into it. "Zeke just did that. He's a whiz with the engraver, but it was my idea. We

used to just do famous people. Sold a lot of Trumps and Rush
Limbaughs. Then I got the idea that hey, you know how people
get their baby's faces tattooed on their arms? What if instead they
got it tattooed on their guns?" He looked at Zeke. "Ain't that
right?"

"Now they can shoot their baby at people if they want," Zeke
said.

"You got any babies, lady cop?" Bubba asked.

"No."

"Well, keep us in mind when you do."

Carrie kept looking. The display case next to the register had
rows of noise-suppressors and attachments people could add on
to their firearms. Flashlights and laser sights and the like. There
was even a grenade-launcher attachment for an AR-15 on the bottom shelf for a thousand dollars and a sign next to it that read FOR
SIGNAL FLARE USE ONLY! ATTENTION UNDERCOVER FEDERAL AUTHORI-
TIES, THIS PRODUCT NOT TO BE USED FOR ARMED PROJECTILES! WE AU-
TOMATICALLY INVOKE OUR RIGHT TO AN ATTORNEY!

"Get a lot of undercover feds in here?" Carrie asked.

"That's the kind of thing you don't know until it's too late, ain't
it?" Bubba tapped on the glass and said, "You want to see something cool? It just came in and I haven't had the chance to show
anybody yet."

"Sure. What is it?"

Bubba reached under the counter for a black plastic case. He
laid it in front of her and popped the snaps on either side. Carrie
leaned forward to see what was in the case and said, "Wow."

He reached into the thick foam and got his fingers around the
gun's silver frame. It was as large as his hand. "This right here's a
Colt 1911 forty-five caliber in chrome. It's their top-of-the-line
model, made right here in the United States up in Hartford, Con-
necticut. Everything you see on this gun is from authentic natural
materials. I'm talking about steel. I'm talking about wood. Every
component. One hundred percent real, no plastic. Every component fitted by a master gunsmith, by hand. You know how rare
that is nowadays? Zeke, how rare is that?"

"That's rare," Zeke said.

"That's right. So, you got one of the finest guns made in the world, but that's not what makes this piece so special." Bubba tapped the black electronic device mounted beneath the gun's frame, it looked like something from science fiction. "What you're looking at right here is something nobody else has. We're the only ones. This baby is a prototype designed by Australian Special Forces."

"What does it do?"

Bubba smirked. "Zeke, come on over here so we can show the lady cop what this does."

"No, thank you."

"Come on now."

"No!" Zeke said, and he ran around the corner for the door that let him into the back room.

Bubba watched him go, then leaned closer to Carrie and said, "He's still mad at me from the last time. I used it on him and he wound up on the floor rolling around in his own piss."

"Is it a laser sight?" Carrie asked.

"It's got a laser sight and a flashlight," Bubba said. He tapped a button on the side and said, "But it's also got this. A special high-intensity strobe that can cause a seizure if you look at it. I didn't believe it when I heard it, but then I used it on Zeke, and sure enough, he went straight down. Pissed all over his self."

"Jesus," Carrie said. "Keep that thing away from me."

Bubba closed the case and said, "You don't even want to know how much it costs."

"More than I can afford, that's for sure," she said.

Bubba slid the case back under the counter. "You ever need anything, come on back. We give a law enforcement discount."

"I'll be sure to do that," Carrie said. She called out, "See you later, Zeke!" but there was no response from the back.

The trailer was better than she'd expected. She'd assumed Bender was talking about some dilapidated mobile home like the one Brenda Drake had. The kind that was seized in a drug bust and still smelled like a meth lab. At worst, she feared they'd rent some ancient Airstream trailer made of aluminum that cooked you like a turkey on a hot day.

Instead, the county had borrowed a foreman's trailer from Meditz Construction, a local company that bought farmland and turned it into high-end housing developments in the area. The trailer had windows and a wooden porch with steps leading up to the front door. There was a large heating and air conditioning unit mounted to one side, and as Carrie walked up, she could hear it humming along nicely.

The trailer was parked off the highway next to a closed gas station. The land surrounding it was nothing but high yellow grass that glinted with broken glass from all of the trash people tossed out of their windows as they drove past. An old wooden sign for the Carver Dam and Reservoir stood on the side of the road and Carrie couldn't see any water through the thick grass, but she could smell it. It was rank and stunk of rotting vegetation.

They were out in the middle of nowhere, with no reason for anyone to want to come visit them, and that was fine by Carrie. She wasn't the kind to need people around her to do her job. She didn't crave the company of others or need human interaction at the water cooler. As she walked up the steps to the trailer's front door, she thought, I could get used to this.

She knocked on the trailer's door before she twisted the knob and opened it. She heard papers scatter and shoes slam down on the floor. Carrie poked her head in and saw Sal Vigoda sitting there, rubbing his eyes, trying to look like he hadn't been sleeping. His fedora had been draped across his eyes and had left a circular ring around his face.

"You all right, Sal?" Carrie asked.

"I'm good," he said. "You here to check up on me? I wasn't sleeping. I had a headache, so I just shut my eyes for a second to see if it would go away."

"I'm not here to check up on you," Carrie said. "We're both assigned to this trailer until they get us back into the office."

The trailer had a workstation large enough for one person

where Sal was sitting. There was a county laptop and a desk phone. Toward the back of the trailer was a couch, a kitchenette, and a tiny bathroom.

Sal looked around the trailer. "It's not really big enough for two people to work in."

"Not with just one computer," she said. "Do you have anything you need to work on right now?"

"I'm not good with that damn thing anyway. I can barely even turn it on. Back in my day, the dispatcher ran everything. You gave them the tag, they ran it. You gave them the guy's name and date of birth, they told you everything you needed to know. Now, you gotta do everything yourself. It's like the automated tellers at the supermarket. A bunch of employees standing around staring into space while I'm there trying to figure out what code to enter for a goddamn tomato."

"So, you don't mind if I use the computer then?"

"I'll be better off sitting on the couch anyway," he said. He got up from the chair and moved. "I've got a medical condition I picked up during all those years working midnight shift in a patrol car."

Carrie raised the lid on the laptop and turned it on. "Yeah, what's that?"

"Whenever I'm seated in an upright seated position, I fall asleep," he said.

Carrie laughed as she typed in her password. "Let me ask you something. You did how many years on the street?"

"Forty-five," he said. "All in uniform. Never wanted to be a white shirt, never wanted to be a detective, nothing. Just a road dog, the entire time."

"Forty-five years," Carrie whispered. "What the hell made you come to the county detectives?"

"My brother. At the time, he was real big in politics and thought he was going to be a big-shot county commissioner. He got me the job. Just do five years, Sal, he says. At five years you get a county pension, on top of your township pension. Maybe it makes up for the half you had to split with your ex-wife. You'll never have to touch a case. You'll be my driver, that's all. We'll go fishing every day. So, I say okay. What's five years, right?"

Carrie thought for a moment. "I've never heard of your brother, so I'm guessing he didn't get elected county commissioner?"

"Nope. He died right before the election of a heart attack. Two weeks after I took this fakakta job."

"Shit," Carrie said. "I'm sorry."

"Ah," Sal said, waving his hand. "He never took care of himself. Always smoking cigars and drinking martinis at these political events. Mr. Big Shot. Meanwhile, I'm stuck here pulling cases just like the rest of you."

"You've got to be close to the five-year mark now, right?"

"Six months, two weeks, three days, and four hours to go," he said. "Not that I'm counting or anything."

"If it makes you feel better, I have to do over twenty more years before I reach a full pension. I left my first job way before I vested, and this place won't count my time from there."

"Twenty years is nothing," Sal said. "It goes by like that," he said, snapping his fingers.

"I hope so," Carrie said. "Somedays it feels like I'm stuck in quicksand."

"You got any kids?" Sal asked.

"No," Carrie said.

"That's why. Kids make it all go by fast. Always needing to go the doctor, or play practice, or football games, or all the other things that go along with it. You spend so much time running around, before you know it, they're grown up and you're almost retired. But, there's nothing better than family. I mean that. Even my ex-wife, as much time as we spent hating each other, she's still the mother of my children. Last year she got cancer, and I drove her to every single radiation treatment. She beat it, thank God. Never a word of thank you to me, of course, because I'm still the prick who cheated on her with her cousin, but still. You know why I did it?"

"Because you felt guilty about cheating on her?" Carrie said.

"No, her cousin was superhot and my wife hadn't come near me in ten years. I don't regret it at all. But that's besides the point."

Carrie laughed and said, "Okay, so why'd you take her?"

"Because we're family. Nothing can change that. Not even her hating my guts and taking half my pension." Sal leaned his head back against the couch and dropped his hat over his face. He yawned and smacked his lips together. "Get yourself some kids and start a family, Carrie. Before you get old and it's too late. It's the only thing you really have in this world. Trust me."

The laptop was slow and old. Two of the function keys were missing on the keyboard. After ten minutes of running, Carrie could feel the heat emanating up from beneath the thing. She imagined it bursting into flames as she typed.

Even the interface was old. Her monitor at work had sleek icons and a crisp, bright display. This one looked like an operating system from the 1990s, with cartoonish graphics and ugly gray boxes every time she opened a new folder.

Still, it let her into the county database. She typed *Brenda Drake* into the master list of all names associated with all investigations ever conducted by the county detectives. There were multiple Drakes in the system but none of them were named Brenda.

There was a database for known aliases, and she opened that and typed the words *The Master.* No results.

"The Master," Carrie whispered. "Hey, Sal, you awake?"

"No."

"Who has a master?"

"A dog."

"No, I mean, what kind of lifestyle is someone involved in if they have a master?"

"I dunno, a kung-fu person?" Sal asked.

"I don't think my girl was into kung-fu," Carrie said. "Maybe it meant for sex."

"Someone can be a sex master?" Sal asked. "Is that something you go to school for, or what?"

"No, I mean, like, people into whips and chains and stuff. BDSM. I think they have masters."

"BDSM. Since when did people need costumes to be intimate?" Sal said. "It's crazy now. I hear they get dressed up in bunny suits and leather masks and capes. When I was young, you didn't need accessories for lovemaking."

"Well, in all fairness, when you were young, everyone was still getting over the shock of having just invented fire," Carrie said.

"Oh, that's very funny," Sal muttered from beneath his hat.

"Go back to sleep, Grandpa," Carrie said. She kept digging through the database, when it occurred to her that she was only searching adult names. She opened up the juvenile database and searched for contacts with Brenda Drake.

"Bingo," Carrie said.

Brenda's name popped up associated with a fifteen-year-old abduction case, with her listed as the victim. Carrie clicked the link to open the report, and groaned. There was hardly anything there. Back in those days, everything was still being done on typewriters, and the secretaries would enter only the bare minimum information into the computers. There was the victim's name, the type of case, and a location.

Carrie clicked the link to read the list of charges and had to wait for it to load. She tapped her fingernails on the laptop's edge as she stared at the cursor, waiting for it to unfreeze. The charges appeared, and they were no joke. Kidnapping. Aggravated Assault. Aggravated Assault of a Law Enforcement Officer. The last one made Carrie lean closer to the screen. Attempted Homicide. "What the hell, Brenda Drake," Carrie whispered. "Who'd you piss off?"

It said there was an arrest made, but when she clicked the suspect box, it was empty. There were no investigative reports and no detectives listed as being assigned to the case. It was a dead end. Her only hope was that the physical case file was still in the archives and hadn't been lost or destroyed when the suspect turned eighteen.

She felt her phone vibrate in her pocket and pulled it out. She smiled when she saw the name *Bill Waylon* on the screen. "Well, hey, stranger. How are you?"

"I've been better, kiddo," Waylon said.

She could hear the strain in his voice to speak. "What's wrong?" she asked.

"I need to see you. Now."

6

*H*e'd lost a hundred pounds since the accident. No, that wasn't right, Carrie thought. It wasn't an accident and it was wrong to call it one. A psychopath had cut his throat from ear to ear because he was trying to save her and Nubs. That's no accident. But Bill Waylon survived and that was no accident either.

On the night they found the Omnikiller, they'd all nearly died horrific deaths, completely at his mercy. Carrie and Nubs were locked upstairs in a torture room with no way of escape. Waylon and Jacob Rein were knocked unconscious in the basement. The Omnikiller chained Rein's left hand to the basement wall and made Rein watch as he slit Waylon's throat.

By rights, that should have been it. The Omnikiller should have been able to take his time carrying out his sick fantasies for as long as he liked. But Waylon, through an incredible act of determination, survived. He dragged himself across the basement floor close enough to give Rein a weapon. As for Rein, well, he'd taken it from there with an act of determination as well.

Carrie had been in the waiting room that night when Jeri Waylon and the girls arrived at the hospital. The girls were distraught as they embraced one another and pleaded to God for their father to be okay. It wasn't possible, Carrie remembered thinking. He'd had his throat cut. The odds of surviving that are next to impossible.

Jeri Waylon didn't cry. She didn't plead. She didn't move. She did nothing except stare at the operating room door and wait. "He won't die," she said. "My husband will not allow that son of a bitch to kill him. He just won't."

Hours later, the doors opened and an exhausted doctor emerged to tell them she was right. Bill Waylon had survived. He'd live. The girls screamed with joy and Carrie wept into her hands with relief and then the doctor said, "He'll live, but things won't be the same for him, not for a long time."

Two years had passed and they still weren't.

In the years Carrie had worked for Waylon when he was chief of the Coyote Police Department, he'd always been a large man with a robust stomach, but he'd always been a stickler for uniforms. He was one of the few chiefs in the county that bought all his officers new uniforms and paid to have them tailored. He believed a police officer's appearance went a long way. Even as chief, when he could have worn anything he wanted, he still showed up to work every day in a uniform, wearing a clean and crisply starched white shirt with creases down the arms so sharp, you could almost slice bread with them.

When they went to training and he dressed down, he wore polo shirts and always buttoned all the buttons up to his chin. On the rare occasions when she'd seen him in a T-shirt and shorts, he'd worn the T-shirt tucked into the waistband of the shorts, no matter how much she made fun of him. She'd never seen him unshaven, except for his carefully manicured mustache that was long out of style, but he thought it made him look like some kind of Old West sheriff.

The man sitting at the kitchen table in front of her was gaunt and dressed in pajamas in the afternoon. He was wearing a bathrobe that hung loose off of his withered frame. The scar along his neck was thick and purple, a jagged length of gnarled flesh, hidden only by the strands of his long gray beard. The beard itself was an ugly thing. It grew high up on Waylon's bony cheeks, just an inch or so below his eyes. Hairs grew out of his nose down into his mustache and blended in with them. She could no longer see his mouth.

"Is Jeri around?" Carrie asked.

"No," Waylon said. He touched his neck and forced himself to swallow. "She finally went back to work. It was either that or we had to—" He winced and stopped speaking to massage his throat again.

Carrie got up and filled a glass of cold water for him from the refrigerator and handed it to him and sat back down. He took a long sip. "Or we had to sell the house."

"I know the girls are doing okay," Carrie said. "Abby texts me from school sometimes. Seems like she's enjoying college, but not too much, so don't worry. Kate, I don't hear from as often, but that's normal. You know how high school kids are. She's afraid I'll rat her out to her dad."

"She's a good girl," Waylon whispered. He took her hand in his. His fingers were bony and thin compared to hers. "All my girls turned out great. I'm very proud of all of you."

Carrie smiled and covered his hand with hers. "What's wrong, Chief? Did something happen?"

His hand started to shake inside of hers. He reached into the pocket of his robe and pulled out a folded letter. He set the letter on the table and slid it toward Carrie. "This came in the mail three days ago. I had to wait until no one was around to call you."

My Dearest Detective,

I so look forward to seeing you at our reunion.

You are a lucky man to have such a beautiful family. A wife and two lovely daughters. Perhaps I will get to meet them someday.

Until Then, I Remain,

The Master

Carrie read the letter again, trying to control her anger. Now her hands were shaking. "Who is this prick, Bill? He sent the same letter to a suicide victim I just handled."

"Which one?" Waylon asked.

"Brenda Drake."

Waylon nodded, and then his eyes went to a faraway place. "That poor girl. We saved her except I guess maybe we didn't."

Carrie had to lean forward to get Waylon to focus on her. "Bill, who is The Master?"

"Some maniac teenager from back in the day," Waylon said. "Christ, he's got to be over thirty now. Tucker Pennington. Had all these crazy religious ideas. Made up his own Bible, but it was full of spells and incantations that he created. Or read about somewhere. Hell, I don't know. He wanted to set this girl Brenda Drake on fire to purify her, from what I remember. Had her all tied up in the woods after he snatched her off the street right in front of her mother."

"And you caught him?"

"Right after he poured gasoline all over her," Waylon said. "Me and Jacob. Christ, Pennington was just a kid. Where's that evil come from? How's that kind of thing get into someone so young?"

It was as if she could see through his eyes into his mind, at all the swirling ghosts there.

"Can you tell me anything about the other victims?"

Waylon took another sip of water and touched his throat and closed his eyes. It hurt him to speak, but he forced the words out anyway. "Pennington had a cousin. I can't recall her name. Real shy and emotional. Hard to talk to. He'd been sexually abusing her ever since they were little. We never got the full extent of what he did to her, because she couldn't hardly speak about it without shutting down. Her parents weren't any help. They hired their own lawyer and I couldn't talk to the girl without them or the attorney present."

Carrie grabbed a pen off the table and asked Waylon for something to write on. He handed her a junk mail envelope. "Their daughter was a victim, and her family wouldn't let you or Rein talk to her without an attorney?"

"Just me," Waylon said. "Jacob was too busy with more important things, I suppose. We ended up not letting her testify because the DA thought she was going to have a nervous breakdown on the stand."

"Do you remember that victim's name?" Carrie asked.

"No, I do not."

Carrie drew a line under those notes and said, "Was there anyone else?"

"Alexis Dole," Waylon said.

"You remember her name."

"I'll never forget it, either," he said. "Alexis was a cheerleader. Class president. Beauty queen. Everything. Back then, the high schools had this dance called the Winter Ball, and they'd build these big bonfires outside. Been doing them since I went to school, and probably longer than that. A group of kids were standing around the bonfire, and Alexis Dole was standing with them. Tucker Pennington crept up on the group and hurled a bottle of sulfuric acid at the group. It hit Alexis right in the face. He'd stolen the acid a year before and had it waiting, all that time. This kid wasn't just sick. He was a mean little bastard too."

"Holy shit."

"Scarred her bad, for life. Took one of her eyes. She went through skin grafts, hair transplants, everything. The skin was too ruined. She wore this big wig and sunglasses to the hearing, trying to hide her face, but by the end, she got so angry she ripped them off and threw them at Pennington."

Waylon took a break to massage his throat. Carrie offered him more water, but he waved it away.

"She pulled off her eye patch and made everyone look at the hole in her eye and see what he'd done to her. She stood up in the witness box and forced the judge to look right into it. I'll never forget that. It was her testimony that sent him away for the rest of his life, or so we thought at the time."

"Did you try him as an adult?" Carrie asked.

"Nope. Pennington was such a maniac, they committed him to a mental facility for sadists and sexual offenders after he turned eighteen. People sent there aren't ever supposed to be released until they're medically cleared, which doesn't happen. How can you cure that kind of crazy? The state was supposed to keep people like Pennington confined for the rest of their lives. I guess that's all changed now."

Carrie looked at the letter from The Master again.

I so look forward to seeing you at our reunion.

"Is he being released?" Carrie asked.

"Could be. I read the government is cutting the budget for all their mental health facilities. People like Pennington are suddenly declared fit to return to society." Waylon pulled another letter out of a stack on the table and showed it to Carrie. It was a hearing notice. "This came a few weeks ago. I suppose they want me to testify as to why Pennington shouldn't be set free."

"No one's ever going to let him out. Come on. After what he did? They can't."

"This is the government we're talking about, kiddo."

"Have you heard from Jacob?" Carrie asked.

Waylon took a long sip of water. He cleared his throat and grimaced in discomfort. "No. We haven't spoken in some time."

"Did something happen between you two?"

Waylon pointed at the scar on his neck. "Besides this?" He picked up the letter from The Master. "Besides this?" He tossed the letter aside and pounded his fist on the table. "I'll be paying for being Jacob Rein's partner for the rest of my life, Carrie. But I won't let it anywhere near my family. Not ever again. If Pennington so much as dreams about showing up here, I'll put a bullet in him and everyone who looks just like him."

Carrie picked the letter up from the floor. She folded it and put it in her pocket. "Well, Jacob has to know about this. Both of you need to be there to keep this maniac from going free. I'll find him and make sure he knows to be there."

"I'm not going," Waylon said.

"What? Of course you're going."

"I'm not."

"What the hell are you talking about?"

"Exactly what I said."

"Chief," Carrie said.

"I'm not Chief anymore. They fired me after the long-term disability ran out. Now, you'll have to excuse me," Waylon said. He got up from the table. "I need to go lie down. Please see yourself out. And I'd appreciate it if you don't say anything about this to Jeri or the girls. It would just worry them."

She watched him shuffle down the hall, going away from her. The sound of his bathrobe sweeping the floor grew distant, until she heard his steps going up the stairs toward his bed. It wasn't yet ten in the morning.

The Vieira County Children and Youth Services building was crowded with all the extra staff from the DA's office. All the intake workers who answered the phones for incoming reports of abuse and neglect were stuck sharing desks with unhappy-looking Child Protective Services personnel. All of the DA's and county detectives scattered around the office were relegated to the rear and sides of the main floor. The walls were covered with paper signs that told people where to go to find whoever they were looking for.

The front lobby now had two desks. The Children and Youth Services secretary's desk and the DA's office secretary's desk, which was only a card table and folding chair with a laptop and phone.

Carrie got off the elevator and walked toward the card table. "Good morning, Miss Mabel."

"Can you believe this nonsense?" Mabel asked. "Where'd they put you?"

"Out in a trailer with Sal Vigoda."

"Be glad you aren't stuck in this mess. We're all tripping over each other," Mabel said.

"I'm guessing we still can't get back into the old office?"

"Nope. I asked them to bring my old chair over so I'm not stuck sitting in this uncomfortable thing, but they won't unlock the doors or nothing. This place is a dump," she said. She looked at the Children and Youth Services secretary seated across the way and said, "No offense."

"Can you look up a case for me? There's a hearing coming up, and I'm wondering who hearing notices were sent to. The defendant's name is Tucker Pennington."

"Pennington," Mabel repeated as she typed. "Here we go. Looks like hearing notices went out a little while ago. Brenda Drake. Patricia Martin. Alexis Dole. Dr. Linda Shelley. Here's your buddies, Bill Waylon and Jacob Rein. Detective Rein's came back undeliverable, just like everything else we've sent him, of course."

"Of course," Carrie said. "Can you print me out that list of names? There's a few follow-ups I'd like to do."

"Who assigned you to do follow-ups on this rusty old case?" Mabel asked, surprised. "This is a civil hearing, it looks like. There won't even be an ADA there. Is somebody giving you busywork? You're too good for that, you hear me?"

"This is just something I'm doing on my own," Carrie said.

"Oh, I see. You know this is how people get in trouble, right? Looking into old mess," Mabel said as she leaned forward to find the print button.

"I sure do," Carrie said.

Carrie ran intel on Tricia Martin and Alexis Dole from her phone in the parking lot. Martin's digital footprint was nothing. She had a driver's license and work history, but no social media at all. No photographs of her appeared in any search engine when you typed in her name. She wasn't listed on any school alumni sites or property listings.

Alexis Dole was a different story. Dole's scarred face was everywhere. She'd been interviewed on survivor websites and featured as Shooter of the Month at various local firing ranges. There were pictures of her holding guns and trophies. Her, smiling with her deformed half mouth, her one remaining eye gleaming. Carrie watched videos of her teaching kali, a Filipino martial art fought with knives, and she spun people around and slashed the inside of their thighs and necks with a dull-edged training blade with ghoulish precision.

She came to the last name on the hearing notice list. Dr. Linda Shelley, address, the Vieira County Juvenile Detention Center. It took her a minute to put Shelley's face to the name. "Oh right," Carrie said, remembering the last time they'd met. "This should be fun."

"Detective Carrie Santero, here for Dr. Shelley, please," Carrie said at the front window.

The secretary looked up. "Is she expecting you?"

"No, but she helped me two years ago and should remember me."

"Let me see if she's in." The secretary moved away from the window to talk on the phone. She came back and said, "I'll buzz you through the door. Do you know where you're going?"

"Straight down the hall, if I remember," Carrie said.

"Stay to the center of the aisle," the secretary said. "Don't get too close to any of the doors."

Carrie stood at the large metal door and waited to hear it unlock. When it clicked, she pulled it open. Fists pounded against the doors when she entered, like caged animals demanding to be fed. High-pitched voices screeching at her. The first three rooms were crowded with teenagers in jumpsuits. At the second window, a boy pulled down the front of his pants and thrust his penis against the glass at her.

She could hear guards shouting, "Get the fuck back from the door!" and "Quit that fucking banging!"

Many of the rooms were dark and unoccupied. The security station at the first intersecting hallway was empty. No orderlies or nurses patrolled the halls. The trash cans were overflowing with coffee cups and wadded-up papers. Bags of trash sat next to the cans in a row that no one had taken out yet.

Carrie passed the gymnasium and it was filled with children. Children who should have been home getting showered and ready for elementary school the next day were mixed in with older boys who towered over the security guards. Dozens of children stood on the parquet floor and none of them were moving. They swayed like trees, staring in her direction through the window but none of their eyes tracking as she walked by. Against the wall beneath one of the bare basketball hoops, orderlies counted racks of trays filled with paper cups on a large metal cart. The shelves around the bottom of the cart on one side were labeled CLOZAPINE, RISPERIDONE, ARIPIPRAZOLE, CARIPRAZINE, and TOPIRAMATE.

A door opened at the far end of the hall and Dr. Linda Shelley emerged. Carrie walked faster, wanting to get out of the hall. She shook Dr. Shelley's hand at the door. Shelley's grip was harder than Carrie had anticipated, and Carrie found herself having to squeeze back to keep her finger bones from being ground together.

"Doctor," Carrie said.

"Detective."

Shelley led her into the office and told her to have a seat. Shelley's office was unchanged from two years prior. Ornately framed diplomas and certificates decorated her walls. Papers and binders covered her desk. A coffee cup was balanced on top of a thick report next to her computer keyboard and had left a damp brown ring on the paper beneath it.

"I'm here about Tucker Pennington," Carrie said.

"He has a hearing coming up."

"That's right. I was wondering if I could ask you about him. You were such a big help to us last time."

"I have no idea what you're talking about."

"Of course," Carrie said, nodding that she understood. "What I meant was, you're listed as a witness, and I wanted to know if there was anything you could tell me about his victims."

"I never met them."

"Well, several people connected to the case have received letters from someone calling themselves The Master. Real threatening. Have you gotten one?"

"No."

"It could have been sent here or to your home."

"I don't get mail at my house, Detective Santero. I use a PO

Box. After all the years I've spent treating prisoners and sex offenders, I prefer not to use my home address very often. I'm sure
you can understand. Now is there anything else? I'm extremely
busy here."

"Smart," Carrie said. "Before I go, can you tell me anything
about Pennington? What was he like when you treated him here?"

"I didn't treat him here."

"But you're listed as a witness. What, are they just having you
bring his records or something?"

"If you'd done your homework, you'd know I wasn't working
here back then. If you'd done your homework, you'd know I
treated Tucker Pennington after he was committed at Sunshine
Estates."

Carrie set her pen down. "Hey, did we get off on the wrong foot
or something? I apologize for not knowing any of that, but I can't
access the old case file because there's black mold in the building."

"I'm sorry to hear you're having problems with your building.
I'm currently working with half my regular staff, and the county
won't free up any funds to hire more personnel. Over the summer, they only allowed the air conditioner to run in the morning,
which meant the temperature inside this facility reached ninety-
five degrees each day by three P.M. The budget for recreational ac-
tivities has all been reallocated into drugs, in hopes that by
turning all of the children here into overmedicated zombies, we
won't need to hire any more guards. Shall I go on?"

"No, I get it," Carrie said. "You've definitely got it rough out
here, but Pennington sent one of his victims a letter, calling himself The Master and that he can't wait to see her again. She killed
herself. My old boss, Bill Waylon, the one I was here with last
time? He got a letter too. All I'm asking is, what can you tell me
about Pennington that might help me understand what I'm dealing with here?"

"It would be illegal for me to disclose anything related to any of
my patients, Detective. I will be at the hearing as required, and
give any answers while under oath, but that's it. Now, if you'll excuse me, I have a lot to do."

"I'm just looking to talk," Carrie said. "To stop what might be coming this way, before anyone else gets hurt."

"And you think what? I'm supposed to break the law to help you?"

"You did it before. And I'm grateful every day you did."

"Well, the only reason I did it before isn't here right now, is he?"

Carrie leaned back in her chair. "Oh. I knew there was something between you two. I could see the way you were looking at him back then. Is that what your problem is?"

"You have no idea what you're talking about."

"I know petty jealousy when I see it."

Shelley slammed her hand on her desk. "Jacob was out! Maybe he was lost, okay, but at least he was free, until you came along with your little, I don't know, white girl lost in the woods routine. I hold you responsible for every single thing that's happened to him since then. And if anything is, as you say, coming this way, I suggest you stop it long before it gets to him, because if not, your newest problem will be me."

Carrie got up and left. She shut the office door behind her and stayed to the middle of the hall past the gymnasium and empty rooms and other rooms where people were shrieking. She came to the metal door at the end of the hall and banged on it with her fist, over and over until someone heard her and let her out.

II

LINDA

7

*L*inda grew up in Norristown. That's the bottom of Montgomery County, Pennsylvania, just outside of Philly. Her mother had six children and Linda was the youngest. Her four sisters had ten children combined and all of them were older than Linda. The house had three bedrooms. Linda's bedroom had two sets of bunk beds with two children in each bed who slept inverted from one another.

By the time she was twelve years old, she'd been molested six times. Four times by one of her mother's boyfriends. Once by her fourth grade teacher. Once by her older cousin Antoine when he ordered the sister Linda normally slept with to move and he crawled into the bed instead.

When she was seventeen she took a bus to the nearest army recruitment center. There was a desk in the center of the office and three flags. One for the United States, one for Pennsylvania, and one for the army. The soldier said, "Can I help you?"

Linda had a folded-up pamphlet in her back pocket that she'd taken from her school's library. "Is it true you give people a place to stay in the army?"

"Yes, ma'am."

"Is it true they go all over the world and don't stay here?"

"Yes, ma'am."

"Do you have to fight and kill people?"

"No, ma'am. Our soldiers do a lot of different jobs."

"Is it true they experiment on black people in the army?"

"Say what now?"

"I heard that's what they do."

"Who'd you hear that from?"

"Just around."

"Well, back in World War II, some doctor did an experiment on black soldiers in a place called Tuskegee. Is that what you heard about?"

She shrugged.

"Well, nobody does those kinds of things anymore, I promise you."

"How you can promise that?"

"I'm black and nobody ever did any experiments on me," he said. "It's not allowed."

She looked around the recruitment center and put her right hand against her mouth and bit her nails. "Do you have to wear your uniform the whole time you're in the army or do you still get to wear regular clothes?"

"You only have to be in uniform when you're on duty."

"How come I see people wearing they uniform to dinner and on the bus?"

"I guess they're getting some kind of discount."

"What's that mean?"

"Sometimes people do nice things for you when they know you're serving your country. Out of respect."

Linda bit her nails. "How you get in?"

"You take the ASVAB, that's the written test, then a physical, and then if you pass all that, you're in."

"How much do that cost?"

"What, the test and physical?" he asked.

She nodded.

"It's free." He watched her, and she just stood there, biting. "You have any more questions you want to ask?"

She wiped her fingers on her shirt. "Can I take the test now?"

Five years later Linda was asleep in bed and woke up to find the side next to her empty. She lay there a minute, listening. Trying to figure out what had woken her up. There wasn't any light on in the hallway bathroom. "Jerry?" she called out.

She rolled out of bed and walked across the bedroom floor. She stopped at the door and leaned her head out. "Honey? You okay?"

The tall, narrow, window on the staircase landing was black. No lights on downstairs, either. She went down the steps, holding the handrail. She stopped at the landing and said, "Jerry? Are you down here?"

A car drove past the house, its lights coming through the staircase window first, moving across the wall and Linda, then glanced off the large windows of their living room. Even after three months, the house was bigger than she was used to. They'd bought it with Linda's salary and housing allowance combined with Jerry's salary and housing allowance, plus all the money Jerry had banked each time he'd been deployed to fight. Linda had been deployed twice. Once to Japan and once to Germany. Her Food Services job never took her close enough to the fighting to get her the combat deployment bonus.

The car was up the road and gone by the time she stepped onto the living room's wooden floor. Her weight made the slightest creak, but it was the only sound in the room. She stood there, listening to herself breathe, then held her breath and tried to listen even closer. Nothing.

She felt the pressure of his hand around her face long before she heard him coming. His palm tasted like sweat against her open mouth as it muffled her cry. He dragged her backward from the living room, into the darkness of the kitchen and onto the floor. His left hand covered her mouth and nose, not letting her take a full breath or speak. His right arm was wrapped around her torso, pinning her arms to her sides and keeping her tight against him.

"They're here," he whispered.

"No, they aren't. Baby, listen."

"Quiet!" He squeezed her face harder. "We can't let them take us."

"Get off of me!" She kicked the floor and beat her fists against his thighs. He bore down on her, squeezing harder, whispering that they couldn't be taken alive. She bit his hand. She felt the fat skin on his palm give way beneath her front teeth and the warm gush of blood in her mouth.

He cried out and slapped her across the back of the head to get her to let go. She spun on the floor and punched him square in the face, her knuckles cracking him just beneath his nose and just above his teeth.

He covered his face with both hands and she scurried across the floor to get away. She waited, crouched in the darkness, ready to run. She called his name, asking if he could hear her.

Jerry looked up at her in confusion. Blood dripped from his fingers onto the floor. "Why did you hit me?"

The commanding officer waited for her to finish speaking. "Linda, do you still love your husband?"

"Of course, I do, sir."

"Do you honor your commitment to him?"

"Yes, sir."

"Then you have to be there for him during this difficult time. I've been married thirty years, and my wife will be the first one to tell you that it hasn't always been easy. When I came back from my first deployment, she told me she couldn't do it. The stress of not knowing if I was alive or dead from day to day was too much for her. Jerry's on his, what, his second combat deployment?"

"Third, sir. It's his second since we've been together."

"What you're feeling is totally understandable. Tell you what. When Jerry gets home, I'm going to arrange something special for the two of you. Everything is going to be just fine."

She opened her right eye. The left was swollen shut. It ached when she touched it. It felt obscenely large and strange against her fingers. Other parts of her ached too. The monitor to her right beeped steadily, measuring her pulse and respiration.

The military policeman standing in the corner of her room came forward, holding his hat between his hands. "Specialist Shelley," he said.

She sat up and cringed at the pain in her ribs. It forced her to lie back down. She was out of breath and had to steady herself. "Where's Jerry?"

"Ma'am, I'm supposed to ask you a few questions when you feel up to it. Are you up to it?"

"Where is my husband?"

"Lieutenant Shelley is in custody, ma'am."

"I need to see him. This wasn't his fault."

"Ma'am, I'm supposed to ask you some questions."

She sat up. The room was spinning. "This wasn't his fault!"

He pulled a notepad out of his uniform's breast pocket. "Just a few questions. Okay. Let's see. How many times did he hit you?"

"I don't know."

"Do you remember how it started?"

"I'm not sure. I'm not feeling good. Can you get the nurse?"

"Just a few more questions. How did it start?"

"I don't know! He just got back. We were celebrating. Everything was fine until we got home."

"What happened when you got home?"

"Nothing happened. He just went crazy."

"Well, did you say something to make him upset?"

She sat straight-backed in the chair with her knees together. Her camouflage hat was folded in her right hand and both of her hands were resting on her knees and her uniform shirt and pants were ironed so that there were sharp creases along both arms. Her nails were short and clean and unbitten. She looked at them while she waited.

"How is my friend Tim Williams?" Dr. Shorn asked without looking up.

"Major Williams is good, ma'am. He sends his regards."

"Tim and I went to high school together."

"Yes, ma'am. He told me."

Dr. Shorn pushed her glasses up the length of her long nose as she looked over the stack of paperwork assembled on her desk. The papers were tabulated and ordered and bound together by color-coded fasteners. "I'm sure you're aware, your high school transcript does not meet our traditional standards for admittance."

"Yes, ma'am," Linda said.

"You never even took the SATs."

"No, ma'am."

"And you work in Food Services?"

"Yes, ma'am."

"Why did you pick that career path?"

"That's what they had available for me, going in, based on how I did on my ASVAB."

"I see." Dr. Shorn folded her hands on top of the paperwork. "However, I can also see that you've been applying yourself. The major tells me you've been taking whatever training classes the army offers. He seems to think you'd be a good fit for our school."

"I'd do my best, ma'am."

"And you're still on active duty?"

"I separate in two months. It's my intention to use the GI Bill to pursue a degree in psychology, ma'am. I'd prefer to do so at this university, ma'am."

"Can I ask why?"

"Your psychology program has a fine reputation, ma'am."

"I know that. What I meant was, why are you interested in it? Most military people who come here pursue criminal justice degrees. However, with your training in the kitchen, you could get a degree in the culinary arts in half the time and be a real chef. They're both good careers. You'd make money doing either."

"Thank you, ma'am, but I intend to study psychology."

"And I asked why."

Linda looked up, unsure of how to answer.

"Let me just cut to the chase here. To become a licensed psychologist in Pennsylvania, first you need your bachelor's degree. That's four years. Then your master's. That's another two. Then you move on to get your Ph.D., and before you graduate, you have to log two thousand hours of supervised practice. Do you understand what I'm saying? It will take you ten years of full-time, non-stop, unwavering commitment to pursue this. You barely graduated high school."

"Yes, ma'am. I understand."

"Work ten years as a cop instead and you'll be almost halfway to retirement."

"I appreciate your suggestion, ma'am. No, thank you."

"Let's cut the *ma'am* shit for a second. You want me to help you get into a school that kids apply to from all around the country. You want me to use my resources and connections to get you in here. So, I want to know why. I've made psychology my life's pursuit. What makes you think you want to make it yours? And don't bullshit me. I'll know."

"Ma'am," Linda began, then stopped. "I suppose it's just an area I'm interested in."

Dr. Shorn gathered up the stack of papers. "Thank you for your time, Sergeant. I'm sure someone from Admissions will be in touch with you soon. Now if you'll excuse me."

"Wait," Linda said. She took a deep breath. It was hard for her to speak. "Please."

The professor set the papers down and leaned back in her chair. "Take your time."

"I'm hoping that it will help me understand."

"Understand what?"

It was hard and it took a while, but Linda eventually got it all out. About her mother's boyfriend, and her cousin. About Jerry. Things she'd never told anyone. The tightrope of living with someone who was packed like a pipe bomb. The craving to be a part of something, and the panic of having it taken away. Everything.

Dr. Shorn listened. She passed a box of tissues across the desk. And when Linda was finished, Dr. Shorn got up and put her arm around her and said, "Come on. We're going down to Admissions to get you enrolled."

* * *

It was dark out and she'd only been home long enough to set down her schoolbag and kick off her shoes when someone knocked on her apartment door. Panic seized her body like she'd stepped on a live power wire. It ran up from her feet up into her legs. It travelled down her arms to the tips of her fingers and locked all of her muscles in place.

There was a second of silence and then they knocked again. She forced herself to move close enough to the keyhole to peek through it. She saw it wasn't Jerry and so much air escaped from her chest, it left her light-headed.

Tim Williams looked older than the last time she'd seen him. He was the only man she knew who had a full head of hair and still shaved it so short, it looked like little more than a shadow. He was wearing his dress uniform. The dark green jacket and olive green shirt and dark tie one. His hat was tucked under his left arm.

She undid the chain and turned the latch and opened the door. "Tim, how are you?" She hesitated, unsure if she was supposed to salute or not. She did anyway.

He saluted her back. "I'm sorry to barge in on you like this, Linda. Can I come in?"

"Of course," she said. She stepped back to let him in, then closed it and locked it behind him. She'd lived there a year and there were still boxes stacked next to the couch that she hadn't unpacked. There were textbooks and photocopied newspaper articles and rough drafts of term papers stacked everywhere. "I'm sorry about the mess."

He looked around the living room and kitchen area. There were two windows high up on the wall with blades of grass sticking up over the bottom frame. "It must stay cool down here in the summer, being beneath the ground," he said.

"It's not bad. It's cheap."

"No hassle of worrying about anything breaking down, though. I wish I could just call the landlord when my roof starts leaking."

"Do you want some coffee or anything?"

"No, I'm fine. I'm actually here on official business."

"Is that why you got all dressed up?" She sat down on the couch and curled her legs up under herself. "I'm not re-enlisting, if that's what you're about to ask."

He sat down on the couch next to her. "I came to talk to you about Jerry."

"No. My answer is no, and that's final. The papers are already signed, Tim. I'm not backing down this time."

"Hang on."

"No, you hang on. That man put me through hell. I stood by his side and begged him to get help, but what did he do instead? He went back over there for another combat tour. You people won't be satisfied until I'm dead. Is that what you want?"

"That's not what I meant," he said. "I'm sorry to have to tell you this, but Jerry was killed in action this morning."

She stopped moving.

Tim ran his hand across the top of his head, giving her time to process it.

"How?" she asked.

"He was searching a house for a high-value target and the bad guy was hiding in the back. Jerry got hit in the chest and didn't make it."

"I'm sorry to hear that," Linda said.

"Are you all right?"

"He died doing what he loved."

"Okay," Tim said. "Listen, since you're still technically married, there's some paperwork that needs to be filled out. There's money too, since he was killed in action."

"Send it to his mother. I don't want to be involved with any of it."

"You're his legal next of kin, Linda."

"I already signed the divorce papers."

"Well, it isn't through the court yet, so it doesn't mean shit." He brushed his pants leg and looked at the stack of textbooks on the table. "It's a hundred grand. Tax-free."

"So what?"

"So take the money. Use it to pay for grad school. Be smart."

"You honestly think I want one single penny from his death?"

"I honestly think he'd want you to have it and finish what you started. He loved you. He really sucked at it, but he did love you. If death gives us the chance to examine our lives free of all the, I don't know, whatever the hell he had wrong with his mind, then yeah. He'd want you to have it." Tim fit his hat on his head before standing up. "The paperwork will come in the mail. If you need any help filling it out, just call me."

"I will. Thanks for coming over. I know you could have sent someone else."

"I mean it. Anytime."

"I know."

After he left she leaned her head back on the couch and looked up at the ceiling. She rubbed the inside of her ring finger with the pad of her thumb. It still felt bare to the touch. She hadn't grown used to there not being a band of warm metal wrapped there. The ring itself was sitting at the bottom of an old water jug in the corner of her bedroom under a year's worth of spare change.

"Okay, a quick disclaimer before we show you the next slide. These are the crime scene photos from Anton Ola's first victim. They've been edited to cover up anything too sensitive, but there is still a fair amount of blood in the background." The FBI agent looked around the class, waiting for permission to go on.

Dr. Shorn held up her hand and said, "Anyone who thinks they can't deal with this, please avert your eyes. Self-care is the first step to providing care for others."

The agent clicked the remote and the screen behind his head lit up with the image of a young white woman. There was a black bar over her eyes to conceal her identity. A large black square covered most of her torso. She was lying on a kitchen floor. The linoleum around her was smeared with blood. It looked like she'd rolled around in it before rolling over on her side and dying.

"This was in a row home in Northeast Philadelphia. For whatever reason, historically there aren't many serial killers on the East Coast, if you don't count Florida. I do not count Florida. If you told me I had to find a serial killer somewhere in the United States, and I had absolutely no other information to go on, I'd tell you that it's most likely going to be in Florida and it's happening near a Walmart. That's some FBI humor, if you couldn't guess. Still pretty true though."

He clicked the remote to take them to the next photograph. There were audible gasps from the students sitting near her. Whoever had placed the black square had not aligned it properly. This woman was flat on her back with her legs splayed open. The flaps of her stomach were on either side of her waist like a dissected frog pinned to a foam board in some high school biology class.

"This is the second Blue Worm homicide. This was an alleyway in Kensington. For anyone who doesn't know, that's a real bad part of the city. Lots of drug murders and shootings. Not usually anything like this, though."

Linda raised her hand. "Were both women prostitutes?"

"The first one wasn't. She was a housewife. This one was a crackhead. I'm sure she prostituted herself, but that was just one of the thousand things a crackhead will do to get money. Not your typical prostitute victim of this kind of crime, if that's what you mean, though. No."

Linda made several quick notes and raised her hand again. "Why were they called the Blue Worm homicides?"

"Did I say that?" He tapped himself on the forehead with the remote. "My apologies. Disregard that." He clicked the remote. "This is Anton Ola's third victim." He looked at the class with one eyebrow raised. "See any differences?"

The victim was dead in the street, her body twisted and broken. Behind her, a station wagon with a crumpled front end and blood smeared across its white hood. It looked like an accident scene with fire truck and ambulances in the background. There were police officers in the photograph dressed in black uniforms, not Philly blue.

"This is Norristown, PA," the agent said. "Markley Street, to be exact. Norristown is no stranger to murders. That place is a dumpster fire, to be honest. But for all intents and purposes, this looked like nothing more than a regular struck pedestrian." He stepped away from the screen and used the remote's laser pointer to aim at the victim's stomach. He drew a neon line up and down the curvature of her stomach and said, "Except for one thing. She's pregnant."

He clicked back to the second victim and said, "So was she."

He clicked back to the third one and said, "And so was she."

The next screen showed Anton Ola, a bald, scared-looking man, being stuffed into a police car in front of a field of news cameras and reporters. Surrounding Ola were special agents in suits, detectives in windbreakers that said HOMICIDE, Pennsylvania State Police troopers in wide-brimmed Smokey Bear hats, and the mayor.

He admired the picture of Ola's arrest, then glanced back at the class. "You see all those people in the picture from all those agencies? Not one person there had anything to do with figuring out who the killer was. Nobody from any of those units, even. It all came down to one regular detective in the city, assigned to the Northeast division. He wasn't from Homicide, he wasn't from the district attorney's office, he wasn't even from any of the task forces. Just a regular detective who worked cases for his district, and he figured it the hell out."

Linda raised her hand again. "How?"

"It wasn't public knowledge that the first two victims were pregnant. Norristown PD had no reason to suspect their victim was related to the other two, so when a pregnant woman got killed by a car, it was just chalked up to a local tragedy. This detective took it upon himself to drive out to Montgomery County and canvas the neighborhood where it happened, just talking to people sitting on their stoops. An old lady said she saw the victim being chased down the street. She lost sight of them in the alleyway, but she heard the car crash on Markley, and saw him come running back out of the alley and jump into a purple van."

"Did she get the tag?"

"She got the first two digits," the agent said. "That's all it took. Anton Ola was in custody before he could ever hurt anyone ever again."

"Our main focus is to try and understand the mind of someone like Mr. Ola, maybe not so much the mechanics of how he was captured," Dr. Shorn said. "Can we move forward into the study of him that was done by Cambridge?"

"Sure," he said, clicking through several more slides.

Linda raised her hand again. "What was her name, sir? The one in Norristown."

"The victim? I can't remember off the top of my head," he said.

Dr. Shorn looked across the room at Linda, wanting her to shut up. Some of the people in the class around her were looking at her as well.

"You're very interested in this," the agent said. "If this whole psychology thing doesn't work out, you want me to get you an application to the Bureau?"

People laughed, and Linda did as well. "No, that's fine. I just grew up near Markley Street, that's all. I was wondering if I knew her."

And then they were quiet.

She had not seen him since she left Norristown and was not sure how she'd react when she did. There was inch-thick glass between them and several prison guards on either side of the divider. They'd searched her at the entrance. She'd known they would, and was glad for it, because otherwise, she might have tried to bring in a gun.

In basic training, she'd learned how to use pistols and automatic rifles. She'd always scored high. She'd never told anyone that the paper targets were Antoine.

Two guards led him through the door into the visitor section. He was shorter than she remembered. His skin was ashy now, like gray dust. He was balding. Strange that her most vivid memories of him were of him constantly brushing his hair with a flat brush he always kept in his back pocket. She didn't remember the specific events of him molesting her. She'd used the trick she'd learned when it happened before. The trick of going to a far-away place and leaving behind whatever was happening to her body.

The anger came from the betrayal. Her mother's boyfriend

and her teacher had been adults. Linda knew she could not have fought back if she'd tried. They used their authority over her and physical strength over her to do what they wanted, and she'd learned it was better to lie there motionless and pretend nothing was happening than to fight back.

She and Antoine had grown up together. They'd played together, and listened to music together. He'd protected her around the neighborhood. She trusted him so much that she told him what had happened with the other men. He was the first and only person she did tell.

"I couldn't move," she'd said.

"What do you mean, like they held you down?"

"It was like my mind went to some dark place and didn't come back until it was over."

"Every time?"

"The second they start touching me."

In a way, she fantasized he'd go beat the shit out of them and be her protector. Instead, that night he crawled into bed next to her and stuck his hands between her legs. When she tried to push him away, he put his hand around her throat and said, "Go to your dark place and forget all about this, or else."

Now, Antoine sat down opposite her and picked up the phone next to the protective glass. He waited for her to pick up the phone on her side. "Hey, Lin. I'm glad you came. You're all grown up now."

She didn't speak.

"I didn't think you'd come."

"I came to ask you what the fuck you wanted."

"Just to talk. Had a lot of time to think about things while I was in here. They've got this therapy group I've been going to."

"You? You been going to therapy?"

"Yeah. It's nothing big. This counselor comes in once a week and a bunch of us sit around and talk about stuff. Really helped me see a lot of things."

"Like what?"

"Like how much I fucked up. How bad I hurt the people in my family. My mama and grandmama. And you."

"I'm fine," she said.

He frowned against the phone. "I heard you went into the army and married some white dude and now you're in school. Doing real well for yourself. What are you in school for?"

"I'm just in school."

"All right. You got any kids?"

Her fingers clenched the phone receiver so hard, she thought its plastic housing might crack. "Why, you want to know if I have any daughters?"

She wanted anger back from him. For him to rise up in his chair so she could scream at him until the guards came and dragged them both away. So he'd be so enraged he'd fight those guards and they'd kick the shit out of him then dump his broken body back inside his prison cell. Instead, his mouth opened and he let out a puff of air like he'd been punched in the stomach. Tears came into his eyes and he covered his face with the phone.

She watched his shoulders shake as he wept. The guards near the door watched also. Some of the prisoners walking past looked over. A few of them laughed.

"This punk ass over here crying like a bitch," someone said behind her.

Antoine wiped his face on his arm, leaving a long, wet trail of slime. He kept his eyes closed as he pressed the phone against his face once more. "I'm sorry. I'm sorry for what I did. I don't expect you to forgive me. I just wanted you to know it's true."

"So why did you do it?"

"I don't know. We talk about it in therapy a lot." He wiped his face again and opened his eyes but couldn't look at her. "It had happened to me a few times and I guess I did that shit to you to prove I wasn't—I don't know—it don't matter."

"Who?" Linda said. He asked her what she meant, and she said, "Who did it to you?"

"Your mom's boyfriend. Same dude that did it to you. He was doing it to most of the kids."

"I never knew that," she said.

He shrugged and looked over his shoulder at the people standing around him, eyeing them. His knees were bouncing nervously as he held the phone. "Anyway, everybody's got some kind of sob story in this place. Lots of excuses here and nobody guilty of shit. I just wanted you to know I apologize. Thank you for letting me say it."

He hung up the phone and signaled for the guards. He was led back through the door and gone a long time before she moved again.

Linda placed her keys, purse, watch, and the metal pen in her breast pocket, in the plastic tray on the counter in front of her. The guard wrote down each item. "Do you have any money on you?"

"Just what's in my purse." She patted her pockets to double-check. "Nothing on me."

"No weapons or drugs?"

"No."

"Phones, pagers, or recording devices of any kind?"

"No, nothing."

The guard pointed at a blue sign on the wall behind him. "You'll be going through that metal detector. It's a criminal offense to bring contraband or the below listed items into a Pennsylvania State correctional facility. Doing so will result in you being arrested and charged. Do you understand?"

"I understand."

The guard passed her a visitor's badge and told her to keep it displayed at all times. "Pass through that metal detector and stand on the other side in front of the door."

Linda clipped the badge to her shirt and walked through the machine and it did not beep. She looked back at the guard. He reached under the counter and pressed a button. The thick metal door in front of her clicked and the guard said, "Go on through."

The floor and hallway were fashioned from smooth, polished, concrete. Both were gray. The floor and ceiling were darker shades than the walls. No doors or windows. She followed the tunnel to a set of metal bars with a hinged gate in the center of them and stopped. She wondered if anyone monitoring the security cameras could see her waiting. An inmate walked past her pushing a tray of dishes. He was draped in what looked like a plastic from a garbage bag. His afro was covered in plastic. His shoes were covered in plastic booties. His legs swished together as he walked.

When she was growing up, people in her neighborhood would cut armholes and head holes in garbage bags and wear them when it rained. She remembered her fat neighbor shuffling along the sidewalk in her bedroom slippers, with dirty water going over her bare ankles, draped in the largest size Hefty bags they sold.

A group of inmates walked past Linda in a single file, all of them dressed in dull orange jumpsuits and plain white sneakers. They looked at her but did not speak.

The gate clicked. Linda pulled it open and stepped into the hallway. There were red lines painted on either side of the floor, forming narrow lanes that ran the length of the wall. Another group of prisoners was coming toward her, this time led by a guard. She saw that all of the prisoners stayed inside the red line closest to them, but the guard stayed out of it and walked in the middle. She stepped out of their way. "Excuse me," she said. "Can you tell me where to find Dr. Harmon's office?"

"Ask at the main station," the guard said. "Go down till you see it."

There was nothing but gray tunnel in either direction. She waited for the prisoners to pass and moved to the other side of the hall, safely behind the opposite red line, out of reach.

"Prisoners only in the red zone!" a voice barked from behind her. She turned to see a guard leading another group of prisoners from the opposite direction, headed her way. Linda stepped into the middle section. The prisoners laughed quietly as they walked past. "Where are you headed?" the guard asked.

"The main station."

"Follow us after we go past and stay outside of the red zone."

She did as she was told. As they reached the main hub, the red lines stopped and prisoners roamed the area freely. There were interview rooms along the hall for prisoners to meet with their attorneys. They were small rooms with two plastic chairs and a table bolted into the floor. There was a well-lit barber shop where inmates used electric clippers on other inmates, only able to cut their hair short, very short, or shaved, because they weren't allowed to have any scissors. Opposite the barbershop was an empty lunchroom. She could smell beef and tomato sauce cooking inside.

Noise filled the hub. Voices all around her echoed off the concrete walls. The wheels of a cart carrying a stack of empty lunch trays squeaked so loudly she winced.

In the middle of the hub was the guard station. An octagon-shaped, walled-off structure, with shaded windows. Inside, she could see computer monitors and computer consoles that blinked green and red. She saw the shadows of several guards moving within. One came to the window in front of her and the speaker next to the window crackled. "Can I help you?"

She had to lean forward to hear it over the noise in the hallway. "I'm Linda Shelley. I'm here to meet with Dr. Harmon."

"He's in admin. Go around to your left and take the ten o'clock corridor. What I mean by that is, go past the first hallway on the—"

"I know which one you meant. Thank you."

She went around the station and passed the hallway to her left. That was the nine o'clock. She'd come down the six. The next major hallway was the twelve. In between was a more narrow corridor marked ADMINISTRATION ONLY. There were no lines on the floor and the walls were painted canary yellow.

A guard sat on a plastic chair ten feet down the hall, leaned back with his arms folded across his stomach and his feet crossed. His eyes flicked toward her badge, making sure it was there, and then he went back to staring at the corridor. "Hello," Linda said.

"How you feel?"

There were offices on either side of the hallway. Dark wooden doors set within the yellow, and no windows on either side of any of them. She came to the last door on her left, marked DR. DANIEL HARMON, MENTAL HEALTH SERVICES. She knocked on the door. "Dr. Harmon?"

"Come in."

She put her head into the office. "I'm Linda Shelley."

"Welcome!" Harmon was a middle-aged, burly man, with a full gray beard. He wore a purple sweater vest over a striped blue button-down shirt, under a brown blazer. He glanced at the time on his computer monitor. "You're early."

"It's a habit from the army," she said. "Early is on time and on time is late."

"You're former military?"

"Yes, sir. Were you?"

"God, no." He smiled. "Please, grab a seat. You know, I've never actually had a student ask to do their supervised visitation here, before. I read your essay on why you want to study in this environment, though, and I have to say, this is a breeding ground for the type of trauma you're interested in. Most of the people here have PTSD of some sort, and I'm not just talking about the inmates. You know, I once gave a psychological test to a volunteer police officer in Florida. They have them, down south, you know. People who are given guns and badges and uniforms and they go out and be cops but don't get paid for it."

"I never heard of that," Linda said.

"Florida has them. Louisiana has them. Probably other places too. Anyway, this guy had been a volunteer police officer for five years and decided he wanted to make it his full-time job, so he took the written test and passed all the interviews with flying colors and got hired. They send him to me and I give him the psych and he fails. He fails bad. Like lock him up in the funny farm on the spot, bad."

"You're kidding," Linda said. "And he'd been carrying a gun all that time?"

"Here's the thing. He never told me he was a cop for five years. I thought he was a brand-new hire. I based my whole test on him having all the baseline normalcies and mores of a regular, upstanding citizen. When I found out, I retested him, and he passed easily."

"What changed?" she asked.

"My scoring. You can't score someone who's been exposed to

that level of humanity the same way you do everyone else. The same as you can't score any of the correctional officers or staff here the way you do anyone else. You have to remember, they're all in prison too. They just get to leave for a few hours each day. You have to be careful of that during your time here."

Linda laughed. "There's nothing these corrections officers can do to me that men in the army didn't try. I can handle myself, no problem."

"I wasn't telling you to be careful around them. That just goes without saying. I was telling you to be careful about what it does to you."

She closed her folder and set it on the floor next to her chair. "That's all for today, gentlemen. I'd like to thank each of you for sharing. Please remember to write down anything you want to bring up at our next session. Let's close out with our breathing and affirmations."

She laid her hands on her thighs and sat up straight. She closed her eyes and took a deep breath and held it in her chest.

The seven prisoners sitting in a circle around her did the same.

"I'm in control of myself. I'm in control of what I say and do," she said. They repeated the words as she spoke them. "My mind is a train station, and my thoughts are just trains, passing through. If I find myself on the wrong one, I can just get off, anytime I choose." They repeated the words as she spoke them.

She opened her eyes. "Thank you so much."

The prisoners stood up to leave. Linda grabbed the chair nearest her and slid it against the wall, under a long row of windows. When she turned to pick up another one, one of the prisoners was standing behind her with two chairs at his side. "I thought I'd help you clean up."

"That's very nice of you, Miguel, but I'll be fine. It's time for you to go to lunch."

"I'm not too hungry." He was taller than she was by a foot or more. *Jesus* was tattooed across the top of his forehead in cursive, along with two large black crucifixes beneath each of his eyes. They were cover-up tattoos. The black teardrops he'd once worn, for the length of his prison sentence and the people in his family who'd been killed and the people he'd killed, were now hidden beneath each cross. The cursive scrawl of the word *Satan* on his forehead could still be seen underneath the word *Jesus*. Miguel said he liked it that way. It was his way of showing that the power of Christ had overcome the devil.

He stacked the chairs against the wall and she bent over to pick up her folder. When she stood up, his eyes were fixed on her. "I wanted to ask, are you married?"

"Miguel, as your counselor, it's not appropriate for me to talk about my personal life. You know that."

"I bet you're not married," he said. "Otherwise your husband would never let you in here with us animals."

"I don't think you're animals and I am ending this conversation now, Miguel. Go to lunch. I hear they're serving hot roast beef today."

After Miguel left, she collected her things and opened the door. The hallways were filled with prisoners making their way to the cafeteria. Lunch was a main event for them. It helped mark the passage of yet another day. For some, it was a significant step toward freedom. Short-timers, with only a handful of days left before they'd go home. They each knew how many more lunches, how many more hours in the yard, how many more times they'd have to wake up in prison before going home.

It had been the same in the army. People coming to the end of their contract talked about all the things they were going to do once they were free. All the places they'd visit. For them, the army was like a leash around their neck, only ever letting them get so far away before yanking them back. The bizarre thing was, the ones who complained the loudest were the ones who most often reenlisted. The money to reenlist was too much to pass up.

Just like in prison, many of them were institutionalized, just in different ways. For the prisoners, the prison was the most structure they'd ever had in their lives. What a sad fact, she thought. For the soldiers, especially kids like her, the army was their family. Maybe their only family.

She'd done studies on soldiers, cops, gang members, and now

prisoners. All of them possessed the same tribal instinct. We are This and the rest are Other.

She turned down the admin hall and said hello to the guard as she walked past. "How you feeling?" he said, the same as he said it every other time she walked past, without looking at her.

Dr. Harmon's door was shut but unlocked. She checked her watch. He was on his lunch break. She was allowed to use the office computer for her schoolwork, and it would not be unusual for her to do research on the prisoners who'd signed up for her program. It would be unusual for her to pull up files on anyone else. All activity on the computer was monitored and recorded, or so they said, she thought.

She logged into the prison database and did a generic search, starting with last names that began with each letter of the alphabet. Her explanation, if asked, was going to be that someone new had asked her to participate, and she wasn't sure how to spell his name. She did a few cursory searches and scrolled down just enough to make it look believable, until she came to the *R*'s. It didn't take long. The man she was looking for, the one she'd come to that specific prison to meet and study, was near the top.

Her next session was not for another hour. Plenty of time, she thought.

She went down the corridor toward the main station, past the cafeteria and barbershop, and down the three o'clock corridor. No one needed to tell her to stay outside of the red zones any longer. Some of the prisoners greeted her and she said hello back. There was one room on the right side of the corridor, almost as large as the cafeteria, with windows that had been obscured by racks and racks of books. She opened the door and went in. The prison library was completely silent. Strange, after the cacophony of the hallways just outside the room. Its blue industrial carpet was worn but clean. There were tables and chairs, all mismatched, set up along the floor. All the chairs were pushed in. It was empty except for the prisoner sitting at the desk.

The man looked different than she'd expected. His head was

shaved and he wore a goatee. He looked the same as many of the other prisoners, and she thought that was intentional. He watched her come in, then went back to the book he was reading.

"It's so quiet in here," she said.

"Well, it is a library," he said.

She stood near the front of the desk. "What are you reading?"

He held up the book to show her the cover.

"*Accounting For Canadians For Dummies.*" She raised an eyebrow. "Are you planning on moving to Canada and becoming an accountant?"

"All our books are donated. This came in last month, and it's the only thing I haven't read yet."

He went back to reading and she turned to look at what books were on the shelves. Several variations of the Bible and other religious texts. The biography of a vaudeville performer. How-to books that looked like they were printed in the seventies. Half an encyclopedia set. Thick paperback books with no cover and nothing but the glue on the binding of the spine. She glanced back at him. "Can I ask you a question?"

He turned a page in his book and kept reading.

"I'm Linda Shelley. I work in the psychology department here. You're Jacob Rein, the police detective, aren't you? Don't worry, I won't tell anyone. I know the guards sure won't. They probably love you for what you did to Krissing. A lot of the prisoners too, from I've heard about their feelings toward child rapists."

He glanced at the clock on the wall behind her and closed his book. "The library is closed."

He waited for her to her to leave before he flicked off the lights and pulled the door shut behind him.

She showed the paper bag to the guard and said, "Do you want to go through these, or can I just take it through the metal detector?"

"What is it?" He peered in and scowled. "Books?"

"I'm making a donation to the library."

"None of these mutts can read the ABC's let alone any of this. Just go through."

She carried the bag past the main station and made a right instead of her usual left. She clenched the bag to her chest tight with one hand so it didn't fall and opened the door with her other to let herself in.

She set the bag down on the desk in front of Jacob Rein and put her hands on her hips. "I heard you all were in need of some books."

Rein picked the first book off the top of the bag and looked at the cover. It was a red softback with a bear holding a balloon. "*The Tao of Pooh?*"

"I read all the rules online," she said. "No hardcovers. No romance novels. Nothing with weapons on the covers."

"No textbooks," he added.

"Shoot. I sell all my textbooks back to the library. Are you kidding? Those things are expensive as hell."

"Thank you for your donation," he said. He put the bag on the floor next to his desk and picked *Accounting For Dummies For Canadians* back up and continued to read it.

"You're seriously still going to read that? I brought you real books."

"I'm almost finished with this one. I feel like it's going to get good any minute now."

She laughed and he didn't, but he did almost smile.

She came back for him the next day and was pleased to see him reading one of the books she'd brought. "This is starting to become a habit," he said without looking up.

"I was hoping we could talk."

"You can't find other people to talk to?"

"None in this place."

"I'd say it's odd, then, that you chose to work here."

"Listen, I just want to ask you a few questions. A short, short, interview, I promise."

"I see," he said. "You want to ask me about Walter."

"Actually, I'm more interested in you. They mentioned your name in the Cambridge study on Anton Ola. You were the detective who figured out he killed the woman in Norristown, weren't you?"

"Doesn't sound familiar."

"Did you know he was sexually molested by multiple family members growing up? So was Walter Krissing."

"What a shame." He licked his thumb and turned to the next page on his book.

"I've heard Anton Ola referred to as The Blue Worm several times but it's not in any of the paperwork and no one will say why. It's like an inside joke or something. Will you at least tell me why they called him that?"

"I have no idea. Please leave."

"I just want to ask about your work with—"

He slammed the book shut so hard, it sounded throughout the quiet library. He closed his eyes and went still. When he opened them again, he said, "My work has ended."

"Well, mine hasn't," she said.

"Is your work annoying me?"

"My work is preventing people like Walter Krissing and Anton Ola from ever existing. I want to figure out how to identify them from the earliest stages, to stop them before they hurt anyone."

"Not possible."

"What do you mean it's not possible?"

"Because a lot of kids are abused and molested. Only one in a hundred thousand, maybe a million, of them will grow up to be a Krissing or Ola. There aren't enough indicators early enough to stop them before they develop a fetish for killing."

"Then I'll figure out what to do with them after they've been identified and make sure they never hurt anyone again. Not too long ago, society viewed schizophrenia as demonic possession. They thought exorcism was the proper treatment. All I'm saying is that maybe if we tried a new approach, we could save lives. I'm asking you to help me."

Rein leaned back in his chair and considered her more carefully. Reading her. Whatever decision he needed to make about her, it was over in seconds. He went back to his book. "Do yourself a favor and stay as far away from these people as possible."

"I'm not leaving until you help me, so I can help them."

"Anton Ola thought alien worms were infesting the human

species with their own kind. He was convinced that pregnant women had been abducted and implanted with worms. It was actually the women's intestines. He cut their stomachs open and pulled out the fetuses then ripped all of their intestines out and chopped them to pieces. Have you ever seen intestines when they're emerging from the human body?"

"No."

"That's why they called him The Blue Worm."

"What did he do with the fetuses?" Linda whispered.

"He ate them," Rein said.

The muscles in her jaw tightened. "How interesting," she said. Rein smirked and went back to his book.

"How did you wind up in Norristown looking for Anton Ola?"

"I tried to tell Homicide they needed to go, but no one believed me, so I went."

"Were they mad when you proved them wrong?"

"Very. It ruined my career in the city."

"Can you tell me why you felt strongly enough about catching The Blue Worm that you risked your career?"

"I think we've talked enough."

"That's my last question. Honest."

Rein looked at her over the top of his book. "I was married at the time and my wife was eight months pregnant with our son. So was the first victim. I guess you could say I took it personally."

"I suppose I would have too," she said. "That must have been hard for you to see."

He didn't answer.

"Fine, I'll go," she said. "But just so you know, you're wrong. People like Anton Ola and Walter Krissing can be helped. Just because no one has figured out how to do it yet doesn't mean it can't be done. I'm going to do it."

"You go ahead and do it," Rein said.

"I will."

"You know what?" Rein said. "I think maybe you're right."

"Of course I am. I'm also a lot of fun to hang out with and talk to. See how much better this is than just sitting here by yourself all day?"

Rein smiled at her. "You know, all this talk about the old days reminds me of some good stories."

"Oh really?" She tucked her hair behind her ear. She liked the way he looked when he smiled. "Tell me one."

"You won't be bored?"

"Not at all!"

"Okay," Rein said. "This is the weirdest call I ever had. I was still on patrol, right out of the academy. You know how people rescue dogs?"

"Of course."

"Well, this lady rescued boa constrictors."

"Say what? That's different. Was she taking them from laboratories that experimented on snakes or something?"

"No, from houses where people bought them as exotic pets and couldn't take care of them. The snakes started getting so big, the owners would release them into the Pennypack River and it would cause a huge commotion. So she'd go around and rescue boas from people who couldn't take care of them. She must have had a dozen giant snakes in her house."

"So what was the call you got there?"

"This part's comical. Ready? Her neighbors found her on her front yard with one of her boa constrictors wrapped around her entire head."

"Oh my God! That's insane. Did you have to pull it off of her?"

"Eventually." Rein's eyes narrowed on her. "There was no rush. She was already dead."

"What?"

"It attacked her at feeding time. She ran through the house and managed to get outside, hoping someone would see her and get help. But it was too late."

"That's awful," Linda whispered.

"Her neighbor saw her pounding it on the sides with her fists, her legs kicking like crazy, but then she just went limp. Can you imagine? Trying to breathe against all that slithering flesh while it constricts around your throat, your face? It must feel like steel cables cinching down on you. You die listening to the sound of your own skull cracking. See, she rescued these snakes. She fed them. She loved them. Then one killed her."

Rein got up from the desk and headed toward the door.

"My mind is a train station, and my thoughts are just trains, passing through," she said in unison with the group of prisoners seated around her. Their voices filled the meeting room. "If I find myself on the wrong one, I can just get off, anytime I choose."

Linda opened her eyes and pressed her hands together to thank them. "Today was an excellent session. Everyone did wonderful. Thank you so much."

Miguel put his hands together and bowed his head back at her. She dismissed the group and all the prisoners stood up to leave. Miguel stood up with the others, but hung back as the rest filed past him. He picked up two of the chairs and carried them to the wall before she could stop him.

"Thank you, Miguel," Linda said. "But you know you have to go when I dismiss you."

"I know," he said. "I just wanted to show you something." He reached into his pocket and pulled out a small and intricately folded butterfly made from purple paper. "My grandfather was Japanese. He used to do these paper cuttings and sell them at festivals. He taught me origami. I forgot most of it, but I've been practicing in here." His fingers trembled as he held it out for her to take.

"It's beautiful," Linda said. She turned it over in the palm of her hand to inspect it. "You're very talented."

"You think?"

"Thank you for showing it to me," she said and tried to hand it back to him.

"I made it for you."

"I can't accept anything from you, Miguel. You know that."

"It's a secret. Nobody will know, and it's just paper, so it won't set off any of the alarms or anything. See? I thought it through."

"I really appreciate it, but I can't."

He winked at her as he backed toward the door.

"I could get fired and never be able to come back here. I'm serious, I can't accept this."

The crucifixes tattooed on his face grew straight and rigid. "Then throw it the fuck out then. Fuck it."

"That is enough!"

"Fuck you, black bitch."

She aimed her finger at the door. "Get out of this room, right now! I will have you written up."

He stood between her and the door. A hundred people in the hallway behind him walked past. None of them could hear her over the noise in the corridor. He threw his arms wide. "You think I care, *pinche idiota?*"

"Miguel," she said. "Listen to me."

He grabbed his crotch with one hand and shook it. "*Métetelo por el culo, puta.*"

There were cameras in the corners of the room. They were monitored by the guards in the main station. If they weren't too short on manpower to staff the main station that day, she thought. And if they weren't too distracted by all the prisoners in the hall to notice.

Physically, it was in her to fight. Her hands tightened into fists. She had the ability to scratch and claw and bite and scream her head off until the guards came rushing in like a sea of gray uniforms and batons.

Her mind betrayed her, as it always did. It threatened to drag her off to that same faraway place she'd found as a child. That distant island in the dark sea that wrapped its sickly tentacles around her and would not let her act or move or cry out for help. In the end, all she did was stand there, staring at him, unable to move.

Miguel clicked his tongue against his teeth. He pulled the door open and stepped into the stream of prisoners rushing past. He grinned at her, the corners of his mouth touching the underside of each long black crucifix and then vanished into the sea of orange jumpsuits.

* * *

Rein didn't look up from the book on his desk when she walked into the library. It was an old thesaurus she'd donated. The book was nearly a thousand pages and heavier than a brick. Rein licked the tip of his thumb and turned the page. "I've always loved old reference books," he said. "If you have any others, I'll take them."

Her lips trembled. She ran her fingers across her forehead to move the wet strands of hair away from her face. She took a quick, sharp, breath, and said, "Okay." Another breath. "I'll check."

Rein closed the book. "What's wrong?"

The word *Nothing* squeaked out of her as she fanned her face. Sweat was coming down the small of her back. She was shivering.

Rein came around the desk and took her by the elbow. He guided her into his chair and helped her sit down. "Something happened."

"It's nothing," she said. "I'm fine."

He went to the library door and peered through it. There was nothing but prisoners and guards outside. He went back to the desk and picked up a Styrofoam cup and carried it to the water fountain next to the entrance. He filled the cup and carried it back to the desk. "Drink," he said.

She wrapped her hands around the cup and raised it to her mouth, spilling some of it on her chin before it reached her lips. "Shit," she said. She blinked sweat out of her eyes and wiped her face with her palm. "I think I'm having a panic attack."

Rein opened one of the desk drawers and found a roll of paper towels. He ripped off a few sheets and dampened them with water. "Press this against your forehead and breathe." He walked over to the fountain and refilled her cup.

She held the wet towels to her forehead with one hand and reached for the cup of water with the other. She sipped it and set it down. Her breathing was getting more regular. "Thank you," she said.

"Tell me what happened."

"It was nothing."

He peeled the wet towels off her forehead and tossed them into the trash. He pulled off several more sheets and trickled less water than before, just enough to make them moist, and handed them back to her. "I've been thinking about what you said."

"Which time?"

"About men who grow up to be like Walter Krissing and Anton Ola. You won't find any answers here. I may have someone you can talk to, though."

She tossed the paper towels aside and grabbed her notepad and pen. She laid them on the desk and said, "Tell me."

"Tucker Pennington," Rein said. "He called himself The Master. I arrested him when he was a juvenile. He's a sadist, but he hasn't killed. At least, not yet."

There was excitement in her hand as she wrote. Excitement in her voice too. "Where is he?"

"Sunshine Estates."

"What is that? It sounds like some kind of retirement community."

"It's a psychiatric facility where they house certain offenders under a civil commitment."

"Will Pennington talk to me?"

"Of course not."

"So why are you telling me about him?"

"To prove to you I'm right."

Linda smirked. "Just for that, I'm going to get him to talk. I'm going to study the shit out of him and write a big paper and get on TV."

"Good luck," Rein said.

"What did he say to you during your interview with him?"

Rein rocked his head back and forth, listening to his neck crack. "I never gave him the chance. It was not my best night. Just one of my many mistakes."

"No worries, I'll interview him enough for the two of us." She stamped her pen to dot the period at the end of her last sentence. "This is exactly what I've been looking for. Thank you so much."

She came up from the seat to where he was standing, their faces only a few inches apart. She breathed him in. The prison soap and shampoo and laundry detergent had no fragrance. There was nothing except the scent of him.

"What are you doing?" he said, but he did not pull away from her.

She touched his face. She ran the tips of her nails down the sides of his cheek, and his hands came around her waist. He found the way around her hips toward the high, rounded curves of her backside.

She heard the library door swing closed before she realized there was someone standing in the entrance, watching them. Rein yanked his hands away from her and spun around.

Miguel sneered at them. "So now I know everything you said to me was bullshit."

"Listen to me," she said. "It's not like that."

"You telling me I don't see what I see? You think I'm stupid because I'm not like this faggot surrounded by books, huh?" Miguel's hand dipped into his right front pocket and emerged holding a jagged piece of metal. The handle was wrapped with masking tape. Its blade had been sharpened against the prison's concrete floors until its edges and point gleamed. He aimed the shank at Rein's face. "*Ya te quedaste, pinche joto.*"

Miguel circled around the desk toward Rein and Linda shouted for help. It was useless. There were too many people in the hallway outside. Too much noise.

"Guards!" she cried.

"You shut the fuck up, whore! I'll cut out your fucking heart after I cut his throat. See if you even have one."

Rein picked the thesaurus up from the desk and held it against his chest with both hands.

Miguel waved the blade in front of Rein's face. "You going to read to me, pussy?"

Rein smacked him in the mouth with the book. The corner of the book's spine caught Miguel with his mouth open and impaled his lower lip on his bottom front teeth. Rein grabbed Miguel's wrist with one hand and struck him with the book again, this time on the side of the head. The impact sounded like a softball hitting the leather of a catcher's glove. Rein raised the book high in the air and brought it down on the same place, harder. Miguel's knees buckled. Rein snatched the shank away. He pressed the metal tip against the white meat in the corner of Miguel's eyeball. "Imagine being blind in prison."

"Get off of me!"

"I can't think of anything worse," Rein said. He ran the blade across Miguel's eyelashes. "They leave you in general population. There's nowhere else to put you."

Linda wrapped her hands around Rein's arm. She pulled at him, but his muscles were coiled tight. "Let him go, Jacob. That's enough."

Rein withdrew his forearm but kept the shank pressed against Miguel's face. Miguel slid sideways to get out from under it and rolled off the desk. He scrambled to his feet and ran for the door, throwing it open and racing down the hallway to get away.

Rein laid the shank down on the desk. He bent over and picked the thesaurus up from the floor and laid that on the desk as well. She reached for him, but he pulled away from her. "If you have good to do in the world, go do it, but leave this place and don't ever come back," he said. Then he walked away.

Dr. Linda Shelley had three small dark black growths under her right eye that looked like tiny moles.

They aren't moles, the dermatologist had told her. They're seborrheic keratosis. Nothing to worry about.

Can you remove them?

There's no need to, he'd said. It's just part of growing older.

She touched the moles with the tip of her finger, feeling how large they were. They weren't easy for anyone else to see. Someone would have to be close to her to even notice them. To really look into her face. That hadn't happened for a long time.

There was a knock on the door. "Come in," she said.

Mr. Darryl stuck his head in. He was dressed in an all-white uniform with a black leather belt. He had a bright white beard and wild, kinky, hair. "Morning, Dr. Shelley."

"Good morning, Mr. Darryl."

"You heard about them two boys fighting last night?"

"Which two boys were that?"

"Tucker Pennington, and that other one. The creepy white boy."

"I'm afraid you'll have to be more specific than that."

"What's his name." Mr. Darryl snapped his fingers and said, "Gregory Moon."

Linda picked up a pen and wrote both of their names down. "What were they fighting about?"

"Nobody say. All I heard was there was some kind of commotion in Pennington's room and they found him whooping on Moon. You ask me, Moon probably deserved it."

Linda kept writing. "Would you mind bringing one of them to my office, Mr. Darryl?"

"I'll go see who I can find. Moon might still be in the infirmary. Be okay with me if he stays there awhile."

"I'll take whoever you can find, Mr. Darryl," Linda said.

The door closed and Linda opened the drawer in her desk to pull out a fresh notepad. She laid it on her desk and wrote the time and date and Report of Disturbance Between Patients on the top line. There was another knock, and Mr. Darryl opened the door and said, "I brought you Mr. Pennington, Dr. Shelley."

"Ah, yes," Linda said. "Thank you, Mr. Darryl. Hello, Tucker. Please come in."

"Do you want me to stay?" Mr. Darryl asked.

"No, that won't be necessary. I'll call you when we're finished."

Mr. Darryl guided Tucker toward the nearest chair. Tucker's hairline was receding. The skin under his eyes sagged. He looked at her with the slow gaze of the overly-medicated.

There was something on his lower lip, either from lunch, or it had fallen out of his nose. He didn't notice it. She didn't mention it. Tucker watched her, staring as if he were trying to make sense of her. "Hello."

"Hello, Tucker." She pulled out his file. "How have you been this week?"

"Okay."

"That's good. The pastor says you've been a big help to him at the chapel this week."

"Yes."

"What else have you been doing this week?"

"Praying."

"Anything else?"

He squished his eyes together in thought. "Eating."

Shelley smiled gently. "Has anyone been bothering you?"

"No."

She pulled a report out of the file on her desk, looking it over before she spoke again. "The orderlies told me that Gregory Moon and you were fighting last night."

"No."

"Their report said he was found in your room and they heard screaming. When they came in, you were on top of him, punching his face."

Tucker shook his head in confusion. He touched the side of his head and tapped it with his fingers, each tap making a soft thud against the bone there. He rocked back and forth as he continued tapping and said, "Gregory is bad."

"How is he bad?" Shelley asked.

"He wants me to do bad things."

"What kind of bad things did he ask you to do?"

"I told him no. She told me to tell him no."

"She? Was there a girl in the room with you?"

"No," he said, looking away.

Linda closed the file and slid it out of the way. She leaned her head back against her chair, eyes cast down at him. They'd drugged both him and Moon with super doses of phenothiazine and thioridazine since the incident. Talking any further was useless. Tucker clutched himself around the chest with both arms and rocked back and forth. "Do you remember what I told you when we first met, Tucker?"

"No."

"I told you I'd taken this job to meet you."

"Okay."

"That I wanted to help you."

"Okay."

"We've been doing this ever since I came here and you know what? It's always the same old thing. Nothing I say even matters, does it?"

"Okay."

"I could tell you at night I grow wings like an angel and fly around the sky."

"Okay."

"Because you and all these other people are really just nothing but goddamn fucking lunatics, right?"

"Okay."

Linda closed her eyes and took a deep breath. When she opened them, Tucker was picking his nose. He was really going for it. His right index finger was buried up to his knuckle. It was hardly the worst thing she'd seen during her interviews. Half of the patients liked to masturbate during their sessions. They could do it just talking to her, carrying on normal conversations. It had gotten so routine, she knew when to pass them tissues before they finished.

She pressed the button that called for the orderly. "Mr. Pennington is ready," she said.

Mr. Darryl arrived and helped Tucker to his feet. "Do you still want me to bring Gregory Moon, ma'am? He's out of the infirmary, they say."

"No," she said. I'll talk to him tomorrow, she thought. Or the next day. Or next week. Or never. It didn't matter. It was always the same. They were radios transmitting nothing but static. She'd run out her thread as far as she could carry it, and she knew it. Deep within, it was all for nothing. There were no answers to be found in the human mind. No solutions. Some people functioned and some were defective. Some had families and went to work and some thought aliens had implanted worms inside pregnant women. It was that simple. Everything else came down to pharmaceuticals. Trial and error, route experimentation, until you found the exact formulation to deal with that specific patient.

But if it ever stopped working, or the patient ever forgot to take their meds, it was back to square one.

She picked up the phone and dialed the number she'd written on her notepad. The same one she'd been looking at for three days. The phone rang, and the woman who answered said, "Vieira County Juvenile Detention Center."

"This is Dr. Linda Shelley," she said. "Can I speak to the director?"

"Yes, one moment please."

The phone rang once before it was picked up. "Linda!" the voice on the other end said. "I was starting to think I'd never hear from you."

"I gave it some serious thought," Linda said. "Five thousand dollars more and I'll accept the position."

8

*T*he woman with the half face entered the courtroom. Alexis Dole's remaining eye glared at everyone, wide and blue, as she walked down the aisle toward the witness stand. She glared at the ones who looked at her. She glared at the ones who looked away. Her other eye was nothing but an empty black socket surrounded by ruined flesh. Her scalp on that was side was bald from scarring. She wore the other half short in a buzz cut like a boot camp recruit. Scars curved around the right side of her mouth, pulling her lips permanently taut in that direction. Her right ear was malformed. The scars ran down her neck and disappeared inside her black T-shirt. The T-shirt was tucked into a pair of camouflage pants. The pants were tucked into shiny black combat boots.

Dole stopped at the table where Tucker Pennington sat with his head lowered. Tucker's parents were in the row behind him. Thad Pennington was trim and spry for a man in his fifties. He wore a custom-fit suit. His gray hair was swept back and parted. He looked young and his wife looked old. Grace Pennington's face was lined and hard. She wore a form-fitting dress that showed off her bare arms and legs. They were muscular and too tan.

A priest sat next to them. He was a tiny man whose torso did not even fill out his extrasmall black shirt. He wore his hair short, bright silver against his olive skin. He closed his eyes and bowed his head toward Alexis Dole but she ignored him. Her gaze fell on Tucker himself and she did not move.

Both sheriff's deputies sitting behind Tucker leaned forward in their chairs. One of them lowered his hand to his holster.

"Miss Dole," the judge called out to her. "Please be seated in the witness box."

Judge Roth waited for her to sit and instructed one of the court staff to fill her a glass of water. "It's my understanding you had a little trouble at the security gate."

"No trouble," Dole said through the good side of her mouth.

"It's not often someone carries two guns and four knives into the courthouse."

"I have a permit."

"So I was told," the judge said. "Apparently you set off so many alarms when you walked in, it sounded like D-Day all over again. That's okay. These boys were probably getting complacent anyway." He winked at the deputies. "Do you know why you're here today, Miss Dole?"

"You're going to let that diseased piece of garbage go free."

"Well, the Commonwealth has petitioned the court to release Tucker Pennington from his civil commitment. I should advise you that this isn't a criminal hearing. There's no prosecution and no testimony about his previous crimes. Mr. Pennington was tried and convicted as a juvenile in a different court, so there is no need to retry his case. The reason you were asked here is to help us determine the impact Mr. Pennington's release will have on the community. I realize you were one of the people most significantly affected by his crimes, so I'd like to put your thoughts on the record. Do you understand?"

"I understand," Dole said.

"Excellent. Now, I'm sure you're aware that Mr. Pennington has been locked in a mental health facility since his release from the juvenile detention center. He's been under constant psychiatric care, and according to the facility's records, has been a model patient."

"I'm sure."

"After all these years, can you please tell the court what your opinion is of allowing Mr. Pennington to return once more to his home?"

Dole's eye fixed on Tucker. His head was still lowered. "Look at me," she said.

Tucker was rocking back and forth and muttering. His hands were clasped together under the table in prayer.

"Make him look at me," Dole said.

The attorney looked to Judge Roth. The judge only shrugged.

"Tucker," the attorney said. "Can you please face the witness."

Tucker raised his face toward her. He was gaunt and pale. Sickly looking. Alexis Dole's mouth twitched in anger. She grimaced in disgust at him. Then, her ruined face twisted into a bizarre shape. Half of her mouth curled upward into a mortician's facsimile of a grin. "Believe me," she said. "I want you to let him out."

After that, the judge dismissed her. He waited for Alexis Dole to get down from the stand and make her way back up the aisle. Tucker's head lowered as Dole walked past. She loomed over him. Even Tucker's attorney looked unnerved. He picked up his pen and began doodling on his notepad until she moved past him.

"Next witness," Judge Roth called out to his clerk. He looked at his list. "Patricia Martin?"

One of the court staff stationed at the back of the room left to fetch her, only to return seconds later and say, "Miss Martin isn't ready yet, sir. It might be a while."

"What do you mean she's not ready?" Roth said.

"They are trying to convince her to come in."

"Well, we don't have all day," Roth said. He pushed his glasses up on his nose and peered down at the list of witnesses. "Is Dr. Linda Shelley present?"

"I'm here, Your Honor," a voice called out from the rear of the courtroom.

Tucker Pennington raised his head as Linda made her way down the aisle toward the witness stand. He smiled benignly as she walked past.

Linda placed her hand on the Bible as the judge read her the oath, then sat.

"Dr. Shelley, it's my understanding you treated Mr. Pennington for four years while you were employed at Sunshine Estates?"

"That's correct, Your Honor."

The judge reached up and pinched the bridge of his nose with his fingers, squeezing hard. "It's been a long day, Doctor, so I'm going to cut to the chase. In your opinion, is it advisable for the Commonwealth to release Mr. Pennington into society?"

"No."

There was an audible gasp from Tucker's mother. Tucker's father squeezed his wife's hand hard.

"Why?" the judge asked.

"Because he'll never be cured, Your Honor. He can be stabilized with the proper amount of medication, but that's it. If he goes off his medication, or if they stop working, he'll be a grave danger to himself and everyone around him."

The judge pointed at Tucker's attorney. "Do you have anything you'd like to ask, Counselor?"

"I do, Your Honor. Dr. Shelley, how long did you work at Sunshine Estates?"

"Approximately four years."

"And during that time, was my client ever a threat to you or any of the staff?"

"No."

"Does he appear to be properly medicated at this time?"

Linda looked Tucker over. He was hunched forward, eyes wet and distant. "He does," Linda said.

"So at present, he poses no threat to you, to me, his family, or anyone else in this courtroom. Is that correct?"

"Not that I can see," Linda said.

"Dr. Shelley, I'm sure you're aware the Commonwealth has been releasing multiple citizens who've been detained outside of the judicial system under the auspices of civil commitments. Is that correct?"

"Yes, it is."

"In your opinion, is Tucker Pennington any more dangerous than the people who've already been released?"

Everyone was silent. From the back of the courtroom, Alexis Dole's eye bore through her. Toward the front, Carrie Santero leaned forward in her seat.

"No," Linda said. "He's no more dangerous than any of the others."

The judge dismissed Linda and called out for Patricia Martin again. The staff said she wasn't ready again.

"Well, Miss Martin either wants to make a statement or not. We haven't got all day." He looked at his list again. "How about Brenda Drake? Is Brenda Drake available?"

A hand shot up from the back of the courtroom and a young woman stood. "Miss Drake is deceased, Your Honor."

Roth leaned forward and squinted. "And who are you?"

"Detective Carrie Santero."

He checked his list. "I don't see your name on here, Detective."

Carrie hurried down the aisle, holding her case file in the air. "I'm here on Brenda Drake's behalf."

"Objection," the attorney said. "The detective is not on the witness list. She can't speak for someone else."

Carrie stopped at the wooden gate. "I have information regarding Brenda Drake's death that will help the court make its decision, Your Honor."

"I'll allow it for now," the judge said. "But don't get comfortable."

Carrie set her case file on the witness stand ledge as she laid her hand on the Bible and raised her right hand to be sworn. After she said, "I do," she sat and opened the file. "Your Honor, the reason Brenda Drake could not be here to testify is because shortly after she received notice to appear, she got a second letter." Carrie held up the letter from The Master and said, "I believe this was sent by Mr. Pennington as a way to intimidate her. It worked, because she killed herself."

"Excuse me, if I may, Your Honor," the attorney said. "Was this letter signed by my client?"

"No," Carrie said. "It was signed by The Master, a name he called himself when he assaulted his victims."

"Was the envelope it came in postmarked near Sunshine Estates?"

"I didn't see the envelope."

"I'm sorry, but is there any proof at all this letter was sent by my client?"

Judge Roth looked at Carrie.

"Not physical proof, Your Honor."

"So you have, what, mental proof?" Judge Roth asked. "Spiritual proof? Exactly what kind of proof did you bring us today, Detective?"

"That wasn't the only letter, Your Honor. Retired Detective Bill Waylon received one also."

"Objection."

The judge looked at her. "Do you have anything else?"

"The second letter threatened a police officer's family, sir."

The attorney raised both arms in the air in exasperation. "Your Honor, I object to every single thing this witness has said to the court so far. Unless the detective can offer some kind of foundation linking these letters to my client, then I fail to see how this is doing anything but wasting the court's time."

Judge Roth turned toward her. "Can you?"

Carrie couldn't find the words to tell him she could not.

"You're dismissed, Detective," the judge said. "Is Miss Patricia Martin ready yet?"

"No, Your Honor," the staff person called out from the back.

The judge stroked the sides of his mouth with his thumb and forefinger as he mulled over his decision. Finally, it was made. He picked up his gavel and said, "Release Mr. Pennington from custody."

Tucker raised his head from between his hands. He looked stupefied. His mother and father burst from their seats to clutch him from behind. Grace Pennington's sobs of relief were loud and guttural, like screams.

Carrie asked the court staff where she could find Patricia Martin. They told her just go down the hall and you'll hear her.

The corridor was nearly empty at that end of the courthouse. The rooms were meant to be set apart from the proceedings. They were a safe place where attorneys met with clients, or witnesses were kept with their families. Patricia Martin's parents were sitting outside of the room. The husband was fatter and balder than he looked in his driver's license photo, Carrie thought. He had his arm around his wife. She sat with her back straight. Both of their faces were blank. Drained. They didn't look up as Carrie walked past.

Carrie could see shadows moving behind the frosted glass within and leaned her head to the door. There was a sharp cry inside the room at the sight of Carrie's shadow. "Someone's here! No. They're trying to take me in there. I don't want to see him! Don't make me go in there, please. Please, I can't, please."

Someone whispered quietly to her and told her it was going to be all right.

Carrie knocked softly on the door. "No!" Carrie turned the door handle and opened it just enough to put her face in. Patricia Martin was curled in a ball on one of the chairs, shivering and frail. Linda Shelley was bent down beside her, trying to calm her.

Patricia clutched Linda in terror at Carrie's appearance. Her feet slid across the chair's polished wooden seat, scrambling to get away.

"It's okay. Listen. Hang on," Carrie said. "It's over. You don't have to go in. You don't have to see him."

Patricia stopped moving. Her eyes opened wide and blue. "I don't?"

"No," Carrie said. "Just take a deep breath, all right?"

Patricia clutched the sides of her face and wept with relief. "I don't have to see him. Oh my God! Thank you!"

Linda hadn't let go of her yet. She stayed kneeling next to her, with her head down, eyes cast to the floor.

"They're putting him back in jail," Patricia said. She was weeping and laughing at the same time. "I knew they would. I knew they couldn't let him out. Will they keep him forever now? They have to, right?"

Linda didn't look up.

Carrie cleared her throat. "Well, you see, Miss Martin. Here's the thing."

* * *

Both doors on the ambulance slammed shut. They were still able to hear Patricia Martin screaming as it drove away. It had taken four medics and both Carrie and Linda to strap her down to the gurney before loading her onto the ambulance. Patricia's mother was in the back of the ambulance with her and her father was following behind them in a station wagon. He gave both Carrie and Linda a withering look as he drove past.

"So that didn't go as well as it could have," Carrie said.

"No shit," Linda said.

"Oh, I'm sorry. If only there'd been a licensed psychologist around to break the news to her in a more productive way instead of sitting there with your thumb up your ass and letting me do it!"

Linda came within inches of Carrie's face. "Do not yell at me."

"Or what?"

Behind them, Tucker Pennington emerged from the courthouse. He turned his face upward toward the sun, basking in the warmth, like a reptile. His mother was wrapped around his arm, clutching him tightly. She'd finally gotten her son back and nothing in the world was going to let him get taken from her again. Tucker's father guided them down the steps as a shining black Cadillac came around the bend and stopped. Their driver got out to open the rear doors and let the Pennington family inside.

Linda put her hands inside her coat pockets as they drove off. "I'm assuming you're going to keep tabs on him."

"You're damn right," Carrie said. "How soon before he does it again, do you think?"

"Who knows? With the right treatment maybe never. It's impossible to say."

They walked together toward the parking lot, the heels of both of their shoes clacking against the concrete in near unison.

"You want to get a drink or something?" Carrie asked. "I could use one."

Linda stopped to get her car keys out of her purse. "You want to drink with me?"

Carrie shrugged, "I've drunk with way worse people. I don't know. What the hell? Why not?"

"Are you one of those people who has a lot of friends?"

"No."

"Me either."

"If we went out for a drink and then we became friends, we could fight crime together," Carrie said. "I'm the hard-ass detective and you're the older psychologist."

"Easy. I'm not that much older than you."

"Let's say, more seasoned, then."

Linda laughed. "Listen, I can't get a drink right now. I have somewhere I have to be. Some other time, maybe?"

"Sounds good," Carrie said. She reached in her purse to get her keys as Linda walked away.

9

*T*he bar was an hour away, but she didn't have to be there until seven P.M.

There was time. Linda was excited and impatient, but it wouldn't do her any good to arrive early. Her showing up was supposed to be a surprise and she didn't want to ruin it.

She drove to the post office. She went through the front door and went right to her PO Box, hoping none of the clerks saw her. It had been weeks since she collected her mail and they were sure to be annoyed at her for letting it get so full. It wasn't full at all. She opened the door and saw a yellow Postal Service index card with the words *Overstuffed Box* written in Magic Marker.

She lowered her head and went around the corner to the counter, holding the yellow card of shame. "Hi," she said when she reached the front of the line.

There were three registers but only one was open. The duty clerk was an Asian woman with a thick accent. She eyed Linda and said, "Box One-sixty-one?"

"Yes."

"You're here for your mail finally?"

"Yes."

"You haven't been here in a long time."

"I know. I've been busy."

"We had to put it in the back."

"I'm sorry."

The clerk vanished into the rear of the building and came back holding a plastic bin piled with mail. She set it down on the counter and started going through it, looking for any parcels that needed to be scanned. It was crammed with junk mail, catalogs, bills, circular ads, and dozens of other envelopes.

The clerk pulled out a large yellow package. "You shop a lot online?"

"Sometimes," Linda said. There were people standing in line behind her then, waiting for their turn. Other postal clerks walked behind the counter but never stopped to open any of the registers.

"People who shop a lot online need to come in more often."

Linda looked over her shoulder again and smiled sheepishly at the person behind her. He looked annoyed. She looked back at the clerk. "Do you want me to go through that and find the parcels for you so you could help these people behind me? I don't mind waiting."

The clerk ignored her. She scanned several more packages and typed on her computer and put them back into the bin, one by one, until she'd finished. The line was all the way to the door by then. The clerk slid the bin across the counter and said, "Take the bin with you. Bring it back when you come in next time, and don't wait so long."

Linda picked the bin up with both hands and carried it toward the door. She apologized to everyone in the line and used her back to open the door. She walked across the parking lot with the bin of mail toward her car with the wind rustling across the top of the open box, threatening to snatch up loose pieces of mail and send them into the wind.

Linda made it home with time to toss the bin on her kitchen counter but not look at it. She raced up the bedroom steps. She needed to be naked and in the shower fast, so she undid her earrings and left on her necklace. She kicked off her shoes. She slid out of her blazer and undid the buttons on her purple shirt, then tossed the shirt onto her bed as she entered her bedroom. She undid her pants and pulled down her underwear and unsnapped her bra. She tossed it all at the hamper.

She pulled open her closet door. There was a long line of dress suits and business casual wear and shirts emblazoned with the Vieira County logo on the upper left breast, but there, nearest to her, was her dress for that evening.

She'd gone out and bought it the same day she received the phone call inviting her out to the bar that night.

She laid the dress on the bed flat so it didn't crease. She put her shoes on the floor next to the bed. She went into the bathroom and turned on the shower and didn't wait for it to get hot. She slid a shower cap over her hair and got in. The water was cold. She didn't pay attention to it.

It occurred to her that she didn't remember locking the door when she came in. She thought about it as she scrubbed the lengths of her arms and the sides of her neck and beneath her breasts. She'd come in the door, carrying the tote, and dropped it on the table, and come upstairs. The door was shut. That much she was sure of. Whether or not she'd locked it, she couldn't remember.

She scrubbed her legs and hips and stomach and worked the washcloth into the recess of her belly button and made quick work of her legs and lower torso.

Of course I locked it, she thought. It was the same feeling she had when she cooked breakfast in the morning and then, as she was driving to work, couldn't recall if she'd turned off the stove's burners. When she came home, they were never on. On the rare occasions she'd turned around and gone home to double-check, they were never on either.

She tossed the washcloth into the corner of the tub and ripped back the shower curtain. The bathroom was filled with steam. The mirror was opaque and dripping. She grabbed a towel and wrapped it around herself and pulled off the shower cap and opened the door to her bedroom.

It was quiet. Her dress was still lying on the bed. Her shoes were still positioned near the bed on the floor. Time was still slipping away before she'd get stuck in rush-hour traffic on the way to the bar and wind up being late. Whether or not the door was locked would have to wait.

The dress was mid-length and hugged tight to her body. She stepped into it and wiggled it up over her shoulders, then twisted and turned and flapped her arms around, trying to get it zippered up the back. When it was done she closed her bedroom door to see herself in the full-length mirror mounted on the wall behind it. She saw the reflection of the bedroom wall and closet door behind her and she stopped.

Linda knew that the psychic phenomenon of knowing when you are being stared at is untrue. A psychologist named Edward B. Titchener had studied it in the late 1800s, debunking the idea that it was caused by any sixth sense. The latest research had shown that it was largely due to confirmation bias. The subject believes they are being stared at and suddenly looks around to see who is looking at them. Someone else detects their sudden movement and turns to see what caused it. Now, everyone was looking at one another, and the person who thought they were being started at initially feels they are proven correct.

It was all just an illusion that people believed in. Meaningless superstition. Linda stood in front of the mirror, searching the room around her in its reflection.

There was nothing there. She forced herself to turn and look and saw nothing but her laundry and bed and dresser and closet door and the steam escaping from her bathroom.

"This is what I get for spending my entire life surrounded by maniacs," she said.

She went to her dresser for her makeup bag and carried it back over to the mirror. She bent close to put on her lipstick and eye liner, stopping only a few times to check the room behind her, before telling herself it was all in her imagination.

Linda drove toward the bar and didn't hit any traffic. The GPS on her phone guided her toward the shopping center with ease and stayed connected the entire time. She drove listening to music and tapped the steering wheel as she sang along with it. She followed the GPS into the parking lot and pulled in.

The bar was at the far end of the shopping center, with a large blue neon martini glass mounted over the entrance. She grabbed her purse and hurried across the lot toward the door. She went inside and made her way past the people crowded at the entrance, waiting to be seated in the restaurant section. She raised her head to look across the bar, and there he was.

Jacob Rein, holding a margarita in one hand and staring at his phone with the other. Rein, like she'd never seen him. Dressed in an expensive suit and undone tie, casual and fashionable at the same time. His hair, carefully unkempt and styled. Jacob Rein, no older than the day the she'd met him. Younger even. Undamaged.

He looked up from his phone and saw her standing there. "You must be Dr. Shelley."

"That's right," she said. "You must be Jacob Junior."

Jacob Thome put his drink down on the bar and wiped his hand on his suitcoat before holding it out to shake hers. "I tried to call you to keep you from coming all the way out here."

Linda's face fell. "He's not coming, is he?"

"I'm afraid not. He sent me a message an hour ago saying something came up."

"Did you tell him I was coming?"

Thome could see the hurt in her eyes. "I wanted it to be a surprise. I'm sure if he knew you'd be here, he would have come." He moved aside to clear her path to the bar and said, "Here, let me buy you a drink."

Linda set her purse on the bar. "I'll take a glass of red wine. I might as well, right?"

Thome flagged the bartender down and ordered her wine and another margarita for himself.

Linda tried not to stare. "You look just like your father. It's amazing."

"I hope that's a good thing."

"It is. Why did you change your name?"

"He asked me to. After his legal troubles, he didn't want me associated with him. I regret it."

"So why did you pick that one?"

"When I was a kid we lived in Philly. Jim Thome was our favorite baseball player."

The wine arrived and she took a sip. "I'm trying to imagine him taking you to Phillies games and I can't. I guess I always pictured him sitting at home brooding, waiting for darkness to fall so he could go out and look for bad guys."

Thome laughed. "No, it wasn't always like that. He kept work at work, if that makes sense. He did a good job when I was growing up. I can't complain."

"I really wish I'd gotten to see him tonight."

He looked at her. She was a beautiful woman, with rich dark skin and fierce eyes. He turned back to his drink and shook his head. "I'll make sure he knows what he missed out on."

Linda took another sip of her wine. "So, what are we celebrating? You invited me out here for a surprise celebration for your dad, and since he's not here, you might as well tell me. What's the occasion?"

Thome raised his glass. "My dad's no longer a criminal."

"What?"

"We won the appeal. His conviction got overturned. He's no longer a felon. Whole case got dismissed. I kept begging him to let me work on it ever since I graduated law school. It wasn't until recently he agreed. Sure enough, we won."

Linda massaged her temples with the tips of her fingers. The wine was hitting her harder than she expected. The music in the place was too loud and she felt uncomfortable in wearing such a tight dress surrounded by such younger people. "I imagine he'll be going back to his old life, then, in some form or another."

"I hope not," Thome said.

Linda turned toward him. "Really? Why do you say that?"

"Because he has a fresh start. He's a brilliant person. He could do anything he set his mind to. It doesn't have to be tracking down maniacs and staring at dead bodies all the time. You can only deal with so much of that stuff before you start taking it home."

"Yes!" Linda said, smacking the bar with the flat of her hand. "That is exactly what I always said about your father. Thank you! He could go back to school or start a business or become a teacher. I don't know. Anything. He could live."

Thome nodded and said, "Damn right." He raised his margarita glass to her. "To living."

"To living," she said, and clinked her glass against his. She swallowed the rest of her wine. She said good evening and thank you for a lovely evening and went home.

The house felt cold and alien as she stepped through the front door. She shut it and made sure she locked it behind her. The dining room light was on. She tended to keep it on when she was out, so that no ever knew if someone was really home, and because she hated walking into a dark house.

I wasn't supposed to come back here alone tonight, she thought.

There was a point where someone was supposed to stop chasing a dream. To stop injuring themselves over the expectation of a thing that was never going to happen. She told herself she was at that point and had probably been at it for a long time. It was time to move forward. There was a difference between facing up to pain and wallowing in it.

She slid out of her shoes and walked barefoot into the kitchen to get a bottle of water from the refrigerator. The aftertaste of wine had left her mouth dry. She twisted the cap and drank as she turned to lean back against the counter. The post office mail bin was sitting across from her, its contents piled high enough that she could see the items scattered across the top. A utility bill. An advertising index card. A letter addressed to her in handwriting she didn't recognize.

Linda set the bottle down. She didn't remember seeing any letters before when she carried the bin out of the post office, or when she'd carried it into her house. You'd been in a rush, she told herself.

She picked up the envelope and saw her name and post office box address, and in the left-hand corner, printed in elaborate script, the name and return address for Sunshine Estates.

She ripped it open, careful not to tear the letter inside. She unfolded the page and glanced at the name printed on the bottom. She flung it across the room like the paper stung her fingers, watching it float through the air, side to side, until settling on the floor.

She stood over the letter, hands clenched into fists, and read it.

> *My Dearest Doctor,*
> *I hope this letter finds you well. Safe and warm within the comfort of your home.*
> *Perhaps I will find that comfort as well. Indeed, I intend to try.*
> *Until Then, I Remain,*
> *The Master*

Linda pulled a paper towel off the roll and used it to pick the letter up from the floor. She set it on the counter, then picked up the envelope it had been sent in and laid that on the letter as well. There were chemicals the police could use to develop fingerprints on paper. They could also swab it for DNA. First thing in the morning, she'd call Carrie Santero at the county detectives' office and ask her to come over to pick it up. Linda would have called her then, but they'd never exchanged cell phone numbers. I guess we may turn out to be friends after all, she thought.

The letter from The Master did not bother her all that much. She was not afraid of Tucker Pennington. The man she'd seen at the courtroom that day was too pathetic to frighten anyone. She had spent her professional career looking into the eyes of the crazy and the cruel, and had gone through far too much in her personal life to waste any time being afraid of someone like

Tucker. Anyway, the letter had come to her PO Box. It wasn't like he knew how to find her home.

She walked over to the front door and made sure it was locked. She pulled back her front curtains and checked the windows there, making sure they were locked as well. She checked the rear sliding door and it was locked, and the wooden plank she kept along the base of it to keep anyone from sliding the door open even if they broke the lock was there as well.

The house was secured and there was no question in her mind about it this time. She reached behind her back and unzipped her dress, pulling the zipper down to the small of her back, and shimmied out of it until it was pooled at her feet. She laid it across the back of one of her dining room chairs to remind her to take it to the dry cleaner's when she went out the next day.

She walked up the stairs in her bra and panties, feeling warm air blowing from her vents across her stomach and thighs and the tops of her feet. When she reached the landing, she heard something above her and stopped moving. It was nothing loud or ominous. The creak of a beam. Something on her bedroom floor or on the wall outside. Houses creaked. They creaked with age, or when the heater kicked on, or when an animal scurried across the top of their roofs.

She listened and heard nothing. If she hadn't been alone, it would have meant nothing at all to her, she thought. She went up the rest of the steps and flicked off the lights when she reached the top, leaving the staircase and hallway in darkness.

The light from the bathroom was still on. She crossed in front of the large mirror and shuddered, feeling like scalding hot water was dripping across the center of her back. Something foreign there. Something watching.

She turned on the lights in the bedroom and looked around. Nothing was disturbed. The closet door was closed. The bathroom shower curtain was open. The bed frame was too low for anyone to be hiding under. Stop being ridiculous, she told herself.

She turned off the lights and jumped into bed, using the knob at the end of her bed's headboard to vault off the floor. It was an old childhood need to be safe under the covers instead of standing vulnerable in the pool of darkness on the floor. All of it silly and irrational, she knew, but there was comfort in the familiarity of her bed. That much the letter had been right about.

The house settled, and she settled, breathing steadily until everything else fell away from her like loose pages from an old book. There was a point to stop chasing dreams.

She was a young girl again, floating downstream in a small boat. She looked down at a worn book sitting in her lap, between her hands. She opened it and saw that each page was a different scene from her life.

Her family. Her childhood. Even Antoine. All of it was there. Her crowded bedroom at her mother's home. Boot camp. The army kitchens. Her marriage to Jerry, both the love and the fear. Dr. Shorn helping her get into college. All the hours she'd spent studying. One of the pages was a picture of Jacob. As she flipped through each page, she realized she did not need to keep the things she no longer wanted.

She pulled pages out by the handful and sent them into the wind. They floated gently down toward the water and were taken away, swallowed by the current. Page by page, until the book was almost empty.

She heard that same creak from before, coming from the dark woods along the shore, but she was in her boat and too far away to worry. The last few pages came away freely in her hand and it felt so good to let them go.

A sudden wind rose from the woods that rustled its dark leaves and sent them scattering. Sticks and rocks came flying past her, and one of the rocks struck her in the chest. It hit her so hard, she gasped aloud and could not breathe.

An inescapable warmth flooded through her being. It spread down from her chest and spilled over her arms and legs. The river rose around the boat until water came up over its sides.

Water pooled around her body, surrounding her in its warmth. The boat sank.

Linda slid below the surface of the water where the pages of her life still floated. They were her want and hurt and love and regret and she slipped beneath all of them. She left them behind as she descended toward that final place. There was a flickering light at the bottom of the river, and when she reached it, it went dark.

III

WEST, SOUTH, AND EAST

10

*D*ave Kenderdine never had a really good answer to the question, "What's the most fucked-up thing you ever saw?"

Most rookies ask that question of their sergeants and field training officers and other senior cops. They ask it as a way of preparing their brain for something they'll someday encounter that exists far beyond the scope of normalcy. A way to gauge what the job can show you, far beyond the textbooks and movies and stories they've heard.

With almost twenty years on the job, he'd seen some crazy shit, of course. He had a few decent stories, but none of them were showstoppers. In a coffee klatch of other cops who were standing around sharing war stories far better than his, he'd always had to shrug and say, you know, just the usual.

Hansen Township ran three-man squads during the day shift. Kenderdine as the sergeant and two patrol officers. A kid fresh out of the academy they called Howdy on account of his red hair and freckles, and another kid with fourteen months on the job named Wallace. Being the junior guy, it was Howdy's job to bring coffee and Dave sipped his while the two patrol officers took turns reading the incident reports out loud.

"They had a domestic last night. Check this out. Lady reported her out-of-control seven-year-old wouldn't go to bed."

"So she called the cops?" Kenderdine asked.

"She called the cops," Howdy said.

Kenderdine shook his head. "Children and Youth should start a file right now. If Mom needs police intervention for a seven-year-old, that whole family is doomed." He took another sip. "What else did they have?"

Howdy flipped through the next few incident reports on the clipboard. They were nothing but vehicle lockouts and streetlight checks. He turned to the last page and laughed. "Eighteen-year-old kid with a brand-new Mustang was stopped at red light. It turned green and this dumbass decided to stomp on the gas and peel out to show off for everybody. He lost control and went right into a tree. Car's totaled. Moron."

"Insurance won't cover that one," Kenderdine said. "Not if it was from negligence. Hope he didn't owe too much on the payment."

Wallace sipped his coffee. "Guess what I saw on my way in. I never saw anything like it before in my life. I thought it was something out of a horror movie."

"What was it?"

"This huge buck with antlers wide as my arms. I mean, trophy antlers. The kind they hang in the gallery at Cabela's. He was all scraped up and bloody, right? Gashes on his sides, all the way up to his neck. It was dark, but I could see something hanging from them antlers on the one side. I get close enough with my high beams and it's the head of another deer."

"You're shitting me," Howdy said.

"I shit you not. It's the severed head of another deer with its antlers all locked up in this one's. I couldn't believe it."

"You get a picture?"

"No, he ran off."

"You're lying. Sarge, you think he's lying?"

Kenderdine shrugged. "It happens. Two bucks in rut decide to duke it out over some pretty little doe. They start fighting and get entangled. Bigger one starts twisting and turning and yanking to get free. Next thing you know, one of their heads pops off and the other one has to carry it around for a while. I've heard of it."

"If I saw that I'd shit my pants."

"No, you wouldn't," Kenderdine said. "When you see things like that, it takes a while for your brain to figure it out. You're there in your car, driving along, safe in your own little world. Your music's going. You got your coffee. Everything is normal. Then you see this deer, and that's normal too. Even when you see it's got a second head dangling from its antlers, it will take your brain a little while to process the horror of it. It's not till later on when you realize how fucked-up it was. Same way with the stuff you see on this job. When it's all going down, it's complete mayhem, but you're just in there trying to get through it. It won't be until later on, when you're far removed from it, when you're lying in bed there trying to fall asleep, that it hits you."

Wallace nodded sagely at Howdy, like he knew exactly what the sergeant was talking about. "He's right."

"Shut up, dipshit. You've only been here three months longer than me and I handled the last crash because the lady had a bone sticking out of her leg and you said you were gonna throw up."

"I told you my stomach was queasy from all the beer I drank the night before. That's all it was," Wallace said. "Sarge, what's the most fucked-up thing you ever saw?"

Kenderdine tossed his empty coffee cup in the trash. "Has to be the two of you sitting here instead of doing police work. Let's roll out."

He'd seen a few things, sure. Bad crashes with mangled bodies. A fight between two women in the Dollar Store parking lot, a real fight, with punching and kicking and hair pulled from each other's scalps right at the roots, all while both of them were holding babies.

He'd seen a suicidal guy jump off a bridge and land on the rocks below. Kenderdine was talking to him, trying to get him to come off the bridge, and the guy just stepped out into the sky and dropped. He didn't scream or anything. He fell straight down and made a splattering sound when he hit.

Twenty years dealing with the public meant you were bound to see some messed-up things. But none of it had been too much to cope with. Nothing that kept him up at night or made him regret being a police officer or afraid to raise kids in this world. Nothing truly pants-shittingly terrifying. He hadn't seen anything too much to take in twenty years.

He saw it that day.

They received the call that morning as a check-the-well-being. County to any available Hansen Township car. Linda Shelley hasn't shown up for work at the Juvenile Detention Center. Can't reach her by cell phone. Available units, please respond.

Kenderdine picked up his radio mic and told them he was en route.

Within minutes he was on the right street, checking the mail-boxes for the right address. Single homes. Three or four hundred grand each. Quarter-acre lots. Some had decks on the back and some had swimming pools. He found the one he was looking for and parked on the street alongside the curb. He was right in front of the house, which was a mistake, and something he'd yell at his guys if they did, but sometimes it shook out like that.

Police training is to park a few houses before the location you're responding to. It's a good habit because cops never know exactly what they're walking into. They don't know who is waiting for them. A routine alarm call could get far from routine real quick. You could be walking up to a house with a deranged sniper holed up on the third floor, zeroing you in on their scope. The idea of parking away from the house and walking up on foot is that you can sneak up and assess the situation before anyone knows you're there.

But sometimes the goddamn addresses are off, or spaced too far apart, or you don't see it until you're right up on it, and then the only thing you can do is just stop in front of the house. So Kenderdine did. He got out, shut his door, and looked at Linda Shelley's house. It was quiet. Well-maintained. No signs of disturbance. A regular house in a regular neighborhood on a regular day.

He'd met Dr. Shelley at the Detention Center a few times. She seemed kind of cold. The kind of woman that's so smart, she gets angry at people who aren't. Looks-wise, she reminded him of Pam Grier. He'd always had a thing for Pam Grier.

A black SUV was parked in the driveway and Kenderdine called it in on his radio and gave them the tag. "Comes back to that address," the county responded.

There were red streaks smeared across the top of the door frame and on either side. She must be in the process of painting the front of the house, he thought. Some kind of weird design choice, maybe, he thought. It was dry and dark against the white paint of the door frame, set against the white stucco front of the house's entrance. It almost looks like blood, a quiet voice in the back of his mind whispered. Yeah, right, he thought. Blood smeared on the door frame of this house in this normal suburban setting where the sun is shining and the wind is blowing and somewhere far off a dog is barking. Cars drive past with people going to work. The mail is being delivered. A morning talk show is being played on a nearby television telling people to get out there and enjoy all that sunshine, folks, winter will be here soon.

He knocked on the door. "Dr. Shelley? Police department."

He pressed the doorbell button and listened to it ding-donging inside for several seconds. He stepped back onto the front yard and looked up to search the windows for signs of movement. He pressed the doorbell again and knocked several times. "Linda Shelley, are you home?" he called out.

He tried the front door. The doorknob turned in his hand and the door came open.

Kenderdine pushed it inward a few inches. "Police department. Anyone home?"

He saw a dress folded along the back of a dining room chair. He saw her shoes kicked off behind the door. He saw the post office bin on the kitchen counter. Her purse and keys were set down nearby. He kept calling out to her, and announcing his presence, as he made his way deeper into the house.

It was important to make a lot of noise in those situations.

The last thing he wanted to do was sneak around some woman's house as she came strolling down the hallway buck-ass naked. Or worse, for her to hear someone in her house and not know it's a cop trying to check on her, so she grabs a gun and comes out shooting. "Police department!" he said.

He made his way up the stairs to the second floor. He stopped on the landing and listened. No shower was running. No hair dryer. "Doctor? Are you home?"

There was a bathroom and two bedrooms upstairs. One bedroom door was open and the other was shut. He looked in the first room. It had been converted into a home office. Books and a computer and large desk. Framed diplomas and awards all over the walls. Nobody in there.

He went to the second door, the closed one, to the large master bedroom, and knocked. He called out her name and then he opened the door.

"County radio to Sgt. Kenderdine, checking your status?" the radio mic squawked.

After a few minutes with no response, they called him again. "Status check, Sarge. You ten-four?"

In the days to come, Kenderdine wouldn't remember them calling him over the radio. Not the first time, or the second. He wouldn't remember responding. Someone eventually played the recording of his transmission from the house that day and he didn't recognize the man's voice on the police radio. It was too high-pitched. Unintelligible. All the man in the recording was doing was screaming.

Harv Bender had sweated through his suit coat. Dark black stains were splattered across his back. His pale blue shirt's collar was translucent from sweat. Carrie could see the length of his dark tie wrapped around his neck below it. There were cops at the front door, and they weren't moving. They weren't even saying anything. That never happens, Carrie thought.

No matter how bad a job was, someone was always making a joke to help everyone else get through it. These guys just stood there now, staring at the house.

Sal Vigoda reached into his jacket pocket and pulled out a tin of thin cigars. He cracked it open and asked, "Does it stink in there?"

"No," Bender mumbled. "I don't think so. I didn't notice."

"Better to be safe than sorry." Sal snapped one of the cigars in half and stuffed the broken ends up his nostrils. He sniffed a few times and loose tobacco flew out of his nose.

Carrie scowled in disgust. "What are you doing?"

"What? You never heard of this? It's an old detective trick." He pushed the cigar end even farther into his nose, until it was almost hidden. "Some guys used to put Vicks VapoRub under their noses thinking it would block the smell of a dead body. All that does is open your sinuses up more to it. This is the only thing that works." He pulled another cigar out and held it out toward her. "Here, you try."

"I'll pass," Carrie said.

"Suit yourself."

"What are we doing about Tucker Pennington, Chief?" Carrie asked.

Bender's eyes were glazed. "When I got the call, I sent two guys over there to sit on him until we figure this out."

"Good call," Carrie said.

Bender wiped sweat from his face with the palm of his hand. "I want you two in there before the crime scene unit and coroner go in. We'll send everyone in separate to get different perspectives on this. Jesus H. Christ, I'm sweating. I need some water. Okay? You both okay?"

"We're okay, boss," Carrie said.

"All right. I'll get you some water for when you come out. There's a bathroom up there. Directly behind you when you're looking at it."

They watched Bender walk back toward the row of police cars parked on the street. There were local cars from different jurisdictions who'd come to assist. Even a state trooper had responded. Yellow tape was strung at Linda Shelley's property lines, from corner to corner, and a line of uniformed cops prevented anyone from approaching too closely.

"All the time I knew Harv Bender, I never seen him like this," Sal said. "It must be pretty bad in there."

Carrie stopped at the entrance, inspecting the front door. "You see that?"

"What, the paint?"

"That's not paint," Carrie said. "It's the sign of the lamb. From Passover."

"What, this Dr. Shelley chick was Jewish?"

Carrie got close to the smears to inspect them. "It's from the Old Testament, when God told the Jews to paint their doors with lamb's blood. Above the threshold and on either side so they'd be spared the slaughter."

"Apparently God didn't get the message this time," Sal said.

The officer standing nearest the door passed them both a pair of black gloves. Carrie and Sal slid them on and Sal stopped to adjust the cigar pieces stuffed in his nose to make sure they wouldn't fall out. Carrie opened the door and went inside. She inspected the lock and the door frame and metal piece that houses the bolt and the keyhole itself. No toolmarks or damage whatsoever. Whoever had done this had not needed to force their way in.

The letter from The Master was on the kitchen counter, where Bender had said it was. She glanced at it before she headed toward the staircase.

She went up the steps. Her eyes were fixed on the bedroom door. It was open.

Black spray paint covered the walls. Upside down pentagrams and crosses and the numbers 666. Intricate symbols she did not understand. On the wall to her left was written, *The Master Summons the Beast.* On the wall above the bed were the words, *Behold, A Blood Angel.*

Sal was directly behind her as they approached the room. She heard him cough and turned in time so see him grab his mouth with both hands. Chunks of wet cigar spilled out in pieces from his nose, splattering his fingers, and he clenched his eyes shut. He gagged and whirled away from the door, diving for the bathroom behind them.

Carrie's eyes were wide. It was something that could not be seen all at once, and yet could not ever be unseen. She stared in wonder at it. It was stunning in its horror.

Linda Shelley was kneeling in the center of her bed, turned

away from them. Both of her arms were tied to the knobs of the headboard in front of her, keeping her upper torso suspended and upright.

The center of Linda Shelley's back was split open, from the nape of her neck to the tip of her waist. Her backbone was bare and denuded of any connecting bones, left to be nothing but a pale white column of exposed, knotted, bone.

Each of her ribs had been pried out of her spine by some tool. A knife or a screwdriver. Carrie could hear the horrific popping noise each rib would make as it was ripped free. Would Linda have heard it too? How much of this had she been alive to endure?

One by one, Linda's ribs had been wrenched backward over her sides, prying her open.

Her lungs were pulled out through the open wound and left to dangle against her lower back. Two useless sacks, shriveled and depleted.

Linda's back was now nothing but an empty cavity, surrounded by a gaping maw of bone. A hideous wide-open mouth formed by her own ribs.

Sal Vigoda was retching in the bathroom behind her. The sound and smell of it was enough to make the acids in her own stomach swirl and threaten to burst up through her throat.

Behold, A Blood Angel.

My God, Carrie thought. He's given her wings.

11

*T*he toilet across the hall from the bedroom flushed. Carrie leaned against the doorway. "Sal? You okay, buddy?"

She heard him run the sink faucet and spit and wash his hands. He came out of the bathroom wiping his mouth. "I'm fine. I'm sorry about that."

"No problem. Listen, somebody was calling for you downstairs. They need you outside for something."

"Did they say what?"

"I didn't ask."

His face turned hangdog. She was lying and he knew it. He looked past her into the room. "I'm supposed to be in there with you."

"I'm good for now," Carrie said.

There were dark circles under his eyes that hung heavy and low. "I'll come back to check on you."

"Sounds good."

Carrie went back in the room. It would be easier to work by herself anyway. She stayed near the door, as far back from the bed as she could, and looked around the entire room like she was seeing it for the first time. Trying to find any details she had missed.

It was daylight outside, but the bedroom's curtains were thick. No one had turned the lights on, for fear of disturbing any trace evidence. Carrie reached in her coat for her flashlight and turned it on, aiming the beam directly into the cavity of Linda Shelley's back.

There were tool marks etched into Linda's spine. Scrapes and divots in the bone where he'd pried the ribs loose. They could take impressions of those marks and the state police lab would be able to match those impressions to the knife or screwdriver or whatever else Tucker had used, once they found it.

As she looked, she saw light reflecting off the headboard in front of Linda's body and stopped. She moved the flashlight to either side of the large wound and realized it was shining through the injury itself. Christ, he cut her open all the way through to the other side, she thought.

Carrie went around the side of the bed and bent forward with her flashlight. There, in the center of Linda's chest, just beneath her breastbone, was a deep stab wound, with a puddle of thick coagulated blood pooled on the bed between Linda's knees. It had soaked through the mattress and box spring and gone through to the floor.

Carrie ran her flashlight around Linda's back and saw very little blood leaking down from the wound there. She ran the flashlight across Linda's shoulders and outstretched arms, seeing purplish bruising on her flesh. She went back around Linda's front and inspected her breasts and belly and the underside of her arms and saw no discoloration there at all.

Blood settles to the lowest point in the human body at the moment of death. Sometimes it can't been seen for a few hours, but it always does, and it's always true. If Linda had died sitting up, bent facedown over her lap, there would be no lividity on her back.

Linda's eyes were closed. Her mouth was open and had filled with the spongy foam or whatever her body had coughed up from her throat at the moment she died. Some of it had come up through her nose as well, but her eyes were closed.

Son of a bitch, Carrie thought. He stabbed her through the chest while she was asleep. He posed her and did all this shit afterward. So how did he get in the house?

She looked around the rest of the bedroom. It was cleaner that her own bedroom, that was certain. There was no dust on the dresser. No hairbrushes with ridiculous amounts of loose hair bedded down in its bristles. No empty water bottles on the night-stand.

All she saw was a tall mirror on one side of the room and an open closet door on the other.

The closet looked immaculate. Perfectly organized. There was a section for work clothes, a section for dresses, and a section for everything else. The shelves above the closet were stacked with boxes. There was a two-tiered rack along the bottom of the closet with all of Linda's shoes. Carrie poked her head in and looked to see how far the closet went, when she realized everything on the far side of it was in disarray. Shoes had been knocked over. Dresses had been pulled down from their hangers. Two of the boxes on the shelf overhead had been moved aside and out of the way, allowing someone to stand upright in that corner without touching them.

From that position, Carrie turned and looked at the rest of the room. She shut the closet door and saw that one of the horizontal slats in the door's surface had been moved, ever so slightly, out of place.

Carrie backed up alongside the closet to where it ended and bent down to the level of where the slat was moved and she real-ized that the killer had been watching Linda from inside her own bedroom the entire time. He'd been able to use the mirror along the far wall to see everything. There was no sign of forced entry, because the killer was already there.

She moved around the rest of the room, focusing on the de-tails. Horror and shock were weapons used by the killer. He wanted anyone who saw what he'd done to be overwhelmed by his evil. It had worked, in some ways. But not on her, she thought. She would not allow it to.

Carrie inspected the strange symbols painted on the wall.

The first was two intersecting triangles, set at inverted angles. One faced down and the other faced up, so that all the points formed into a type of hexagram. In the center, the killer had painted some kind of flower.

The second symbol was a large circle surrounding a triangle.

Within the triangle was a lowercase *h*. Groups of dots were sprayed on either side of the *h*. It looked like there were supposed to be three in each group, but the paint had run and they'd bled together and Carrie could not accurately count them.

The last symbol was larger than the others. It was the most demonic thing Carrie had ever seen. A goat's head, drawn on top of an inverted pentagram. The letters *T-O-L* were written across the top of the symbol.

She knew each symbol had been laid there with purpose. Linda's body had been desecrated in that specific way with purpose. All of it formed arrows pointing toward the killer's unique methodology, but Carrie was helpless to understand what they were.

She needed help. And she knew who to ask.

"No," Harv Bender said. "Absolutely not."

Sal Vigoda was sitting under an apple tree in the front yard, pressed up against it with his back. His suit coat was off, despite the chill weather. His elbows were propped against his knees, and his head was resting on it.

"I need him in there, boss. There's nobody else," Carrie said.

"I assigned Sal to work it with you."

Sal raised his head at the sound of his name. "What's that, Chief?"

"How come you aren't up in the room with Detective Santero?"

"I quit," Sal said.

"When did you quit?"

"Right now. The second I saw that. I don't need to see that. I quit. I'm going home."

"Shut up, you idiot. You're not allowed to quit and you're not going home," Bender said. "You have five minutes to get yourself together and get back in there."

Sal lowered his head again.

"He'll be fine in five minutes," Bender said.

Carrie folded her arms across her chest and swung her foot against the grass, swiping it back and forth. "I just hate to think what happens when Quantico gets wind of this," Carrie said.

Bender raised an eyebrow. "What do you mean?"

Carrie cocked her head at the state trooper standing near the crime scene tape, keeping people away. He was drinking a coffee and talking to the other cops. "You know the state troopers work with the Feds all the time," she said, keeping her voice low. "The Feds will wet their pants when they hear what we've got. Pretty soon, the entire Behavioral Sciences Unit will show up here and turn this into the Famous But Ineffective freakshow. We'll have occultists and profilers falling out of our asses. Hell, you'll be lucky if they even let you stand next to them at the press conference."

"They can't do that," Bender said. "This is my case."

"Not after they get involved," Carrie said. "I've met those guys and they do not share credit. That's why I think it makes sense for you to bring in someone local. Someone who has experience with highly-stylized, ritual homicides."

"I'm not rehiring him as a county detective. Not over my dead body."

"I'm not asking you to do that. Use him as a consultant. His name won't even be on any of my paperwork. We keep this in-house, right where we can control it. It's that, or we wait for the black helicopters to show up."

Bender squeezed the sides of his cheeks and puffed out his lips while he thought. When he pulled it away, he said, "Listen to me, real, real, clear. He touches nothing. He tells no one that he was ever here. He goes in, he sees what he needs to see, gives you his opinion, and he leaves. You are responsible for him. Anything crazy he does. Any trouble he gets into. It's all on you. Understood?"

"Understood," Carrie said. She looked around the front yard, seeing nothing but trees and cops and curious neighbors. She turned to look up and down the street, then just stood there, frowning.

"Well?" Bender said. "Aren't you going to call him or something?"

"That's the thing. He doesn't have a phone. I kind of thought he'd show up here on his own."

Bender turned and looked up and down the street. He caught himself and said, "This is ridiculous. I'm sending the crime scene people in there now so they can get started. If you're not back in there with Rein before they get finished, I'm letting the coroner's office take that poor woman to the morgue."

"I'll go pick him up, boss," Carrie said. "He has to be around here somewhere."

There was an unmarked police car sitting on the street in front of Tucker Pennington's parents' estate. The Pennington house sat a hundred yards back from the road, surrounded by rolling hills of lush green grass. There was a fountain in the center of the driveway in front of the house, and it spurted water twenty feet into the air.

The nearest houses on either side were half a mile away, and there was nothing across the street but dense woods.

Carrie pulled up alongside the unmarked car. "Anything?"

"Nobody's came or went since Bender sent us down here," the first detective said.

Carrie turned in her seat and looked down the road. "Have you seen anyone else?"

"Like who?"

Carrie put her car in park and got out. She stood in the road, shading her eyes from the sun overhead. She peered at Tucker Pennington's house, then turned and searched the woods on the opposite side of the road behind her. "Rein?" she called out. "Are you here?"

"Who the hell's she yelling at?" the second detective asked.

"I have no idea." They came out of their car and stood on the street next to her.

"You guys didn't see anyone? A tall guy, probably looks homeless? Used to be a detective for the county?"

"Does he live in the woods?"

"No," Carrie said. "At least I don't think so. Maybe. Did you see anyone or not?"

"We didn't see shit."

"Rein!" Carrie shouted. "I need to talk to you! It's important!"

A branch snapped above their heads, and all of them turned their heads upward. High in the reaches of an old oak tree, branches shook and leaves fell to the ground as something worked its way down toward them.

Jacob Rein, dressed in black, his face and neck and arms covered in dirt, emerged from the woods. There were pieces of leaves stuck in his beard and he was plucking prickly burrs from his shirt.

"This had better be good," Rein said. "I've been sitting up in that tree since these two idiots showed up and ruined my surveillance."

"Hey!" the first detective said. "We didn't ask to get sent out here. We were perfectly fine back at the murder scene."

"What murder?" Rein asked.

"I need you to get in my car," Carrie said, trying to lead Rein away from them by the arm.

He pulled away from her. "What murder?"

Rein watched the landscape rush past through the window as Carrie drove. "I let him get past me. He must know a back way. I looked at satellite photos of the house and didn't see anything, so I thought. So stupid."

"It's not your fault," Carrie said. "That's a huge property. For all we know they've got underground tunnels or something."

"I should have been there, with her."

Carrie didn't say anything.

"I was supposed to be. My son invited me out last night to celebrate and I knew she was going to be there, but instead, I was in those goddamn woods wasting my time. If I'd gone, this wouldn't have happened."

I guess I didn't get the invite, Carrie thought. It didn't matter, she told herself. "Listen, Rein, before we get there, I have to warn you. It's a bad scene. However, it looks like she was killed first thing. Her eyes are still closed, like she was sleeping when it happened. I don't think she suffered. It's not much, I know, but it's something."

"You're right," Rein said. "It's not much."

* * *

Carrie raised the crime scene tape and waved for Rein to hurry up and come on. All of the cops and detectives there watched as he ducked under the tape. Rein kept his head low, feeling their stares crawling all over him like insects. "They probably think you're bringing me here for questioning," he said.

"Forget them," Carrie said.

Harv Bender was standing by the front door, waiting for the team of crime scene unit investigators to come back downstairs. "We're all done with photographs and measurements, Chief," the lead tech said. "We didn't find any weapons."

"I'll let the coroner know you're ready," Bender said.

Carrie hurried toward him. "Chief. I'm back. We still have time to go up and take a look before the coroner, right?"

Bender turned. He scowled when he saw Rein. "I didn't think you'd make it."

"Well, we did," Carrie said.

Bender put his hands on his hips. "I hear you knew this woman?"

"She was a friend."

"Well, I'm sorry to hear that. No one deserves what happened to her. You going to help us catch this bastard?"

"If I can."

"You know you're not an employee of the county, right? I just need to make sure it's absolutely crystal clear. You're not law enforcement. You're some kind of, what did you call it, Carrie? Consultant. For this case only. This one time only. Understood?"

"I just want to help," Rein said. "I don't care what you call me."

"Well go ahead in there, then," Bender said, stepping out of Rein's way. "Look, everybody, it's the world's first consulting detective."

"Not exactly," Rein said. He stopped at the entrance to the house and stared at the blood smeared across the frame.

"Sign of the lamb, from Passover," Carrie said, coming up beside him. "Right?"

"So it appears."

They entered the house and he started up the stairs before her.

"Rein," she said, and grabbed him by the arm. "I'm serious. It's bad up there, what he did to her."

"All right," he said.

"It's just that you and her were friends and I'm just trying to prepare you."

"I'm prepared." He went up the stairs and stopped when he reached the hallway on the second floor. Carrie knew he could see Linda's body from there. The door was wide open. Her splayed-open, naked back was turned toward him. Rein didn't move.

"You don't have to go in there, Jacob." She put her hand on his back. Letting him feel human contact. "Maybe this wasn't a good idea. We can go. No one would expect you to do this."

"She would." He took her flashlight and went into the bedroom.

Carrie let him go in by himself at first, not wanting to be in his way, and not wanting to invade his privacy as he looked at the remains of a woman he'd once loved. Had he loved her? Carrie wasn't sure. Linda had loved him. That much was obvious. Carrie could see the beam of the flashlight inside the room, scanning the walls in increments, until finally it fell on the center of the room where Linda's body sat. The flashlight flicked off. She heard his breathing catch. A sharp inhalation of air and the knotted struggle of him trying to steady himself.

The light came back on. It kept moving. "Carrie, come in here," he said.

She went in. Whatever effect seeing Linda's body had on Rein, he'd locked it in a basement far at the bottom of his mind. He aimed the flashlight at the symbols and phrases spray-painted on the walls. "What are these?"

"That's your basic satanic and witchcraft iconography. Upside down crucifixes and inverted pentagrams and whatnot. This is all Marilyn Manson one-o-one."

He shined the light at Linda Shelley's body. "And what can you tell me about this?"

"She's obviously positioned in the way that he wants us to find her. "*Behold, A Blood Angel.*,'" She read the words painted on the wall above her. "He's turned her into some kind of Satanic angel. Probably part of an elaborate ritual he concocted in the asylum. Sacrificing her to Lucifer, I guess. Or summoning him. Creepy little asshole."

"Interesting," Rein said. "I'm impressed."

"Really?"

"Inaccurate, but still, an impressive attempt." He aimed the flashlight at the symbols. "You're right about six-six-six and the references to The Beast. That's all basic Satanism. Look at this symbol on the far left, though. That's a unicursal hexagram. Do you see what's at the center?"

"The five-petaled clover thing?"

"It's specific to Aleister Crowley's Mark of Thelema. Crowley was an occultist in the early 1900s, and Thelema was the philosophy he founded."

"Was he a Satanist?"

"No." Rein pointed at the next symbol, the circle with the elaborate lower-cased *h* and the dots. "That second one is the mark of Fraternitas Saturni. An old European order of magicians who worship the planet Saturn."

"They sound like they'd throw kickass parties."

"Technically, they're Satanists, but they do sex ritual magic, not blood sacrifices." Rein pointed at the last symbol, the large one with the goat's head in the middle and the letters written above it. "*T-O-L*," he said. "Temple of Lucifer."

"Finally, some real devil worshippers," Carrie said.

"Not exactly. They're a satirical group dedicated to separation of church and state. Whenever someone wants to hang The Ten Commandments on government property, they show up and demand a statue of the devil be put there as well. When a public high school hands out Christian literature, they show up and start handing out pamphlets for Satanism."

"So why are these symbols here?" Carrie asked. "What do they mean to Pennington that he would use them?"

"I'm not sure. Tucker was never a Satanist, as far as I could tell. He was more inventive than that." Rein turned the light against

Linda's back, reinspecting her injuries and rereading the phrase written above her. "Blood Angel," he whispered. "None of this makes sense."

"The ribs are supposed to be her wings," Carrie explained. "See?"

"Obviously I can see it. Except this is not a Blood Angel. It's a Blood Eagle. An old method of torture the Vikings used. Honor was everything to the Vikings. When a warrior lost his honor, the Vikings would cut his back open, rip out his ribs one by one and splay them backward to resemble the wings of a bird. The prisoners who didn't scream or break down during the ordeal were said to be allowed admittance into Valhalla. There is no such thing as a Blood Angel. It doesn't exist."

"It does now."

"Well, it's wrong."

"Wrong to who? To you and me? You're fucking a-right it's wrong," Carrie said. "But the only person it has to make sense to is the killer, right? Isn't that what you always told me? Maybe he saw these symbols in some book and read about your stupid Blood Bird and somewhere in his mixed-up brain it all got swirled around into something he liked."

Rein snapped the flashlight off. "The blood on the front of the door is from Passover."

"I told you that when we came in."

"That is supposed to make death pass by. Not invite it in."

She maneuvered him out of the room and shut the door behind them. She was tired of staring at the horror of Linda's body. It was even worse that she'd begun feeling desensitized to it. She wanted to be outside on the front lawn and in the fresh air. "Well, if you are turning crucifixes upside down and worshiping the devil instead of God, maybe it means something different. Isn't everything backward with those people? Black Mass. Black Sabbath. Black Led Zeppelin. I don't know. Maybe this is Black Passover."

"Maybe," Rein conceded. "All of it just feels very derivative. Too many unrelated things thrown together. Some kind of effort to confuse us. Tucker was extremely well-organized when I arrested him before. It all came out of his own twisted ideas. He didn't borrow anything from anywhere else, let alone use it incorrectly."

"He also spent fifteen years in an asylum where they medicate the shit out of you. Maybe he read about all this stuff at some point and now he's making it all his own."

"I suppose that's possible," Rein conceded. He wiped sweat from his brow and took a deep breath. "You are absolutely correct. The only person any of this ever has to make sense to is the killer. I must be slipping, trying to force my own point of view into this. That, or I'm just not cut out for this anymore."

She put her hand on his back. "You all right?"

"No. No, I don't think so. She was a good friend at a time when I didn't have any other friends. I should have told her. But I never could."

"She knew," Carrie said.

"Let's go talk to Tucker," he said.

12

*C*arrie rolled down the driver's side window to let some fresh air in and feel the warmth of the sun on her arm and neck. "You certainly knew a lot about Satanists, back there."

"The Night Stalker was the first serial killer I studied, back in the mid-eighties. He was a Satanist. I learned what I could."

"How old were you?"

Rein looked up at the car's ceiling, counting. "I went to California in eighty-four, and he was arrested a year later, so, sixteen?"

"You lived in California? I never knew that. What made you go out there?"

"I was studying the Night Stalker."

The two detectives were still parked on the street in front of Pennington's house. Carrie pulled up alongside them and rolled down her window. "Did anyone come out of the house yet?"

"Nope."

"We're going down there to talk to them. Do you guys want to come with us? We could use a hand."

"Chief said to stay put and let him know if anyone leaves the house. Nobody left the house yet," the first detective said.

"I get that, but we're going down there to talk to them instead."

"Chief said to stay put."

Carrie rolled up the window and turned the car around to head down the driveway. She drove toward the house and pulled around the fountain and parked in front of the house's entrance.

The entrance was a set of double front doors made of richly stained wood and ornate brass handles. The doors parted and Thad Pennington came out of the house and stood on the porch with his arms folded, watching as they got out of the car.

"Detective Santero," Thad said. "We've been expecting you."

Carrie closed the driver's side door. "Really, why is that?"

Thad pointed down the driveway. "There's been two detectives in an unmarked car in front of our house all morning. I assumed someone would be coming to speak with us. Is anything the matter?"

"No, not at all," Carrie said. "The judge forgot to get some information from you yesterday and asked me to stop by."

"I see," Thad said. "So you won't mind if I contact my attorney?"

"Sure, if you want. Or, if you wanted to save time, I could just ask you my questions, and if there's any you aren't comfortable with, you can call him on the phone."

Thad raised an eyebrow at that. "I suppose."

A man came through the doors behind Thad. It was the priest from the courthouse. He was dressed in a collared shirt and black pants. He came to Thad's side and said good morning to them.

"Have you met Father Ihan?" Thad asked.

"You preach at Saint Margaret of Antioch, right?" Carrie went up the steps and extended her hand. "I've seen you there a few times."

He squinted at her and smiled. "You are a member of my church?"

"I take my dad sometimes. He likes to go more now that he's getting older."

"That's very kind of you. Bless you, my child."

"So do you mind if we go in?" Carrie asked.

"You may come in," Thad said. His eyes fixed on Rein. "But not him. My son is in spiritual recovery and has no need to see this man ever again."

Rein stepped backward off the steps and stood in the driveway. "I'll wait here."

As the others turned to go inside, Father Ihan came down the steps. "I'll wait with you. If you don't mind. I could use some fresh air."

Thad let Carrie inside and closed the door.

The priest stretched his arms out and took a deep breath. He held his hand over his eyes and looked up at the thick white clouds above. "When I was a boy, I used to look at the sky on days like this, and I would sometimes see sunlight pouring through one of the clouds. I'd think that must be the doorway to heaven. That all God's angels fly up through the sky and go through that doorway into paradise. I still sometimes think that, if I am honest."

Rein leaned back against Carrie's car with his arms folded. He picked at the rough edge of his thumbnail.

The priest leaned against the car beside him. "During my first year as a priest, I took a confession from a police officer. He told me that he was afraid of having to use his weapon in the line of duty. 'Father, how can I be a good Christian if I am expected to kill?' You know what I told him?"

Rein bit at his thumbnail, trying to make it smooth.

"I told him that in Romans 13:4, the Apostle Paul talked about that very thing. He said to be afraid of those appointed by God, for that man does not bear his sword in vain. He is the avenger who carries out God's wrath on wicked. After that, the police officer never worried about being called to take a life in the performance of his duties again."

Rein spat the piece of nail out and said nothing.

"You think that is untrue?"

"Show me any police officer convinced he was appointed by God, I'll show you someone capable of atrocity."

"Mr. Pennington tells me you were once a police officer. A detective."

"A long time ago," Rein said.

"I see," Ihan said. "In the priesthood, we also have those who walk away from their vows. Of course, what you are never really goes away, does it? There are things that you learn in this life that cannot be unlearned and you carry them forever. Many times, I've wanted to quit."

"So why didn't you?"

Ihan nodded at the door. "Because sometimes someone comes along who needs you. Someone you see great potential in, who, if you don't help, will fail. It's almost like you have failed and you know it, and you are doomed and you know it, but to let them fail would be a sin worse than that. Do you know what I mean?"

Rein didn't answer.

"I know you don't believe it, but young Tucker Pennington has great potential."

"That's why I'm here. His potential."

The priest chuckled at that. "You are a good man, Mr. Rein. You have a sharp mind and a good heart, even if you are uncomfortable with me saying it. I like you."

"Thanks," Rein said. "If it counts for anything, this is the friendliest conversation I've had with a man of the cloth in the past thirty years."

"You have not talked with many servants of God?"

"I've talked with plenty. But they were all child molesters."

"I take it you are not kidding."

"No."

Ihan patted his right front pants pocket and said, "Walk with me, if you don't mind. I need to smoke." They went around to the other side of the fountain where he pulled a pack of cigarettes out and put one in his mouth. He bowed his head to light it and closed his eyes in delight as he inhaled. "The bishop says we are not supposed to smoke in front of the faithful. It diminishes their respect for our purity. Or something like that. I suppose." He finished the cigarette halfway and stamped it out on the fountain and pinched the butt between his fingers. "It is a disgusting habit I picked up in the seminary. Growing up in Venezuela, I lived in austerity, thinking that was the way to become a priest. Then, I go to the seminary and all they do in the evening is drink and smoke and play cards. Now, I only do it when I am stressed."

"From talking to me?"

"From them," Ihan said, pointing at the Penningtons' front door. "They wrote a few checks and now the bishop has me waiting on them hand and foot."

"You're their personal priest," Rein said. "When I was on the street, sometimes people would latch on to you if you were too nice to them, and next thing you know they'd be calling you constantly for every little thing. You became their personal police officer."

Ihan pulled out another cigarette and lit it. "Yes, I am their personal priest." As he smoked, a red robin flew past and he turned to look at it. The priest pointed at it. "Do you know how the robin got his red breast?"

"Evolution."

"I meant, the story. They say that it was burnt protecting the Christ child from a fire, and for its bravery, God marked it for all time." He stubbed out the next cigarette. "This is the truth I have learned after all of these years. Some of it is parable. Some of it is true. All of it is meant to touch men's hearts and inspire them to be better."

"I think we'd be better off telling them the truth than filling their heads up with bedtime stories," Rein said.

"Do you know something? I am like you," Father Ihan said. "I have heard many confessions. I have peered deep into the darkness of men's souls. We are alike."

"I doubt that."

"You have seen evil," Father Ihan said. "You have stared it in the face?"

"Many times," Rein said.

"As have I. I have looked deep into the soul of many men who struggle with the evil within themselves. Alcoholics. Drug addicts. Criminals. All of them have been healed by faith. It sparks a light inside of them that helps them ward off the darkness. It is my observation that those who most fiercely defend the light are the ones who feel the most consumed by darkness. Perhaps what they are fighting most is not what is without, but what is within. This is something you understand also, no?"

A large bird made a wide loop in the sky above them. It was a turkey vulture. A black winged scavenger that looked like its head had been skinned and left raw and bloody. Rein watched it circle, knowing it had been drawn there by the scent of decay. That it searched the ground with its carrion eyes, looking for something dead to feed on.

"If you knew what I understand about evil, you'd run from this house as fast as you can and never come back," Rein said.

Father Ihan smirked and folded his arms across his chest. When he turned his head to reply, Rein had already walked away.

The foyer to the Penningtons' home was shaped into a dome, with a crystal chandelier hanging from the ceiling that was wider than Carrie's arms could stretch. The floor was marble, polished to a mirror finish so fine that she could see herself reflected in it. A spiral staircase wound up toward the second floor. A massive painting of the Pope adorned the wall next to the staircase. There were crucifixes hung over the center of the front doors and the entrances to every room and hallway.

"My wife and son are in the parlor," Thad said.

They walked past a dining room with a round wooden table big enough for eight chairs and place settings. Each setting had actual silver and china, she saw. The centerpiece in the middle of the table was an arrangement of synthetic flowers. All of it was spotless and dust free from regular cleaning, and none of it showed any sign of use.

Carrie followed Thad into a large room on the right side of the foyer. There were two sectional sofas facing each other across a glass table. In the center of the table was a crystal bowl of fake fruit. Beyond the table was a fireplace large enough to fit a tree trunk, with no wood in it. Thad walked over to the fireplace and flicked a light switch set over the mantel. Tiny knick-knacks that read I HAVE A FRIEND IN JESUS, and I AM SAVED—ARE YOU? were placed along the mantel, and statues of different saints sat at either end.

Grace Pennington got up and flicked the fireplace switch on, making the gas jets running along its ceramic basin erupt into flames. "My son has been cold ever since he came home," she said. "It's all those years of that awful hospital food. We'll put some meat on those bones with some good old-fashioned home-cooked meals in no time, won't we, Tucker?"

Tucker Pennington sat on the couch near the fireplace, rocking back and forth. In his left hand he held an ornate crucifix and in his right hand, a length of bright red rosary beads. Tucker made the sign of the cross on the crucifix with the tip of his finger and said, "I believe in God, the Father Almighty, creator of heaven and earth. I believe in Jesus Christ, his only son, our lord, who was conceived by the Holy Ghost, born of the Virgin Mary, suffered under Pontius Pilate, was crucified, died, and was buried."

Grace sat next to her son and draped an arm around his back. She rocked with him. "He hasn't finished his prayers yet."

Tucker finished the Apostle's Creed and selected the next large bead. "Our father, who art in heaven, hallowed be thy name," he said.

"How many does he do each day?" Carrie asked.

"He does them all day and throughout most of the night," Grace said.

Thad sat down on the couch opposite the other two. "What can we do for you, Detective?"

"The judge just had some questions about Tucker's supervision," Carrie said. The heat from the fireplace was too much to stand close to but Tucker was shivering anyway. His hands worked the beads as he continued to pray and Carrie saw that his wrists were thinner than his mother's.

"We are supervising him at all times. He won't be out of our sight, ever," Thad said.

"Except when Father Ihan is with him," Grace added.

"What about last night?" Carrie asked.

"What do you mean?" Thad said.

"Hail Mary, full of grace. The Lord is with thee. Blessed art thou among women, and blessed is the fruit of thy womb, Jesus."

"When you came home from court last night, what did you do?" Carrie asked.

"We went out for dinner at the country club," Thad said. "That was always Tucker's favorite place to get Beef Wellington. They were so happy to see him. They knew he never did those awful things you people accused him of."

"Thad," Grace said.

Thad cleared his throat. "After that we came home."

"What time did you go to bed?"

"We stayed up and watched a movie. Detective, where is this going?"

"I guess I'm just wondering, after you went to bed, what did Tucker do?"

The beads clacked in Tucker's hand. "Pray for us, o holy mother of God. That we may be made worthy of the promises of Christ."

"He fell asleep while we were watching a movie," Thad said. "I woke him up when it was over and we all went upstairs to go to bed."

"What time was that?" Carrie asked.

"I have no idea."

"Around midnight," Grace said.

Carrie pulled a notepad from her back pocket and made notes. "And after that?"

Thad looked at his wife in confusion. "After we went to sleep? We woke up the next morning."

"Where was Tucker when you woke up?"

"In his bedroom," Grace said.

Tucker Pennington made the sign of the cross on the crucifix and started over. "I believe in God, the Father Almighty, creator of heaven and earth. I believe in Jesus Christ, his only son, our lord, who was conceived by the Holy Ghost, born of the Virgin Mary, suffered under Pontius Pilate, was crucified, died, and was buried."

"Did you wake him up or was he already awake?"

"He was awake, lying in his bed," Grace said. Her voice caught in her throat. "He was waiting to be given permission to come downstairs to eat, because, because that's what he had to do." She wiped her eyes. "That's what he had to do while he was locked up in that place."

Carrie made a few more notes. "Does Tucker have access to a car?"

"We have several cars," Thad said. "But it didn't come up. Detective, my son has only been home one day."

"What's your real question, Detective?" Grace asked.

Carrie lowered her notepad. It was the moment of truth.

Another bead. "Our father, who art in heaven, hallowed be thy name."

"Tucker went out last night," Carrie said. "He went to see Dr. Shelley. Didn't you, Tucker?" She snapped her fingers at him. "Hey? Hey! Didn't you?"

Thad Pennington waved his hand to stop her. "Detective, I can assure you, unequivocally, that my son was home the entire night last night."

"Really? How?"

"We had security cameras installed outside of Tucker's room, on his bedroom windows, on the driveway, our backyard, and every square inch of this house and property, minus the bathrooms and bedrooms," Thad said.

Grace's mouth twisted in disgust. "We assumed people would falsely accuse him anytime there was some kind of incident, but I never dreamed it would happen so soon. Luckily, we were prepared for you."

"Tucker never left his bedroom last night," Thad said. "He never left this house. Period. Do you want me to get you a copy of the video?"

He didn't wait for her to answer before he got up off the couch to fetch it.

13

"*E*xcuse the mess in here," Carrie said. She went up the steps and unlocked the trailer's front door. "Sal? You awake in there, buddy?" She leaned her head inside and called his name again. The trailer was empty. "I hope he wasn't serious about quitting."

Rein shut the door behind him. "They put you out here?"

"I guess I don't rate high enough to be in the temporary office with everyone else. I figured you'd appreciate the peace and quiet of having our own workspace."

"You know the dam is contaminated, right? It's been that way for years. People used to pull three-eyed fish and mutated frogs out of there all the time."

"They did? Well, I'm sure they cleaned that up by now, " Carrie said.

"If you say so."

Carrie pulled a thumb drive out of her pocket and plugged it into the side of the laptop. "Let's see if we can get this to work."

Rein stepped aside so she could sit. "In the old days, we had the only multiplex VHS player in the region. The screen was smaller than your cell phone's. Back then only gas stations and larger stores had surveillance. If we couldn't get it to play on our machine, we had to take it back to their store, play it on their machine, and take a photograph of the TV screen."

"You'd literally hold your camera up to the monitor and take a picture?"

"That's all we could do."

Carrie shook her head as she installed the thumb drive's operating software onto her laptop. "Was it scary when the pterodactyls swooped down on you, or were you too amazed by the invention of fire to pay any attention to them?"

The software installed and the system's player appeared on the screen. She pressed PLAY and there was a loud clunking noise from the laptop speaker. Error, it said. "Damn it. I guess I need to update the drivers. This could take a while."

Rein moved a stack of newspapers out of the way on the couch behind her and sat down. "Did you ever hear of Frederick Porter Wensley?"

Carrie clicked through various boxes on the computer screen as Rein spoke. "Can't say that I have."

"He spent forty years in Scotland Yard. Most decorated criminal investigator of his time. His first year on the job, he walked a foot beat in Whitechapel, looking for Jack the Ripper."

"No shit?"

"They wore boots with wooden soles back then, so Wensley nailed small pieces of rubber from bicycle tires to them so he could walk silently on the cobblestone streets."

"That's smart."

"One of the things I like best about Wensley is that he talks about how much technology had changed by the time he retired in the late 1920s. Think about it. The telephone. Cars. Typewriters. Machine guns. All these technological advancements that had seemed like science fiction back when he started in 1888. You know what he said never changed? The job itself. Victims were still victims. Criminals were still criminals. The same socio-economic factors that had caused crime in 1888 were the same ones that caused it in 1929, and you know what? He was right. He was right about then, and he's right about now. It's all the same. It's just the bells and whistles look different now."

The computer dinged and Carrie clicked play again. A time-stamped video appeared, showing multiple camera feeds of the interior and exterior of the Penningtons' house. One of the interior feeds covered the hallway outside of Tucker Pennington's bedroom, facing his door. An exterior feed faced his bedroom with a clear view of his windows. There was an option to watch it at faster speeds. Carrie clicked it and the feeds sped up. The night sky changed in the exterior shots, getting lighter. Nothing about the house changed. No one went in or out.

"Could they have altered the video?" Rein asked.

"I guess anything's possible. But that fast and with no prior warning?"

"Doesn't seem likely."

"All right," Carrie said. "No big deal. Obviously, he's got some sort of underground escape route. A tunnel or something, that comes out in the woods, far away from the video cameras."

"An underground tunnel?"

"Exactly."

"And why would his parents have built an underground tunnel on their property?"

"I have no idea," Carrie said. "Maybe it used to belong to bootleggers. People who ran moonshine. Tucker discovered it, and now he's using it to commit his evil deeds."

Rein picked at a loose thread on the couch's armrest. "We have now entered the realm of wild speculation."

"No, it's called a theory. What if it's true?"

"Is that how murders are solved these days? We just imagine different possibilities and go running off to chase them down until we can prove they aren't true? It's been a while since I worked one. Maybe I forget."

"Oh, shut up."

"Let's make a list of all the theories we can think of. Aliens. Russian mafia. A secret pedophile ring in the back of a pizza shop."

"I said, enough."

"In my day, we just followed the natural progression of evidence until a suspect developed. But who knows, maybe if we'd considered the, what was it, old-time moonshine runners with secret underground tunnels theory, it could have saved everybody a lot of time."

Carrie closed the laptop. "You done? You've made your point."

Behind Rein, a car skidded into the dirt parking lot next to Carrie's car, filling the trailer's window with dust. "Who the hell is that?" Carrie said. She got up from the chair and laid her right hand on her pistol's grip, ready to yank it from its holster if needed. She opened the trailer's front door a crack and peeked through. A thin figure emerged through the cloud of dust, and Carrie said, "Holy shit. It's Bill."

Bill Waylon squinted up at her in the afternoon sun. It was sitting on the horizon, bright and full, just behind the trailer. "Hey, kiddo," Waylon said. "Sorry about pulling up on you like that. None of these lots have addresses and I didn't see it until I almost drove past."

"It's all right, Chief. What brings you out here?"

"I heard about the murder. Dr. Shelley was a good woman. Helped us out that time and I never forgot it."

He was still sickly-looking and his beard was so pallid, it looked almost white in the sun, but he was up and he was moving, and it was all Carrie could do not to come running down the steps to hug him. Bill Waylon was back, she thought. She couldn't help but smile. "Come on in," Carrie said. "I've got Jacob in here. We're getting ready to go nail this Master bastard."

"Yeah, I figured he was here," Waylon said. "Actually, I need to speak with him first. Can you send him out?"

"Sure," Carrie said. She leaned her head back inside the trailer and grinned at Rein. "We're getting the band back together."

Rein moved the trailer's window curtain aside to look at his old partner. "Is that right?"

"He wants to talk to you first."

Rein got up from the couch. He went to move past Carrie and she said, "Be nice."

"I'm always nice."

"Maybe twice in the whole time I've known you."

Rein went through the door onto the top step of the trailer and pulled the door shut behind him. Waylon looked worse than he'd imagined. Withered. Scarred. The injury to his neck had aged the man ten years or more. Something inside of Bill Waylon had retreated into a corner and lain down whimpering. "Bill," Rein said.

"Jacob. Been a little while."

"Every time I called, Jeri told me you were resting. When I finally went to your house, cars were in the driveway and I heard the TV on, but I guess no one heard me knocking or ringing the doorbell."

Waylon ran his fingers around the scar on his neck and squeezed enough to help himself clear his throat. "Can you blame my wife for being angry?"

"No," Rein said.

"The bastards fired me while I was still in the hospital. Can you believe it? All those years, all those killers and rapists we put in jail and then I get my throat slit and they fire me on my deathbed."

"How could they do that?"

"Let's see, first was me being outside my jurisdiction when the incident happened, then failing to tell them about the investigation, then it was nearly getting Carrie killed. They had a whole list."

"I'm sorry to hear that."

"It turned out okay. I sued them and said it was age discrimination and them trying to get out of paying the hospital bills. They let me retire and keep my pension."

"It shouldn't have ended like that for you," Rein said. "You deserved better."

"Yeah, well. Doesn't seem like it ended for you. Looks like you're right back in the mix of things."

"Linda was a friend of mine."

"Friends of yours all seem to pay for it in the end, don't they?"

Rein glanced back at the window to see if Carrie was watching. He couldn't see her through the sun's reflection. He moved away from the trailer, toward Waylon. "Did you get tired of drowning in self-pity at your house and want to come spread it around down here, Bill? You want me to feel sorry for you? Fine, I feel sorry for you. Now, is there anything else or can I go back to what I was doing?"

Waylon's scrawny hands tightened into fists, shaking with

rage. "Fuck you and your pity, Rein. I'm not too sick to knock your ass out."

"Go home, Bill."

"That little son of a bitch Pennington sent me a letter at my home. At my home, Jacob. He threatened Jeri." Waylon's voice quivered, "He threatened the girls."

"We're going to stop him."

"That's not good enough!" Waylon shouted. "Abby, my oldest, she's up at school. You think the security guards there are going to do shit if Pennington goes after her? He could snatch her in the parking lot and do God knows what to her long before we even found out. I've got a family, Jacob. I need your help to protect them."

A car drove past on the highway, close enough to send wind rippling through their clothes. The stench from the dam was enough to make Rein's nose curl. "What do you have in mind?"

"I saved something from when I was chief," Waylon said. He waved for Rein to follow him toward his car.

Waylon opened his trunk. There was a red gym bag inside, sitting next to the spare tire. He looked over his shoulder to make sure no cars were coming before he unzipped it. It was stuffed with a T-shirt, shorts, and a pair of socks. Waylon pulled the shorts out and unfolded them to reveal a chrome snub-nose revolver with black rubber grips.

"I found this in the back of the Coyote evidence room. One of the older cops must have taken it off somebody and stuck it in there. There wasn't even a case file associated with it."

The serial numbers were filed off the gun, leaving nothing but scratches. It was totally untraceable. "Good drop gun," Rein said.

"Perfect drop gun. Now listen to me, Jacob. I'm not asking you to do anything. All I'm asking is that you let me know where Pennington is at and when it's a good time."

"It's a felony for you to even have a gun like that in your possession. You'll lose your pension just for carrying it around, even if you don't go to prison."

"You think I give a shit about that?" Waylon hissed. "I'd do anything to protect the people I love. Wouldn't you?"

Rein glanced back at the trailer, sure Carrie was still trying to watch them. "What about her? You willing to put her in the middle of this?"

"No, I don't want her involved in this. Not at all. This is between you and me and that sick little motherfucker. We should have put him in the ground a long time ago. Saved the world a whole lot of heartache."

"She's smart. What if she figures it out?"

"She won't. And even if she does, well, I have no doubt she will understand. She loves Jeri and the kids."

Rein reached for the gun and Waylon stopped him. "What are you doing?"

"Have you shot it?"

"No," Waylon said. "The thing is clean as a whistle, my friend. I don't think it's ever been fired."

"Then how do you know it works? Let's say I lure this guy out, get Carrie good and distracted, you come along to handle business, you take your gun here and pull the trigger and all that happens is a puff of smoke comes out. Then what? Tucker either kills you or we have to kill him some other way. You didn't think this all the way through, Bill. Nice to know some things never change." Rein held out his hand. "Let me see it."

Waylon looked doubtful but reached for the gun anyway. He wrapped it in the gym shorts and handed it to Rein. "Be careful. We have to make sure to get rid of any fingerprints on it. Not even on the bullets. See, I did think this one all the way through, you ass."

"I take it back," Rein said. "Wait here."

Rein tucked the gun under his armpit and turned around. He went wide around the back of Carrie's car, staying out of view of the trailer window.

"Where are you going?" Waylon whispered.

"Wait here."

As soon as Rein hit the weeds behind the trailer, he started to run.

"Shit!" Waylon ran after Rein as fast as he could. He only made it a few steps past the trailer before he was coughing and gasping for air.

"Stop," Waylon wheezed. He staggered through the weeds enough to see Rein cock his arm back and hurl the gun deep into the Carver Dam's polluted waters. The splash sent a tree full of birds scattering into the air.

Rein wiped his hands as he walked back toward the trailer, past Waylon. "Go home, partner."

"We're not partners anymore, you motherfucker," Waylon hissed. "Whatever happens to my wife and daughters is on your head, you son of a bitch! Your head! And I swear to God, if it does, I'm coming after you." Waylon bent over, coughing and clutching his throat as Rein disappeared through the weeds.

Carrie came out of the trailer as Bill Waylon cranked the wheel in his car and punched the gas, tires screeching as they hit the asphalt road. Dust billowed across the lot, and Rein lowered his head and looked away. "What the hell was all that about?"

"I pissed Bill off again."

"What did you do this time?"

Rein looked back at her. "He wanted to help us. I told him he wasn't well enough and would just get in the way."

"What the hell did you do that for, Jacob? He's been sitting in his house rotting away. Now he finally comes out to be involved in something and you insult him and tell him to leave?"

Rein went up the trailer steps behind her. "I thought you were serious about catching the killer?"

"I am, but Jesus. You ever think life might be easier if you weren't such an asshole to people who care about you?"

He held the door open for her. "Am I an asshole to you?"

"No. But that's because I don't care about you."

"You don't?"

"Not at all. There's no upside to that, Jacob Rein. I learned that the hard way."

He sat down on the couch behind her as she went back to her laptop. There was a stack of printouts on the table. He sifted through them, seeing driver's license printouts for Alexis Dole and Tricia Martin, satellite pictures of their houses, satellite pic-

tures of Tucker's house, Bill Waylon's house, and multiple dupli-
cates of a wide-angle shot that showed all of the houses in the
same image.

Carrie had attempted to draw pentagrams using Tucker Pennington's house as the center, with one of the points connecting
to Linda Shelley's house. She'd twisted and turned the image various ways, trying to get it to connect to the others, but couldn't
make it fit. "It's hard to think crazy, isn't it?" Rein said.

"I'm trying to figure out who he'll go after next. I think it's either Bill or Tricia Martin. They're the two most vulnerable."

Rein slid the driver's license photo of Alexis Dole closer. "Not
Miss Dole?"

"She's not afraid of him. You should have seen her in the courtroom. She looked like she could have killed him with one hand.
She's a complete badass."

"She sounds much different from the high school cheerleader
I met all those years ago," Rein said.

"I guess if a maniac disfigures you for the rest of your life, it
might have that effect."

"Why do you think Bill's vulnerable? He's got guns. He's a career police officer. If he stays in the house all the time, the killer
does not likely know his physical condition."

"He's not just vulnerable because of his health. He's vulnerable
because of the people he loves. Luckily for you, no one knows
Jacob Junior is your son."

"That just leaves you," Rein said.

"Me? What do you mean, me?"

"You were at court today. Obviously you're involved. What
makes you think you're not on the list?"

"Please, I wish he would come after me," Carrie said.

"Well, then," Rein said. "I guess it's good there's nobody you
love."

Carrie stopped typing and picked up her cell phone. She dialed the first number and said, "Penny, it's me. Where's Nubs?"

"You mean Natalie?"

"You know who I mean."

"In her room. She just took her bath."

"Good. Is the front door locked?"

"I think so."

"It's important. Please check."

She could hear Penny walking across the living room floor. She heard Penny jiggle the door handle. "Yes, it's locked."

"Dead bolt too." She waited, listening for the click to make sure Penny locked that too.

"There. You're really getting paranoid, Carrie. I think you need a boyfriend or something to take your mind off your job."

"All the windows too. Even the upstairs ones. And the basement. Sometimes you go outside to smoke from the basement and you might forget to lock it on your way back inside. You can't do that. I need you to go check the entire house and make sure every single thing is locked. Promise me."

"Carrie. Stop."

"Promise me!"

"Fine, for Christ's sake, I promise. What's gotten into you?"

"Tell Nubs I love her," Carrie said, and hung up the phone. She scrolled through the numbers and found her father's name next. She dialed it and held it to her ear, waiting for him to pick up.

"He's not answering," she said. "He probably had a few drinks and passed out in his chair. He's fine."

"Oh good," Rein said. "That's reassuring." He found the same piece of thread he'd been picking at before and went back to picking at it again.

Carrie spun around in her chair. "What does that mean?"

"I guess if there's one thing a lifetime of dealing with homicidal maniacs has taught me is that when you can't reach a loved one, everything is probably fine. There's never anything to really worry about."

Carrie groaned and shoved the laptop lid down. "Let's go. We have to make sure my dad's not being tortured to death, now."

"I think Penny's right. You're starting to sound paranoid," Rein said.

"I take it back. I care about you, Rein. A lot." She followed him through the trailer door and cupped her hand to the side of her mouth, "There's nobody I love more than you in the whole world!"

He waited for her to lock it, then said, "You think the killer heard you?"

"Only one way to find out."

Rein let himself into the car on the passenger side. "Joke's on him. I know you meant it."

"Shut up."

"Kind of weird, telling me in the middle of trying to make sure your father isn't tortured and murdered. The heart wants what it wants, though."

Carrie laughed as she put the car in drive and said, "You wish."

14

*R*osendo Santero lived in a three-bedroom rancher that sat back on a narrow strip of land. It was surrounded by woods. They drove up the gravel driveway and multiple eyes reflected in the high beams from Carrie's car. Deer stared at the car in confusion, then bolted, leaping into the darkness of the trees.

Carrie parked around the rear of the house, by the kitchen door. The kitchen was small and cramped but gave way to a living room that took up two-thirds of the house. It was as large as the three bedrooms combined. Of the bedrooms, Rosendo occupied the main one and used the one next to his for storage. The last bedroom he kept for her in case she ever needed it. She never did.

"I have my own place, Papi," she'd told him.

"I keep it just in case. Maybe you are out working late and need someplace close by to sleep if you are too tired to go home."

"We only live a few miles away from one another."

"It's good to have just in case. Hopefully soon my grandson can use it."

"Oh, I'm giving you a grandson now?"

"A good, strong boy. That is what I ask God for."

"What if it's a girl?"

"The first one can be a girl. Healthy. That is all that is important. A girl would be nice. But then you have to keep trying."

"And what if I don't want kids?"

He'd laughed at that, like she'd said something ridiculous.

Large windows took up the entire living room wall in the rear of the house. There were shades but Rosendo never lowered them. No one could see into his house and he liked to watch the animals.

She saw him lying back in his recliner with his eyes closed and his feet up. She could see his chest rise and fall as he snored. The television was on. Its screen was the only light on inside the house.

Carrie and Jacob got out of her car and headed for the kitchen door. There were two trash cans on the patio. One was nearly empty. The other was overflowing with crushed beer cans and empty liquor bottles.

She turned the door handle and found it was already open. "That's unusual," Carrie whispered.

Rein leaned back and looked through the living room windows again. "Does he always sit in the dark?"

"Only if he starts drinking early and falls asleep before the sun goes down."

They went into the kitchen and Rein put his hand on Carrie's arm to stop her. He lowered his head and closed his eyes. When he raised his head again, he said, "Do you hear that?"

She couldn't hear anything over the sound of the television and her father's snoring.

"There's a window open in the back of the house."

"He never opens his windows," Carrie said. She looked at her father, bathed in the light of the television. The rest of the living room was dark. Carrie drew her weapon. "Let's go."

"I'll go," Rein said. "You stay with him. Keep him quiet."

Carrie crept across the living room floor with her gun at her side. Its tritium sights glowed luminescent green in the darkness. Rosendo was splayed out in his chair. The remote control was cradled in one hand against his chest. His shirt was decorated with pieces of half-eaten hard pretzels and flakes of salt. On the side table next to the chair was his favorite cup, large and green, that he filled every night with bottom-shelf rum and a splash of diet soda. The cup was nearly empty.

She brushed against Rosendo's arm and he jerked awake. He

cried out in surprise, but Carrie jammed her hand over his mouth to stifle him. "Quiet, Papi," she whispered.

She looked over her shoulder at Rein. He was looking at the kitchen counter, searching for something. She could see his form silhouetted by the small windows over the sink. He reached past the microwave oven and coffeepot and there was the sound of something metal being drawn from wood.

Rein emerged from the kitchen with two large chef's knives, one in each hand. He moved in a crouch with the blades extended in front of him.

Carrie felt the smooth warmth of her gun's frame against her index finger. She'd only move it to the trigger when it was time to shoot. She heard the floor creak in the small bedroom. The one Rosendo had saved for her. She listened, forcing herself to listen past the television, past the sound of her father's muffled breathing against her hand, past the sound of the blood rushing through her head. She could hear what Rein heard. A window was open there. Wind rustled through the trees outside. A car splashed through a puddle on the road far away.

She heard Rein move toward the window and braced herself. If the killer was in there and got past Jacob, he was going to come running out of the room toward her and her father. It would be too hard to see him in time. She'd have no idea where Jacob was if she fired blindly. She would hit the killer, but the bullets could go through him and kill Rein as well.

Carrie positioned herself between her father's chair and the bedroom hallway. If the killer did come out running, she was going to launch herself into him and press the barrel against whatever part of his body she could find. She'd jam it under his armpit or against his temple or the small of his back, and then she'd pull the trigger over and over until his body stopped quivering.

Rosendo climbed out of his chair and crouched next to her with his fists raised.

"What are you doing? Get behind me," Carrie whispered.

"I didn't back down from the bastard communists and I don't back down now. If there is a fight, I fight with you."

In the bedroom, she saw Rein lower himself to the floor and look under the bed. She heard him open the closet door and close it again. After he checked the room, he moved into the bathroom and checked, flinging open the shower curtain and looking behind the door.

"Nothing?" Carrie called out.

Rein didn't respond. He turned the lights on in the hall and the bedroom used for storage, taking his time to check the windows and look inside the closet there. He moved into the main bedroom and emerged a few minutes later, still holding the kitchen knives. "There's security locks on all these windows," Rein said. "They can't be opened from the outside."

"Of course not," Rosendo sniffed. "I'm always about the safety. Nobody is breaking into mi casa."

"So the one in that bedroom was opened from the inside," Rein said.

"What? You crazy. Who the hell is this guy? Nobody was in the house except me."

Rein pointed one of the knives toward the kitchen. "There's only two explanations then. You opened the window yourself and forgot about it."

"No."

"And you left the front door unlocked."

"Eso es pura paja. Never."

"You forget things all the time when you're drinking, Papi."

"I wasn't drinking. Who said I was drinking!"

"The only other explanation is that someone broke in. They walked through the house and opened the back window as an emergency escape route."

"What, you think I just lay here while some person came into my house like some cobarde?" He puffed out his chest and balled up his fists. "I kick the ass of anybody who come in here. You saying I can't defend myself in front of my own daughter? I'll kick your ass right now. What's this guy saying to me, huh? Tell him I'll do it."

"No one's saying that, Papi." Carrie holstered her gun. She

pulled her father's head toward hers and kissed him on top of his forehead. "Go pack a bag."

"For what?"

"We're leaving."

"I'm not leaving. You both come in here, acting like crazy people."

"I love you, Papi."

"I love you too," he said.

"I know. Go pack a bag or I'll pack it for you."

There were no K-9's working in the county that evening. There weren't any in the surrounding counties either. Carrie made her father sit in her car with Rein while she processed the scene. She swabbed for DNA and dusted for fingerprints but wasn't hopeful. The never-ending influx of crime scene television shows had instructed even the stupidest of criminals to wear gloves.

She tossed her evidence bag into her trunk and hopped into the driver's seat. Rosendo's arms were folded across his chest and he wouldn't look at her. "What happened?" she asked.

"Your friend back there. He is a goddamn atheist."

Carrie glared at Rein in the rearview mirror and held up her hands.

"I made the mistake of telling him about Linda," Rein muttered.

"That woman's soul needed to be prayed over, to undo all the wickedness cast upon her!"

"Stop," Rein said. "She didn't believe in that nonsense either."

"Nonsense?" Rosendo cried. "You are blasphemy!" He pursed his lips together and pretended to spit. "Pecador!"

"All right, that's enough!" Carrie said. She reached in her coat pocket and pulled out Rosendo's set of keys. "Rein, take these. You're driving my dad's car over to Penny's house."

"Why can't I drive it?" Rosendo said.

"Because you've been drinking. And you can't see at night, anyway." She turned to hand the keys to Rein and said, "You do have a driver's license, right?"

"Of course."

"Is it current?"

Rein scratched the side of his beard. "How long do they last for again?"

"Four years."

He plucked the keys from her hand. "I'll drive slow."

The door closed and Rosendo grunted. "I don't want that atheist driving my car."

"What is your problem, Papi? Jacob is a good man. He saved my life. He might have just helped me save yours."

"He is a bum! Perezoso! Look at that beard. Madre de Dios. You can do better."

Carrie rolled her eyes. "I'm not with him."

Rosendo looked out the window as they drove down the driveway. "Say whatever you want. A father knows."

Penny was waiting for them at the front door with her arms folded. She was wearing her good robe, the silk Japanese one, instead of her pink one with the cigarette burns in it. She'd done her hair and put on lipstick.

Carrie parked her car and told Rosendo to wait a second. "I don't want to scare Penny or Natalie with anything I just told you. I need you to keep an eye on them both. Make sure the house is locked up. Make sure she and Natalie are never out of your sight. If you hear anything, I mean anything, call nine-one-one right away."

"I understand."

"It's very important that Penny doesn't think you're here to protect her. She has too much pride for that, so don't tell her why you're here."

"She is a strong, proud woman."

"Exactly. Listen, I hate having to ask you to do this, but you're the only person I trust enough. They're vulnerable and I need someone I can rely on."

Rosendo patted his daughter on the hand and said, "I know, my love. I will do whatever it takes. You have my promise as your father and as a man."

"Thank you, Papi." She leaned in and kissed him on the cheek. "Let's go inside. Remember, this stays between us."

"Of course," he said. He grabbed his bag from the floor and slung it around his shoulder.

When he got out of the car, Penny put her hands on her hips and called out, "Rosendo Santero, look at you. You haven't aged a day in the past ten years."

"Who is that?" Rosendo said. He shielded his eyes from the porch lights, trying to see her better.

"It's Penny, you idiot."

"That's impossible," Rosendo said. He put his hand over his heart and said, "The woman standing before me is too young and beautiful to be her."

Carrie smacked him on the arm. "Get in the damn house before I puke all over both of you."

Penny greeted him with open arms and he leaned in and kissed her on both cheeks. "Come in," she said, waving him through the door. "Put your bag down anywhere and make yourself at home. Mi casa, su casa. Did I say that right?"

"You most certainly did," he said, and they both laughed.

"Can I talk to you on the porch, Penny?" Carrie asked.

"Sure thing," Penny said.

Carrie leaned in to make sure her father wasn't listening. "Thank you so much for taking him in," she said.

"No problem at all. Was someone really in the house?"

"I think so. I can't be sure, but right now, I can't take any chances."

"I understand."

"Listen, under no circumstances can he think he's here for you to protect him. He's too damn stubborn for that."

"He's got his pride. I understand that."

"Exactly. Until things settle down and we arrest this guy, I need you to make sure he and Nubs—Natalie—God damn it, are never out of your sight."

Penny took Carrie's hand. "You won't have anything to worry about. I didn't get this far in life by backing down from needle-dick scumbags that threaten the ones I love. Matter of fact, you send that little asshole over here and I'll take care of him for you."

"Thank you. You're the only person I trust enough to do this. My dad's vulnerable and I need someone I can rely on."

"Oh, sweetie, you can rely on me. Always."

"I know I can," Carrie said. She embraced Penny and went to go back inside.

"You go run along and take care of business," Penny said, blocking her from the door. "I'm going to go visit with your father."

"I'm sure he's pretty tired," Carrie said.

"What are you talking about?" Rosendo said. "I am as awake as ten men."

"See?" Penny said.

"Keep an eye on him," Carrie whispered.

"Oh, I will. All night if I have to." Penny winked at Carrie and closed the door.

Carrie heard the dead bolt lock in place and saw Penny's shadow move across the room toward the sofa. As she went down the steps to her car, she could hear the two of them laughing.

15

*C*arrie drove slowly past Tucker's house, looking for Rein. Her father's car was parked in a ditch on the side of the road a hundred yards west of the property. No one was sitting in it.

"Is he up in the damn trees again?" She looked through her windows at the treetops as she drove past. There was nothing but darkness. She kept driving.

The handheld radio next to her crackled and made her jump. "Checking up on me?"

She raised it to her mouth and pressed the button. "Just trying to see where you're hiding."

"If you could see where I was hiding, I wouldn't be doing it right."

She pressed the button. "Well, at least I know you've got your radio on."

"Where did you find this thing anyway? It looks older then when I was with the county."

"Did they have radios back then? I thought they sent all their messages by raven."

There was a pause. "Why would anyone use ravens? Homing pigeons would make more sense."

"It was a joke, Rein. It's from a TV show."

"I don't own a television. Sending messages by raven is stupid."

She put the radio down and laughed.

* * *

Alexis Dole lived at the center of a cul-de-sac in a quiet neighborhood. Her entire downstairs was lit. Her porch lights were on. She had spotlights at each corner of the house and they were lit too. The house didn't have motion sensors, as far as Carrie could tell. Everything was just on. Carrie sat in her car a few blocks away from the house. She'd picked that spot because there were no streetlights overhead. She figured Dole would be on high alert after the court hearing and there was no need to antagonize the woman any further.

There was a sign on the front lawn that read NO SOLICITORS, NO TRESPASSERS, YOU ARE BEING RECORDED.

There were no curtains in the house. Just cheap plastic blinds that hung lopsided and cracked from nylon strings. Carrie pulled her binoculars out of the glove box and raised them to her eyes, twisting their lenses until the interior of Alexis Dole's living room came into focus. "Holy shit," Carrie whispered.

The living room walls were barren and the only piece of furniture was a beach chair, folded in the corner. A heavy bag hung from a large metal hook that was screwed upward into the ceiling. There were weights stacked along the walls. No mirrors. A large paper target with a human silhouette was taped to one wall. Carrie zoomed in and saw a dozen throwing knives sunk deep in the head, neck, and groin. As she inspected the knives, she realized something was standing very close to her. Its face was just inches away. Its eyes were level with hers. The only thing that separated it from her was the car door window.

The glass fogged and Carrie lowered her binoculars, and turned her head, very slowly.

The dog's massive head was the size of her own. Its sleek black fur was highlighted by the thick metal chain around its neck. It was a rottweiler and its ears had been clipped so that instead of drooping, they stuck out sideways like devil horns. The dog was growling but somehow made no noise. Its snout was curled back, tight, and quivering. White foam leaked from its sharp, curved, fangs. Carrie put the binoculars down very slowly and leaned back from the window.

"Sentar!" someone behind the dog commanded and the dog's face instantly relaxed. It's tongue unfurled and it panted and sat down. Alexis Dole came up alongside the dog and rested her hand on top of the dog's head. She scratched its ears and said, "Fique. Good."

Carrie cracked her window just enough to speak through it. "Good evening, Miss Dole."

Dole was dressed in a hooded sweatshirt. The hood covered most of her face, leaving her ruined eye in shadow. She kept stroking her dog. The dog was still watching Carrie.

"He's really big," Carrie said.

"I rescued him from a kill shelter," Dole said. "He was found inside a heroin shipment from Brazil. The cartel had severed his vocal chords so no one could hear him. That's why he doesn't make any noise when he growls."

"That's kind of terrifying."

"What do you want, Detective?" Dole moved her hood aside to better see Carrie with her single eye.

"Well, I was keeping an eye on you—both eyes—I mean, I was, you know, just keeping a watch on how you are. That's all." Carrie stopped speaking and took a deep breath. "So, how are you?"

Dole tightened the grip on her dog's chain and said, "Vir!" and the dog stood up. "Go find someone else to babysit, Detective. You aren't needed here."

"Listen, I can't go into too many details, but there's a chance Pennington will come looking for you. If he does, or if anything strange happens, if you find a window unlocked, or something out of place, please get out of the house and call nine-one-one as fast as you can."

Dole smiled at the idea. "If he comes looking for me, I won't be calling nine-one-one, Detective."

Dole led her dog back home. She went up the lawn toward her front door and pushed it open. It wasn't locked. She let the dog in and unchained it. All of the lights went dark inside the house as she disappeared from Carrie's view. The front door stayed open wide.

* * *

Carrie was halfway to Patricia Martin's house when her radio crackled and Rein said, "Pennington's on the move."

She snatched the radio out of the seat and held it to her mouth. "What direction?"

"Stand by," Rein grunted. She could hear branches cracking in the background. "Trying to get out of this damn tree."

Carrie gunned the engine, flying toward him. She started looking for headlights. It was ten o'clock at night and there weren't many other cars on the road. Any car coming her way would likely be Tucker, heading toward his next kill.

What victim was he going for? What would she do if he drove past her? How would she get the car spun around without him seeing it, and still be able to follow him to the next victim's house without losing him?

A thousand questions and scenarios flew through her mind as she drove ninety miles an hour, trying not to hit anyone.

"He's making a right and heading east. I'm getting back to the car now to follow."

"Don't lose him, Rein!" She let go of the button, doing the calculations in her head as she drove, trying to figure where east took Pennington. "He has to be going for Bill," Carrie said.

She could hear Rein's engine start. "Or he's going the long way around trying to cover his tracks. What's your ETA?"

"A few minutes. Coming in hot."

"Well, slow down," Rein said. He sounded so calm, she thought. It was maddening. All she heard was her own voice quavering when she spoke. The raw adrenaline coursing through her veins like quicksilver. "Just slow down and breathe," Rein said. "I can see his taillights ahead of me. If you come racing in, he's going to hear you and know he's being followed. Just hang back until I need you."

"We can't lose him," Carrie said.

"We won't."

Carrie breathed. If they lost Pennington, there could be a dozen mutilated bodies rotting the next day before they were found. Bill and his family. Nubs, Penny, and her father. The other victims.

Other cops and counselors she hadn't heard of. Whoever else Pennington was targeting. No one was safe.

Rein was right. If Pennington realized he was being followed, people might be saved that night, but he'd only reconfigure his plan and find some new crazy way to enact it.

If they stopped Pennington on his way to one of the victim's houses, was that enough? It would depend on what he had in the car, she thought. If he had tools and spray paint and weapons, then definitely. Especially if he had the same screwdriver or whatever he'd used on Linda's ribs with him. The crime lab could match that to the tool marks found on the enamel of her bones. Hell, they could probably match the spray paint from the walls of Linda's bedroom to whatever he still had on him.

That was definitely enough, she thought. Unless it wasn't. Unless he didn't have anything with him. Or had bought all new supplies, because he had something else in mind for his second murder. What if all he had was a flashlight and a saw? Hell, he could have duct tape, a filet knife, and a blowtorch. None of those things are inherently illegal to possess.

If they stopped him before he got to the victim's house, out of an abundance of caution to protect anyone else from being hurt, would there be any way to prove his intention?

No. Not at all, she thought. Not enough for the goddamn courts. Some defense attorney would argue they'd only stopped poor Tucker Pennington because they were setting him up and illegally profiling him. *All Mr. Pennington was doing out that night was driving around trying to clear his mind after the years of awful imprisonment inflicted on him by law enforcement. This was an unlawful arrest, Your Honor.*

She could hear the voice of every police instructor she'd had since the academy, asking her, "Then what happens? You get sued. Judges and district attorneys are all exempt from being sued, but not the cops. They can come after your salary, your house, and your pension. So don't fuck up."

Carrie pressed the button on the radio again. "What's your twenty?"

"Turning onto Main Street in Hansen," Rein said. "Stand by."

Carrie wasn't far behind them.

"He's pulling into Saint Margaret of Antioch's."

"What's he doing there?" Carrie asked. "Is he going after that priest we met at his house?"

"Give me a second," Rein said. After a minute he came back on the radio and said, "Meet me at the diner across the street. No need to rush."

They watched Tucker Pennington carry four large bags of garbage out of the church and take them to a dumpster around back. It was one o'clock in the morning. Each time, Father Ihan followed him outside and waited at the front door for Pennington to come back.

They'd watched Pennington sweep the front lobby. They'd watched him mop. They'd seen him carrying buckets filled with cleaning supplies into the chapel while Father Ihan held the doors open.

When he'd first arrived, Rein saw Thad and Grace sitting in the front of the car when they pulled into the church parking lot. Tucker had exited from the backseat with a small cooler and was summoned back to hug his mother through the window before going into the church.

Carrie took a sip from her coffee mug. She'd only eaten half of the apple pie she ordered an hour earlier. The diner was crowded for that late at night. Mainly it was bar-goers who needed greasy food to absorb all the liquor in their bellies.

"Molly and I would come here for breakfast sometimes after we were out partying," Carrie said.

Rein finished his coffee and set it on the edge of the table to be filled again. "I arrested a serial rapist who used to work here."

Carrie rolled her eyes. "Is that all there is to you?"

"What?"

"*I arrested a serial rapist who used to work here because I have no other context to relate to anything with,*" she said, imitating him. She tilted her head at the church where Pennington was working. "Isn't there anything more to you than sitting here doing this?"

"Of course there is. If you recall, I walked away from this and never looked back."

"Oh, okay. Sure."

"What? I was perfectly content cutting grass and digging ditches. I'd still be landscaping if you hadn't come and found me."

"First of all, I saw where you were living, so don't sit there and tell me you were content," Carrie said. "Second of all, when I found you, you were like one of those divorced dads who lives in a hotel surrounded by pizza boxes and empty booze bottles that cries himself to sleep every night. Except in your case, the thing you were divorced from was being a detective."

"That's ridiculous," Rein said. The waitress refilled his coffee and he pulled it close, holding the warm cup between his palms. "Yes, there's more to me than this. I just think that, when I went to prison, and what my life was like when I got out, I had to bury so much of that so deep inside that I haven't been able to find it again."

Carrie dug into the remaining apple pie with her fork. "Linda didn't want you working with me. She yelled at me about it."

"She yelled at me about it too," he said.

"Is that because she wanted to be with you?"

"I'm not sure what one thing would have to do with the other."

"Come on, Rein. How could anyone be in a relationship with you? You've spent your whole life running off to hunt wackos. Hey, we have dinner tonight. Sorry, I've got to go track down a bad guy. Hey, it's our son's birthday party. Sorry, I have to go track down a bad guy. You put this before everything else and that's why when it went away, you stopped living."

Jacob stared down at his coffee. "I only missed a few of his birthday parties, for your information. And I always tried to make it up to him."

"Hey. That's not what I meant. Come on," she said, poking him in the arm. "Don't get mopey. I'm just busting your balls."

"Maybe you're right," he said. He looked through the window. It was dark enough outside to both see through the window at the church where Pennington was cleaning and see himself reflected in the glass, watching.

"Listen, I'm sorry. I was just teasing. You've helped more people than anyone I know. There are a lot of kids walking around right now because of you. There is nothing else more important than that in the whole world, Jacob."

"I've spent my entire life doing this because it's the only thing I'm good at. I wish I knew how to fix cars or build houses. To create something that's real and exists and people can see it and know there was more to me. But there isn't. This is what I am good at, Carrie. It's a terrible thing to be good at."

At first daylight, the Penningtons returned to the church and waited in the parking lot for their son. Father Ihan opened the doors and let Tucker out. He carried his cooler with him as he slid into the backseat and then they left. There was no need to follow them.

Carrie's stomach hurt from too much coffee. Her body was buzzing from the bizarre combination of caffeine and lack of sleep. She'd worked all-nighters before, plenty of them, especially during her days on patrol, but they'd usually been planned.

She followed Rein out of the diner and yawned into her hand. She thought seriously about sleeping in the diner's parking lot for a little while. Just enough so that she didn't drift off and wreck her car on the way home.

A police siren sounded from far away, approaching fast. The patrol car came ripping up Main Street, coming toward the diner. There was another behind it, following close.

"What the hell's that all about?" Carrie said.

The police cars flew past and a state police car ripped around the corner three blocks away and screeched its tires trying to make a left onto Main Street to follow them. In the distance, two more police cars from different jurisdictions appeared, lights and sirens blazing.

Carrie felt her phone buzzing in her pocket. Harv Bender was calling her. She plugged her finger into her ear so she could hear over the sirens. "Hey, Chief. Is something going on?"

"What!" she shouted into the phone over the sirens. "That's not possible."

Rein put his hands in his pockets and watched the cars whip past.

"We had eyes on him all goddamn night long! Jesus Christ. This is a nightmare. I'll be there in a few minutes." She thrust the phone into her pocket and pounded her fist against the roof of her car. "Son of a bitch!" She ran both hands over her face to collect herself and said, "Patricia Martin is dead. So are both her parents. It sounds like a mess."

Rein went around to the passenger side and said, "We'll go over there together."

"How the hell did he do it, Rein? We were watching him. Did he sneak out of the back of the church and run there on foot? Did he have time to do it during the day? What the hell is going on here?"

"It's simple," Rein said. He leaned back against the seat and closed his eyes. "Pennington isn't the killer and we have made a grievous mistake."

16

"*T*ucker Pennington is absolutely the killer, without a doubt," Harv Bender said. "I want him arrested. I do not give a fuck what he is arrested for. If he tosses a bubble gum wrapper out of the window, I want him arrested. If he jaywalks, I want him arrested. Do I make myself clear? Until further notice, every county detective is assigned to containing Pennington. The FBI is on their way to take over the crime scene. Now go out there and get this bastard in handcuffs."

Carrie raised her hand. There were more cops in the Martins' front yard than had been at her police academy graduation. Bender had called everyone in. Every available local cop from every nearby jurisdiction was there. All the county detectives were there. State Police were there. The FBI were on their way.

"I have a question," Carrie called out. She was standing deep enough in the group that she had to raise her hand to try and get Bender's attention.

Rein pulled her arm down. "Stop talking."

She yanked her arm away from him, "How are we—"

"Stop talking."

Bender clapped his hands together and shouted, "Let's go, people!"

When the crowd dispersed, Rein told Carrie to wait there and maneuvered toward Bender. He was barking commands and directives to the people nearby him. Telling them he wanted to be notified immediately and make it happen now and I want it done yesterday. Rein just waited.

"You two were out watching him all night?" Bender said, once he and Rein were alone.

"That's right. He got dropped off at the church and picked up in the morning."

"Guess the Great Detective got outsmarted after all, then," Bender said.

"I guess so."

"It happens to the best of us."

"I'm sorry to admit it, but you're right."

"What a total goddamn unholy fucking massacre," Bender said. "I hate this little fucker. I'm not a church-going man, but I do have religious feelings just like anyone else, and this fucking asshole is making decent folks into sacrilegious playthings. I won't have it. You hear me?"

"I hear you," Rein said.

"Not in my fucking county. Not on my fucking watch!"

"You'll get him, Harv," Rein said. He clapped Bender on the arm and said, "You've always been the most committed cop I know. I have faith in you."

"I appreciate that, Jacob. I really do."

"Listen, do you mind if Carrie and I have another look at the crime scene?"

"The FBI told me not to let anybody else in there until they arrived."

"Well, that's par for the course. It's okay. I'm sure their people will keep you in the loop."

Bender sniffed to clear his nose, then leaned close to Rein. He kept his voice low. "You see something useful when you went down there?"

"I think so, but I'm not sure. I need a second look. If I'm right, it could help us get a head start."

Bender ran his tongue over his teeth, making sure no one was close enough to hear them. "You go down there and work your magic. Look, but don't touch. If you find anything, I mean anything to help us nail this bastard, I want to know about it like that," and he snapped his fingers.

"Understood," Rein said. He hurried back through the crowd and waved for Carrie to follow him. "We don't have much time."

The Martins' house was a large single home. Not as nice as the Penningtons' but way nicer than any that belonged to the people Carrie knew. It had a large front lawn and the neighbors were far apart and separated by wide stretches of woodland trees on either side. There were statues of lions on either side of the front steps leading up to the house. A large stained-glass window sat above the entrance, filling the foyer with multicolored light.

The large house was silent. The faint scent of decay lingered. Carrie slid on a pair of gloves and said, "Okay. I get that correcting Bender in front of all those people would have been a mistake. But what good does it do to have everyone focused on Pennington if we know he isn't the suspect?"

Rein slid on a pair of gloves. "What do you know about the Freemasons?"

Carrie rolled her eyes. "Can't you just give me a straight answer? You pissed me off back there. I have enough trouble trying to establish myself in the old boys' club without you telling me to stop talking in front of everyone."

"It had to be done."

"Why did it have to be done?"

"Because you needed to stop talking."

Carrie flicked the light on to the basement steps and said, "I really hate you sometimes."

"Duly noted. So what do you know about the Freemasons?"

"Let's see. A bunch of old dudes who secretly run the government. Most of the presidents were Freemasons. Their symbols are hidden all over the dollar bill. They're the Illuminati. They control most of the world governments behind the scenes, and for some reason, all the best rappers in the music industry."

The copper smell of blood grew stronger as they descended into the basement. "That's all part of the popular folklore," Rein said. "Maybe once they had power, but now all the Masons really

do is get dressed up in costumes to put on plays for each other
and have meetings to argue about who's running the spaghetti
dinner that month."

The Martins' basement was an enormous room that had been
finished but never furnished. Its thick plush carpeting squished
under their feet and the walls were painted and tall, but nothing
had ever been hung on them.

Carrie felt herself sag at the sight of the dead bodies inside the
room. She'd seen them already, and there was no more of the
shock or horror their strange positioning was meant to convey,
but as she looked at their vacant eyes and wide-open mouths, she
simply felt diminished. Like the value of human life was lessening
each time she saw another ruined corpse. It was like standing in a
black ocean with the undertow pulling the sandy floor out from
under her. She could feel her footing giving way. No matter how
hard she tried to stay upright, it was only a matter of time before
it took her away too.

"All Masonic temples are set up the same way," Rein said.

Mrs. Martin's naked body was slumped along the wall to his
right. Her throat had been cut so deeply that Carrie could see the
white of the woman's spinal cord within. Mrs. Martin's hands
were cupped in her lap, holding a length of blackened meat. It
was her own tongue, Carrie realized. Torn out at the root. "Did
you notice the sun coming through the stained-glass window
when we came in?" Rein asked.

"I did," Carrie said.

"Where is north?"

"What?" She could not take her eyes off the woman's severed
tongue. What had it been removed by? Had she been alive when
it was done?

"The sun rises in the east and sets in the west," Rein said. "You
said you saw the sun coming through the window. Which way was
it shining and which way is north?"

Carrie thought, trying to orient herself. She pointed at the
staircase behind them and said, "That's north."

"Exactly," Rein said.

In the center of the room was a wooden crate turned upside down. Sitting on top of it was a large, leather-bound, family Bible. There was a clump of something burnt on top of the Bible. It looked like a coil of black sausage surrounded by a pile of charred worms.

There were three black candles placed around the crate. Two on the north side, and the other, facing south. It was only a few feet from where Mr. Martin's body sat on the floor. He was bare-chested, and his round hairy belly bulged over his waist, hanging to the floor. The left side of his chest was ripped open, a long cut that opened him up from his collarbone to the center of his breastbone.

The skin and muscle there had been hacked away and the killer had scooped out the man's heart and left lung. They were tossed over his left shoulder, suspended by a tangle of artery and vein, and left to hang.

At the left side of the room, in the east, where the sun shined high above her but could not be seen in this room, lay both halves of Patricia Martin.

Her naked body had been severed in two at the waist. Her upper torso was laying so that her head faced the wall behind her. The lower half of her body was laying a foot away from her on the carpet, displaying the blue and gray coils of her severed intestines. She looked like she'd been cut in half during a children's magic show from hell, Carrie thought.

What kind of a tool can cut a human body in half? A hand saw, sliding across skin and bone until it cuts all the way through? A chainsaw, filling the room with gasoline fumes, as it splattered Patricia Martin's body in two? Had she been alive when it was happening? How long did it take someone to die when their body was being ripped in half?

The horror was in not knowing.

Carrie thought of all the times she'd been in a hardware store, looking for tools. Things with sharp edges. Implements, designed to cut and angle and work raw materials into shape. To impose order on the chaos of nature. Tools were supposed to be a prized and almost sacred thing, born of balance and mathematics and ancient, proven, design. They'd elevated the apes who'd first invented them into something new. Something that could plan and create entire civilizations. To use those same tools to do something so base as to rip another human being in half offended her on every level.

Patricia Martin's entrails had been cut loose and carried over to the Bible in the center of the room. The killer had lit them on fire there and left them to smolder. Spray painted on the floor in the center of the room, with the crate and Bible at its center, was a large pentagram.

"All prospective masons must go through a series of three degrees to attain the final rank and become full members. The idea is that a mason can visit any Masonic temple in the world, and as long as he knows the secret word or handshake, he will be treated like a brother. Every temple practices the same basic rituals and are all set up the same way." Rein pointed at Mrs. Martin and said, "The Senior Warden, who sits at the West. Her injuries, the severed throat and removal of the tongue, are the penalties for anyone who violates the oath of the Apprentice Mason."

He nodded toward Mr. Martin, sitting across from them. "The Junior Warden, who sits at the south. The second degree is called the Fellow Craft, and if you violate the oath you take during it, you agree to have your heart and innards taken out and cast over your left shoulder."

"So much for only doing spaghetti dinners," Carrie said.

"It's meant to be symbolic," Rein said.

"Clearly, someone didn't get the memo." She clenched her eyes shut and turned away. "Shit, when I said spaghetti dinners, I looked right at all the veins holding Mr. Martin's heart attached to his chest. I'm not getting rid of that mental image for a long time, Rein."

Rein stood in the middle of the room, looking down at the Bible. "The altar is surrounded by the three lights, always formed into a triangle, for the sun, the moon, and the head of the lodge." He pointed at pentagram spray-painted on the floor and said,

"Another clumsy Satanic reference. It doesn't fit, though. Masons used pentagrams and other mathematical symbols centuries before Anton LaVey turned it upside down and adopted it for Satanic iconography."

He circled around the altar and stood looking down at the remains of Patricia Martin. "And here we have the final station. Always set in the east. The punishment of being torn in two and having your organs burned is exactly as described in the third degree oath." He pointed at Mrs. Martin and said, "Apprentice." He pointed at her husband, "Then, Fellow Craft."

Rein turned to regard the display made of Patricia Martin's body. "The mason who passes through all of these degrees to reach the east, who is deemed worthy, is given a title. Do you know what rank you achieve once you reach the east, Carrie?"

She knew. The killer had cut Patricia Martin's body in half and made a desecration of her entire family to make a petty little statement. He was laying claim to his title in the most sickening way. "You become the Master."

17

*C*arrie kept the gas pedal down as she weaved through the highway traffic in front of her. There were troopers hidden all along that stretch of highway, but it didn't matter. If they saw her, they either recognized she was in an undercover police car or just didn't feel like coming out of their hole. She glanced at her GPS. They were twenty miles away from Sunshine Estates.

There was too much traffic in the fast lane. She slid behind a tractor-trailer in the middle lane then cut right to get into the slow lane and speed ahead of him. "So how do you know all this stuff about the Masons? Did you research them when you got tired of learning about Satanists?"

"No," Rein said. "I am one."

"What?"

"Well, I was one. I'm not sure if you lose your status after you leave."

"You did all that? Went through the degree things and promised to get your heart torn out and ripped in half and stuff?"

"What can I say? I always wanted to be part of a secret society."

Carrie laughed and shook her head. "Somehow, I can't picture you wanting to be a part of anything. Did you enjoy it?"

"It was interesting. There is a lot of history involved. The rituals are the same as when George Washington and Benjamin Franklin were members. It was nice to feel connected to something with so much history."

"Why did you leave?"

"There's a question they ask that I could no longer answer. In times of greatest trouble, who do you put your faith in?"

"Jesus?"

"No. It can be any god. It doesn't need a name," Rein said. "But when I knew I could no longer answer that, I left."

"We've talked about this before, but you don't believe in anything? No higher power out there in the universe keeping it all together?"

"Nothing. As an investigator, I committed myself to only following the evidence where it goes. If you observe the world and humanity on its own, without any preconceived ideas about some higher power and you still arrive at that conclusion? I'd suggest you're insane," Rein said. "All I see is chaos. We do our best to stabilize it and maintain it but it's a constant losing battle. If there is a universal higher power, it's an agent of destruction. It's definitely going to win. Stars collapse, worlds go dark, species go extinct. Thinking we're different because some magical being in the sky is our friend is delusional. We will cling to this as long as we can before slipping away into the darkness with everything else."

"I'm sorry I asked. You are a depressing person," Carrie said. She checked the distance on her GPS. "I've never been to a mental institution before. Unless you count police stations." She checked to see if Rein was smiling at her joke. He wasn't. "I've been thinking about this. If the killer isn't Pennington, it could be anyone he knew in here. I mean, first we took all the sickest sickos we could find and grouped them together like some kind of science project. Now, all because nobody wants to pay for them anymore, we're letting them out."

"The killer isn't Tucker," Rein said. "He's an Elmer Hoffman."

"Who the hell is Elmer Hoffman?"

"He was an art forger. A very talented one. He could recreate the style of any artist and pawn it off as an original. Picasso. Rodin. Da Vinci. He made millions of dollars forging their work."

"Why didn't he just do his own paintings if he was that good?"

"He lacked the spark of creativity," Rein said. "He had no imagination of his own. He possessed all of the technique but had none of the inspiration. They said it drove him mad to go without recognition. He started to hide his name within the paintings. No one noticed until he committed suicide and left a note confessing to everything."

Carrie mulled it over. "Just like our killer. He wants us to think he's Tucker Pennington, but because he's just an imposter, he has no original ideas so he's stuck borrowing whatever he can, wherever he can find it."

"Exactly," Rein said. "At some point, like all imposters, he will crave the recognition he feels he deserves. Earlier, you asked why I stopped you from telling Harv the truth about Tucker. We need to let Harv focus on him, because it's going to drive the real killer over the edge. He's out here doing all this work and no one knows it. He'll go into a frenzy."

"It's that easy, huh?" Carrie asked. The satisfaction in Rein's voice when he described his plan to her gnawed at her. She tightened her grip around the steering wheel. "You know, I am trying not to think this, but it's on my mind so I'm going to say it."

"That's for the best. Let it out, whatever it is."

"When you talk about him going into a frenzy, you do realize you're talking about him going after people I love, right? And that if we don't catch him in time, it's my family, or Bill's family, whose asses are on the line."

"We'll catch him."

Anger made her jaw tremble. "Did it ever even occur to you that the only reason my dad and Penny and Nubs are in danger is because of me? Do you have any idea how that makes me feel? Even if everything turns out okay, I'll still have to live with the guilt that for a few days some psychotic piece of shit wanted to torture them to death. Like Nubs doesn't have enough bullshit to deal with because of her mother? I'll be lucky if she doesn't already turn out mentally fucked-up without me adding my own bullshit on top of it!"

"Carrie, none of this is your fault," Rein said. "Nubs is going to be fine. She's a good kid."

"How would you know? How in the fuck would you know? You couldn't even bother to show up for dinner with her the other night. Wait, let me guess. There was something else more important to do."

She cranked the wheel to the right. The sign for their exit was coming up fast.

Carrie laid her file on the counter and badged the Sunshine Estates receptionist. "I'm Detective Santero with the Vieira County Detectives. We'd like to speak to someone about one of your recently released patients."

"Is the staff psychologist available?" Rein added.

"No one's filling that position at the moment," the receptionist said. "Budget cuts. It's just a few doctors and orderlies now."

"Who's been here the longest?" Carrie asked.

The receptionist scrunched up her mouth in thought. "Probably Mr. Darryl."

"We'll talk to him," Carrie said.

The receptionist paged him and said they could wait over there.

"You see that?" Carrie muttered. "No one ever asks to see your ID, do they? They never ask for your badge or your rank. I went to a SANE examination last year and they almost didn't let me into the hospital until I proved who I was. You just waltz in here, the same way you waltzed around the crime scenes earlier and nobody says a thing."

"I guess I look like I belong."

"Or, you just look right. And by that I mean white. And male."

"Is there anything else you need me to apologize for today? The way I talked to you in front of Bender. The way I'm putting everyone in danger. The way I didn't show up for dinner. Now it's that I'm a white male?"

"Older white male."

Someone was coming down the hallway toward them. They could hear sneakers squeaking on the polished tiles. "You know, we don't have to do this anymore," Rein said. "After this case is done, whatever this is, can just be over."

"Fine."

"You go your way and I'll go mine. Then maybe I won't offend you anymore," Rein said.

"Great."

The door opened and a white-haired, bearded orderly waved for them to come along. "Good morning," he said with a smile. "Come on in."

"Thanks, Mr. Darryl," Carrie said. "We'd like to ask you a few questions about some of the patients that have been here. There's been some trouble."

"What kind of trouble?"

"A doctor who used to work here was murdered. So were some other people."

"Which doctor?"

"Linda Shelley," Rein said.

"Oh, don't say that," Mr. Darryl moaned. He pressed his hands to his forehead. "No, please, please, don't say that."

"I'm sorry," Rein said. He put his hand on the man's arm. "We're looking for the man who did it. Can you help us?"

"What do you need?"

"There was a patient named Tucker Pennington," Carrie said. She pulled a photograph of Pennington out of her file. "Do you remember him?"

"Sure, I remember him," Mr. Darryl said. "He killed Dr. Shelley?"

"Actually, we think it might be someone he knew," Carrie said. "The victims were all involved in his case at various stages."

"Tucker kept to himself," Mr. Darryl said. "He was on high doses of medication that really knocked him out. He was like a zombie most times."

"Did he have any friends, anyone in here he spent time with?" Rein asked.

"No, not that I can recall. These folks don't really make friends in here. If they was the friendly type, they wouldn't be in here, if you catch my meaning."

"Is there anyone who's been let out recently who worried you?" Carrie asked.

"Shoot. I'm worried for all them getting out," Mr. Darryl said. "And worried for everybody else too. At least when they was here, they had people to keep an eye on 'em, make sure they got they meds, and didn't hurt nobody. Now, Lord knows what's gonna happen to 'em."

"Who makes you the most worried?" Rein asked. "Who is the one patient you never want to see show up at your house?"

Mr. Darryl scrunched up his mouth in thought, then said, "Gregory Moon. Nasty piece of work. That boy was crazy. I was sorry to see him leave but glad to see him go, if you understand."

Carrie wrote the name down. "Did he and Pennington know one another?"

"They did. They came here from the juvenile detention center together, from what I can recall. Had a few fights. Always ended with Tucker whooping on him, after Moon pushed him too far."

Rein nodded as the man spoke and waited for Carrie to stop writing. "That's good info, Mr. Darryl. Please show us everything you have on Gregory Moon."

"There's not much I can give you. Most of the patient files get archived when they're released."

"There's always a way," Rein said.

"It's in a secure room. Don't you people need search warrants for patient records?"

Carrie looked down the hall. It was empty except for them. She leaned close to Mr. Darryl. "There's not even enough staff here to keep this place operational. Nobody's going to notice. I told you, this is a murder investigation, and more people are at risk."

"I could get in trouble."

"And what, lose your job?" Rein asked. "I've got bad news for you. This job is about to get rid of you and everyone else. Now, we could get a search warrant, sure. By the time we get back, you might already be laid off and a lot more people will already be dead. Or, you help us, and we put in a good word for you at wherever you apply next."

"Mr. Darryl assisted us in a very important investigation. I think he'd be a great asset to your company," Carrie said.

"That's right," Rein said. "A reference like that is worth something."

"I don't need no references," Mr. Darryl said. "What I need is my paycheck as long as I can get it here. We got rules, same as you all."

Rein seized him by the arm. "Linda Shelley was butchered in her own bedroom. Now you say you knew her. Well, I knew her too, and I'm going to find the man who did it and make him pay. I need you to help us do that."

"This is the time you decide which is more important, Mr. Darryl. Rules or what's right," Carrie said. Mr. Darryl's back was pressed against the wall, trying to get away from Rein. Carrie removed Rein's hand from the man's arm. "Linda Shelley always chose what was right. I know that, because I saw her do it myself, even when it broke the rules."

"I'll do it, but only for her," Mr. Darryl said. "It's going to take a little while. Meet me around back in your car and I'll bring it out. Is there anything in particular you want me to find?"

"Everything," Rein said. "We need to see it all."

18

*T*ucker Pennington was kneeling on the floor with his hands pressed together, rocking back and forth as he prayed. His mother, Grace, and the priest were sitting across from one another in the parlor. Grace was making small talk about the people who went to Saint Margaret's. Father Ihan humored her without indulging in gossip. "They are doing their best, I am sure," he said.

He reached for the plate of golden butter cakes on the side table and picked one up. He held it delicately with one hand and took a bite. It melted in his mouth and he sighed with pleasure. "This is fantastic. You are an excellent baker."

"Oh," Grace said, waving her hand at him. "It's mainly just flour and sugar. I was going to make enough for the whole church next Sunday. My pantry is filled with so much flour and sugar I could make butter cake for the Roman legion if they showed up."

Ihan took a drink of coffee to wash the butter cake down. He raised his cup to acknowledge Tucker as he finished his latest prayer. "Well done, Tucker. Come sit." He patted the couch cushion next to him.

Tucker got up from the floor and sat on the couch next to the priest, keeping to the edge of it and rocking back and forth. "You have been praying all day," Ihan said. "Is something disturbing you?"

"The police were here the other morning," Grace Pennington said. "They tried to accuse Tucker of leaving the house unsupervised. Luckily, we had video cameras installed before he came home just for such an event. That really fixed them, I'll tell you. You should have seen the look on that female cop's face."

"Well, they have a job to do too," Ihan said. "We must pray for them to be safe and have good judgment."

"I'll pray for them to have better judgment, that's for sure," Grace said.

Ihan patted Tucker's arm. "You received many compliments on how clean the church is. Everyone noticed."

Grace smacked her hands on her thighs. "I just remembered I forgot to write you that check. Why didn't you remind me?"

"I did not want to make any presumptions."

"Don't be silly. We'd do anything for the church."

"You are very generous," he said.

She laid the leather three-ring binder containing her checks and paged through it to find the right page. "Father, speaking of cleaning the church, I've been telling Tucker that there is more to being a good Christian than just praying."

"Of course."

"He could be working in soup kitchens. He could become a missionary and go visit poor people. You came from Venezuela. Maybe he could go to Venezuela and help the poor people there as a way to give back for you helping him." She tore the check off and held it out toward him. "I think there are more important things he could be doing than janitorial work."

Ihan reached forward and took the check. The woman said the word *janitorial* the way people describe drunks vomiting in alleyways.

"I want people to see him," Grace insisted. "I don't like him scurrying around cleaning bathrooms in the middle of the night, like we're ashamed to have him home or you're ashamed to have him in the church. People need to know that everything they heard about him is a lie, and he has devoted himself to God. They need to see it."

Ihan slid the check into his pants pocket. "If we only believe in what we see, can we call ourselves Christians?"

Grace closed the checkbook and sat back. "You're right. The people who don't believe Tucker has changed must not be true Christians."

He measured his words. "In the book of Corinthians, Saint Paul tells us to look not to the things that are seen, but the things that are unseen. What can be seen is transient. The unseen is eternal."

Before Grace could press the issue, someone knocked at the door. She squished her mouth together and balled up her fists. "So help me, Lord, if that's those detectives again, I'm not letting them in. I'll tell them to call our attorney. This is getting ridiculous."

She looked through the front windows and saw a young man standing on the porch, grinning back at her. He had long black hair, tucked behind his ears and combed flat on top of his head. He wore a faded blue blazer with missing brass buttons and black slacks that didn't fit. His shirt was an awful green floral pattern, tucked in, with no belt. He was Tucker's age but after so many years of confinement, Tucker looked like an old man already with his sagging skin and missing hair. This young man looked awake and alive, and more importantly, he looked glad to be there. "Good morning, Mrs. Pennington," he said through the window.

She opened the door just a crack. "Do I know you?"

"No, ma'am. I'm a friend of your son's. We went to school together, and I heard he was home. I just wanted to come over and say hello."

"Oh!" she said. She broke out into a smile. "Oh well, that is just wonderful. Tucker! Come look. One of your friends has come to visit." She opened the door wide to let the young man in. "Isn't this nice? Please do come in." She waved her hand toward the couch and said, "This is Father Ihan from Saint Margaret of Antioch's. He's been supervising Tucker's treatment."

The young man held up his hand and waved.

Tucker rocked back and forth, not looking up.

"How long have you and Tucker been friends?"

"Oh, we've known each other for years," he said. "We lost touch for a little while, with all the trouble, you know. But I never stopped thinking about him."

Grace was too overcome to speak. It was everything she'd hoped for her son. A friend. A normal person who cared about him and saw the good in him. She rubbed the young man's arm briskly, thanking him without having the words to thank him with.

"Perhaps the boys would like to talk alone?" Father Ihan said. "Fellowship is an important part of all healing."

"That's a wonderful idea," Grace said. "You boys go up to Tucker's room and get reacquainted. I'll make some food and bring it up to you, okay?"

"That sounds perfect," the young man said. He stood in front of Tucker, who did not look up at him, and did not stop rocking. "Come on, Tucker. Show me your room. I have a lot to tell you about all our old friends."

"Go on, Tucker," Grace urged. "Go with—what was your name again?"

"I'm Gregory, ma'am."

She told Tucker to go, and when he didn't move, she insisted he go, and he did.

Tucker sat on the edge of his bed as Gregory Moon roamed his bedroom, picking Tucker's things up and inspecting them. "You have undercover police detectives surrounding your house on all sides," Moon said. He picked up a model airplane that had been put together years ago and turned it over in his hands, inspecting it. "You won't be able to leave without them seeing you. They didn't mind me coming in, though. It seems they only have eyes for you, Tucker."

Tucker's mother had decorated his room for his return home. When he'd left, all the windows had been covered with black trash bags he'd pinned to the wooden corners of the window frame and taped down along the sides. Every inch of the walls and ceiling was covered in posters of death metal bands and women and drawings he'd made of the things he saw. The things that came to him that no one else was blessed enough to see.

In Tucker's time away, the room had been stripped to the

rafters and redone. Nothing he owned past the age of twelve remained. Everything in the room now was a reminder of that time.
A time that, now that he was home, they were all going to revisit
together.

The only new additions were ornate crucifixes mounted above
the bedroom door and windows. Every entrance to the outside
world was now protected by the power of Christ. There was a
painting of Mary holding baby Jesus that hung on the wall above
his bed. Another of Jesus in the garden, his face upturned toward
the sky and glowing, finding resolve in his one moment of weak-
ness.

Gregory Moon set the model airplane down and wiped his
hands on his blazer. "Are you happy to see me, Tucker?"

Tucker didn't respond.

"You should be. I've brought you good news. All your old friends.
Brenda Drake. Dr. Shelley. That whining bitch Patricia Martin and
her parents." Moon smiled thinly. "They're all mine now."

Tucker began rocking back and forth.

"Technology is wonderful. Did you know you can walk into any
library and use their computer to look up anything you want?
Within five minutes, I had satellite photographs of your house
and property. I know every single way into this place and every
way out. I learned all about your case. The people involved. Photographs of your parents. I found everything. All thanks to this
modern world. It feels good to be part of it and not locked up in
that loony bin, doesn't it?"

Moon took a deep breath and scowled at the air. "I'm not sure
you understand the kind of freedom I'm talking about, Tucker.
Seems you went from one prison to another."

"Boys?" Grace Pennington called up the steps. "I'm coming up."

Tucker rocked back and forth so violently the bed frame shook
against the wall.

"I'm going to finish all of the work you never could, while you
sit in your bedroom," Moon said. "I just wanted you to know."

The tray of cookies and milk glasses rattled in her hands as
Grace came down the hall.

"You were always weaker than me, Tucker," Moon said. "Now

I'll prove it to the world. I am the master. The true master. You were always just a pretender."

The door opened and Grace swept into the room with her tray. "Here we are. Are you boys having fun?"

"Oh, we're having the best time just getting caught up," Moon said. He picked a handful of cookies up from the tray and stuffed them in his mouth. Crumbs spilled down his shirt as he told her how good they were. Moon picked up one of the glasses of milk and drank it all the way, tilting the glass until milk spilled down the sides of his mouth. He set the empty glass back on the tray and did not wipe his mouth.

Grace Pennington did her best to keep smiling, even as cookie crumbs and drips of milk landed on the clean carpet in her son's room. "Tucker, it's time for your medicine," she said. She held a rectangular pill box out toward him and he didn't stop rocking or reach for it. "Tucker," she said. "It's time for your medicine. You have to stay on schedule."

"Stay on that schedule, Tucker," Moon said. He reached for the tray in Mrs. Pennington's hands and gathered the rest of the cookies. "It really is important." He stuffed the cookies into his pockets and picked up the second glass of milk. He locked eyes with Grace as he raised the glass and drank Tucker's milk all the way down, gulping and swallowing and spilling and not looking away from her. Moon set the empty glass down and said, "Delicious. You see that, Tucker? I've eaten all your food. You should have been faster."

Tucker reached into his robe pocket and pulled out the length of his rosary beads. He wrapped them around his fingers. "I believe in God, the Father Almighty, creator of heaven and earth."

Moon waved to Grace and said, "I'll be back to see you all in a little while."

Grace stood in the center of the room, holding the tray, as Moon went down the hall to go downstairs. "That boy, he is a friend of yours. Right, Tucker?"

"I believe in Jesus Christ, his only son, our lord, who was conceived by the Holy Ghost, born of the Virgin Mary, suffered under Pontius Pilate, was crucified, died, and was buried."

Grace sighed and said, "I'll go get you some water then, to take your medicine with. Or would your rather have juice?"

Tucker rocked back and forth, holding the beads between his hands as he muttered another prayer.

"I'll bring juice," she said.

Tucker watched her leave. "Did the boys have a nice visit?" he heard Father Ihan ask.

"Oh, it was fantastic," Grace said. "They used to be in Little League together and have stayed in touch all this time. When I walked in they were talking about going camping. Isn't that wonderful?"

Tucker slid his rosary beads back into his robe and opened the pill container. There were four slots. Three of them were filled with the same assortment of colorful capsules. He scooped the ones from the second slot. The first one he'd taken when his mother woke him up that morning. He would have to take another two doses before he went to sleep. He set the container aside and looked at the pills in the palm of his hand. Pale pastel colors, or chalk white. He closed his hand and squeezed them, making a fist so hard, his hand shook. He slid down from his bed and crept across the floor toward the central air duct next to his closet. He listened for his mother, then dropped the pills, one at a time, inside the vent.

When he stood up, the doctor was sitting on his bed. Her long legs were crossed, revealing her pale white thighs. She leaned back so that her long black hair spilled across her shoulder.

It is time, Tucker, she said.

"It is time," he said.

The doctor's eyes turned black.

IV

FAMILY

19

*R*ein flipped through the stack of Gregory Moon's documents as Carrie drove. He stopped at a file with Linda Shelley's handwriting on it and read through it. "This is Linda's last filing before she left the facility. Moon had come up for reevaluation to see if he was fit to leave. Listen to this. '*Moon is a true sadist. He does not appear to suffer any auditory or visual hallucinations consistent with schizophrenia. He is, in my opinion, too dangerous to ever be released back into society.*' Signed, Dr. Linda Shelley."

"If only," Carrie said.

Rein found another document, containing Moon's biography. "Here we go. Moon's mom was a drug addict and lost custody of him when he was ten. His body was covered in cigarette burns and dying of dehydration when they brought him to the hospital."

"Jesus."

"Placed in foster care," Rein said, still reading. "Multiple foster care placements followed due to what they said was an inability to adjust. Allegations of sexual abuse at one of the last houses where he lived."

"Was he the victim or the suspect?"

"Both. He was found molesting one of the other boys and when they interviewed him, it became clear he was being molested by both of the parents."

"What the fuck," Carrie gasped. "No wonder he's a goddamn monster."

"After that, they put him in a residential facility, where he killed a nurse." Rein kept reading and his eyes widened.

"What?"

Rein closed the file. "Don't ask."

"Tell me. I want to know what we're dealing with."

"Apparently they couldn't find the nurse for a few days. She went missing from her post. Moon had killed her in his room and kept the body under his bed. He was doing what he later called experiments on it."

Carrie came to a stop at the next intersection and waited for the light to change. "Moon wasn't that much older than Nubs is when he got taken away from his mom. I can't fathom someone hurting her like that. Or her being bounced around from foster home to foster home. I'm not saying it's an excuse for what he's done. I'm just saying, "

"If you're feeling pity for him, take it and throw it out the window," Rein said. "Bury it far down deep inside yourself. When the time comes, he won't show you any pity. He won't show it to any of us." Rein kept searching the documents. "The state makes you obtain a place to live before you're released. Otherwise they'd be liable if you left their care and froze to death because you had nowhere to go. The hospital must have a record of it."

Rein stopped and flicked one of the pages. "Here it is. The Bridge Motel, Room thirty-seven."

She picked up her phone to activate her GPS and saw two missed calls from Harv Bender. "Shit," she muttered. She called him back and pressed the phone to her ear. He answered on the first ring.

"Where in the hell are you? I've had the same guys sitting on Pennington's house for hours and they need to be rotated out. Get over there and relieve the guys at the driveway."

"All right," Carrie said. "If that's really what you want me to do."

"Why do you say it like that?"

"Because I'm following a lead. A good one," she said, stalling. "Maybe a great one."

Rein pointed at the file in his lap and shook his head. He pointed at her phone and circled his finger in the air, letting her know it was time to wind Bender up.

"If this works, we'll have Pennington dead to rights. You had the right idea containing him. We're closing in on him and he doesn't even know it."

There was silence on the other end.

"Did you want me to break off and come help your guys sit on the house?" Carrie asked.

"What, are you crazy?" Bender said. "They can sit there for the next two days as far as I care. Go nail this little bastard to the wall."

"Nailing him now, boss," Carrie said. She hung up the phone and stepped on the gas. "Is it normal to have to manipulate the people in charge just to get anything done?"

Rein set the packet of papers on the floor behind Carrie's seat. "To be a detective means knowing what people want and using it to your advantage. If you read a person correctly, you learn how to exploit them. It's only natural."

Rein leaned back and closed his eyes, resting while he could. "The only people better at it than us are the maniacs we chase after."

They drove around the Bridge Motel parking lot looking for Room 37. A pick-up truck sat in front of Room 36. Its rear was filled with Mexicans in white T-shirts holding their lunch buckets sitting bunched together. A white man sitting alone in front beeped the truck's horn several times, loud and long. He stuck his head out through the window and said, "Anybody else? Four hours cutting grass, ten bucks cash!"

Two more Mexicans came out of the hotel room and walked around the back of the truck. "There's room in there," the driver said. "Find a spot."

Their friends offered them hands to help them up. There was

no room to sit, so both men squatted in the center of the truck's bed. The truck backed up and turned to pull out of the parking lot, rattling the men in the back as they held the sides to avoid being hurled out.

The rest of the parking lot was empty on that side. They could see Moon's room from there. The blinds were old plastic and cracked. They didn't lay evenly, allowing gaps even when closed. Someone could see out if they stood in the right place. Someone could also see in.

"I guess he's not home," Carrie said. "Unless he parks somewhere else."

"Wait here," Rein said. He let himself out of the car and crept along the sidewalk, past the first motel room. He stopped at Moon's room and quick-peeked, snapping his head into view of the window to see past the blinds, then back out of the way just as fast. He bent lower and did the same thing from a different spot, a quick-peek, and then back. It was an old police tactic for clearing buildings. You were in and out of danger so fast, you didn't have time to register what you saw at first. It took a second. Rein stood with his back against the hotel wall letting what he'd seen form up in his mind. No one was in there. The bed was made. The bathroom door was open.

Rein found a gap in the blinds in the center of the window and covered both sides of his face to shield them from light and see in. He saw clothing. A blazer and floral shirt, draped over the chair in the corner of the room. A pair of dress shoes set in front of the closet.

"Anything?" Carrie asked as she came to his side. Her gun was at her side, down behind her thigh.

"He's not home."

"Are you sure?"

"Unless he's hiding behind the bed."

"Well?"

Rein raised his face from the glass. "Well, what?"

"Are we going in?"

Rein walked over to the doorknob and turned it to test it. It was locked. He glanced over his shoulders to see if any motel staff was in the area. He checked the frame. It was an old motel, with old style doors. The door opened inward. There was no way to secure the room's dead bolt from outside. There wasn't even a strike plate built into the door frame. "Give me your credit card."

She reached into her pocket for her wallet. "Which one?"

"Whichever one you aren't afraid to ruin."

She passed him her wallet and said, "Use my county one."

Rein pulled out the Vieira County District Attorney's Office credit card and wedged it into the slot alongside the doorknob. He pushed the card in as he gently turned. The card bent and creased but did not crack and the doorknob twisted all the way open. He stepped back as Carrie slid past him, her weapon drawn.

"Police," she called out. "You home, Gregory?"

She turned and checked under the window, then dropped down to look behind the bed. She darted toward the closet, then the bathroom, then stuck her head behind the door and shower curtain. "Clear!"

Rein looked inside the dresser drawers and found several sets of clothes, including socks and underwear. The only other items in the room sat on top of the desk. A row of letters with yellow sticky notes attached, and a calendar set beneath them, open to the week. Rein scanned through the calendar's pages and read the writing scattered across the upcoming days and weeks. *Must check in by noon on Sunday. Doctor's appointment. Pay rent for motel— Do Not Be Late. Expect visit from Social Services.*

Carrie holstered her weapon. "Well, he's got a toothbrush and half a tube of toothpaste," she said. "There's a used shampoo bottle in the trash can and a receipt from the Dollar Store. He's definitely living here." She leaned next to him to read the envelopes on the desk. "What's that?"

"A smokescreen," Rein said. "All of this. It's just enough to pass inspection if anyone comes to check on him. Including us."

Carrie looked around the room. "He'd need a work space. Somewhere to plan and do research and store whatever he needs. Maybe he's doing it out of his car?"

"Too risky," Rein said. "He knows if he gets pulled over and they search the car, he's finished. It has to be somewhere else."

Carrie pulled out her phone.

Sal Vigoda was asleep when his phone rang. He jolted awake so hard, his legs flew off the table and sent a stack of papers flying throughout the trailer. He cleared his throat before he answered. "Hello?"

"Sal, it's Carrie. Are you at Tucker Pennington's house?"

"No. The chief wanted me to help the coroner's office with that Shelley lady's body and I told him I refused to go back in there. He dismissed me and told me to report to his office at sixteen hundred. I'm either getting suspended or fired."

"Jesus, Sal."

"It's probably for the best."

"Okay, well, since you're still there, though, I need your help. I need you to look up a suspect named Gregory Moon for me. He's the real killer."

"Moon? Not Pennington?"

"That's right," Carrie said. "I need everything you can find on him. Driving record. Criminal history. Relatives. Whatever we have on him in our system. We have to find him."

Sal looked at the computer on the desk. "I don't know, Carrie. Can't you find someone else who knows how to use this thing better than me? I'm no good with it."

"No," Carrie said. "I need you, Sal. There is nobody else."

"I really don't think so."

"Listen, Sal. I need you, buddy. I don't have time to run all the way back there."

"I'm telling you, I can't do this, Carrie. I was never meant to be a detective. I'm just an old road dog. Seeing the way that lady was butchered, and all the Satanic stuff, and then that family. Forget it. I'm done. I'm sorry, but that's it for me. Even if Bender doesn't fire me, I'm turning in my badge. I made up my mind."

"You serious? You've got what, almost fifty years on the job, right?"

"Just about."

"And this one day is too much for you?"

"Yeah. It's too much. I'm finished."

"You don't sound like much of a road dog to me. You sound like a coward."

"Carrie," Sal said. "Come on."

"No, you come on! You're not a detective? Fine. But road dogs don't run from a fight, Sal. They run at it."

Sal looked at the computer. He wasn't even sure how to turn the damn thing on. "If I was to try," he said, "what would I have to do?"

"It's easy. I'll walk you through it."

The house was located in the outskirts of Coyote Township, where the homes were run-down summer shacks that blue-collar city people used to own. Decades before, when there was nothing in the area to do except hunt and fish, the factory workers in Harrisburg and Pittsburgh would come out to Vieira County for the weekend. The houses were cheaply made and never meant to be full-time residences. Some still didn't have running water. Over time, they'd been purchased by absentee landlords. Florida dwellers who hired property managers to rent the houses to anyone on welfare. They didn't care what happened in those houses because the government always paid well and they paid on time.

Weeds grew up to the windows and buckets filled with cigarette butts sat out front of most of them. There were ticks and tires and broken glass and heroin needles hidden in the tall grass of their front yards. When Carrie had been a cop in Coyote, Bill Waylon had issued a standing order that no one went on any calls there alone.

They found the address. The mailbox sat on a rotted wooden post, stuffed full. There were bundled advertising circulars scattered around the bottom of the mailbox, left when the mailman could no longer force anything else inside it.

Carrie parked the car. "Give me a second. I have to get something out of the trunk."

He got out and went around the back to see her open the trunk lid and lean in. There was an electronic safe built into the rear compartment. The buttons beeped as Carrie pushed them.

The safe's lid popped open and Carrie undid her belt. She slid the worn holster holding her pistol off her belt and stuffed it into the safe. She drew out a much larger pistol with an electronic attachment mounted below the frame. She slammed a full magazine into the gun and jacked the slide back to chamber a round, then she pressed a button on the electronic attachment and lowered her ear to it, listening to it hum.

"What is that?" Rein asked.

"An upgrade," Carrie said. She dug inside the safe for the weapon's thermoplastic polymer holster, molded to fit the weapon and the attachment. She threaded the belt through the new holster and said, "Let's go."

They waded through the grass toward the shack. It swept past their knees. The house reeked of damp and mold as they walked toward it. There were no cars in the driveway. A television was on inside. Some kind of game show. A woman had just won a prize and the audience was cheering.

Rein stayed at the front of the house and Carrie checked around the back. The grass grew taller along the sides, and the backyard was filled with junk. Discarded lottery scratch-off tickets. Rusted lawn mowers. An old Chevy sitting on cinderblocks. Empty Amazon shipping boxes. Bags of glass bottles and rusted cans that were intended to be taken to the recycling center for money, but never were. A huge cat hissed at Carrie from behind the house, then vanished into the grass. There was a barn behind the house, set way in the back, and the cat was headed toward it.

She heard the front door bang open. "What you all doing lurking round my property?"

"Are you Helen Moon?"

"Who's askin'?"

"We're looking for your nephew Gregory," Rein said.

"I ain't seen him. Now you go on and get the hell out of here before I call the police."

Carrie hurried around the side of the house. The woman was

dressed in a large, billowing, nightshirt. It was light blue and see-through in the sunlight. She was bald except for a few lengths of curly gray hair and had no eyebrows. "Good afternoon," Carrie said, fishing her badge out of her shirt. "I'm—"

"We're with social security," Rein said.

Carrie dropped her badge back down inside her shirt.

"We just wanted to make sure the payments for Gregory Moon's housing are coming to the right place. Are you Helen?"

"I am," she said. "What payments?"

"Housing and care expenses for any recently-released wards of the state," Rein said.

"A thousand dollars a month," Carrie added.

"Nobody said nothing about any payments!" Helen said. "That boy showed up out of the blue telling me he's my nephew and begging me to put him up. He said he needed a place to stay and promised to pay me, but I ain't seen nothing of it! Then he ask can he borrow my car. I ain't seen no money, I ain't seen no car, I ain't seen nothing."

"Well, it's a good thing we showed up," Rein said. "All we need to do is verify his living arrangements and we can get you all set up for payments."

"A thousand dollars a month?"

"That's right," Carrie said.

"Shit, you can verify anything you want."

"Excellent," Rein said. "Do you mind letting us in to see his room?"

"He ain't got no room. He just sleeps on the couch when he comes through. Ain't got but one bedroom and he sure as hell ain't sleeping next to me."

Rein looked past her into the house and saw the couch. "Where does he keep his things?"

"I made him put all his stuff out in the barn. Don't ask me what all he has out there. Do I get any extra money for providing him storage too?"

"We'll see what we can do," Carrie said.

"Do you mind if we go out and look at the barn?" Rein asked.

"Go on, see whatever you want," Helen said, and she waved them off.

Carrie led Rein around the house toward the barn. "Watch yourself. There's a feral-looking cat back here."

Rein grimaced at the sight of the tall grass all around them. "I hate cats."

"You do? Why? They're self-sufficient. Cuddly. They take care of rodents. Have you ever seen a cat fight a snake? There's videos of it online. The snakes go crazy trying to strike the cat, but the cat is always too fast. The snakes wear themselves out and the cat just sits there licking its paws until it's time to strike. Cats are cool."

He waded through the grass behind her. "When people die, their cats eat their faces. I've seen it."

"I don't know why I even talk to you, Rein."

"I get that a lot."

They pulled the barn door open and let the sunlight shine in. Most of the barn's concrete slab floor was empty except for scattered hay and rat droppings. There was something else. Carrie pulled her gun and touched a button alongside the attachment. A bright beam of light flared from beneath the gun, illuminating the corner of the barn where she aimed it. There was an antique stone-sharpening wheel sitting upright inside of a wooden frame. A pedal pump was attached to one side of the frame, with a rusted metal bucket sitting next to it. Carrie aimed the gun's light at the cement below the wheel and saw it was still wet.

"Whatever he sharpened there, he did it recently," she said.

The walls were bare plywood nailed to the support beams. Some nails had missed the beams and stuck out from the walls, rusted and sharp. Above them, lying on the rafters that formed the support structure for the roof, was another piece of plywood.

"Do you see a way up?" Carrie asked. There were no stairs or ladder. There wasn't even a rope.

Rein pointed at the rafters. They were at least eight feet up. "He must jump."

Carrie holstered her gun and sprang into the air. She managed to touch the wooden beam above but not enough to grab it. "Here. Lift me up."

He put his hands under her armpits. Carrie flinched and jerked away. "Wait. I'm really ticklish there."

"Well, how do you want me to lift you up?"

"Here." She held her arms out and took a deep breath. "Try again."

Rein put his hands back against her sides and she jerked away again, so hard she nearly hit him. "Nope. Lift me somewhere else."

Rein looked up at the rafters, measuring how high up she needed to be. "Spread your legs."

"Excuse me?"

Rein circled around her and dropped down to one knee and lowered his head. "Walk backward, open your legs and sit down on me."

Carrie laughed as she backed up. "You sure do know how to show a girl a good time, Rein."

"Don't get too excited," he said, as he stuck his head between her legs and guided her backward onto his shoulders. "I used to do this with Bill all the time when we had to reach something."

Carrie said, "Whoa, easy," as Rein came up from his knees and raised her into the air. For one second, she wobbled and would have fallen, until she grabbed the sides of Rein's face and held on tight. When she was stable she said, "You used to lift Bill like this?"

"Of course not," Rein said. "He used to lift me."

Rein cupped the bottoms of her feet in his hands and told her to reach. Carrie raised her arms as high as she could and was able to wrap her fingers around the rafter above. She slowly stood up, lifting herself as Rein pushed. She pulled herself up onto the beam, hanging over it, suspended in the air over top of Rein.

"Be careful," he said.

"No shit."

She worked herself up on the beam, until she was spread out across the next one and had enough balance to situate herself. It was too dark to see more than a few feet in front of her. Everything was cast in shadows except for the few slivers of light getting through the barn's ceiling at the seams. Carrie crawled across the rafter toward the plywood platform and stopped when she saw multiple pages of printed-out photographs scattered there. Each of them had pieces of spent masking tape stuck across the top, like they'd been hung up and cast aside.

There were satellite images of Linda Shelley's house. Patricia Martin's house. Alexis Dole's house. The Penningtons'. Surrounding them were photographs of the people themselves. She picked up the nearest page and saw Linda's picture, taken from her psychology association page. There were several more of her from a charity function she'd attended and the local press had covered.

Carrie heard something move on the platform and froze, able to do nothing except clutch the rafter so she didn't fall off.

The board creaked as the cat from the field crept forward. It opened its jaws wide to show Carrie its curved fangs and hissed at her again. Something was writhing on the platform at the cat's feet, and she saw it had a mouse pinned to the wood with its claws.

"Get!" Carrie shouted. She looked down at Rein. "That goddamn cat again."

"Told you," Rein said.

There was a book on Masonic rituals and customs. The Satanic Bible. Another on Aleister Crowley. Each book had other pages stuffed inside of them of things Moon had printed out. Carrie pulled one out and saw a page on the Blood Eagle Viking ritual. "It's all here, Rein," she said.

"Keep looking."

Carrie pulled herself forward and wiggled onto the platform. There wasn't room to stand, only to crouch. There seemed to be a thousand nails coming through the rooftop boards, aimed at her head, and they glinted in the light coming down through the gaps in the plywood.

At the far end of the platform, she saw a pencil case filled with markers and a roll of masking tape. Pages were taped to the rafters there. The first was a printed-out photograph of Bill Waylon. It was an older picture of him, from when he was Chief of Coyote. Below him was a photograph of Jeri Waylon, standing at Bill's side at a dinner party. The pages below were all of Kate, their youngest daughter, taken from the girl's Instagram page. In some photos, she was flinging her blond hair over her shoulder and posing, looking as mature and beautiful as a supermodel. In others, she looked like a goofy kid, sticking her tongue out and making faces.

Beneath Kate's photograph was a picture of Saint Margaret of the Antioch, the namesake of the church where Father Ihan worked and Tucker Pennington cleaned. *Saint Margaret of Antioch* was printed beneath it. *Renowned for her beauty, she refused to renounce Christ before Provost Olybrius in Rome, AD 291.*

Olybrius ordered her skin torn from her living body. Still she refused.

There was something on the floor, tucked beneath the pencil case. Carrie picked it up and unfolded it. They were medieval paintings of the tortures Saint Margaret endured. Two men were using sharp metal instruments to flay the young woman alive. Her face was turned upward toward heaven.

Something was written in marker along the bottom. Carrie had to raise it into the light to read it.

Careful not to kill her too soon.

Must peel her slow.

Carrie looked at the photograph of Kate Waylon hanging above Saint Margaret of Antioch. She looked down at the stone wheel where Moon had sat, probably only a little while before they'd arrived, sharpening something. She leapt for the rafters and scrambled to get down.

20

Gregory Moon sat in his aunt Helen's car watching Bill Waylon's house. He'd only been there fifteen minutes before some nosy bitch walked her dog past him. She stared at the car and at his face the entire time. A man came past after that, walking a different dog. The postman drove his white truck down the street and parked directly behind Moon so he could feed the mail into the mailbox at the driveway on the right. Moon had to move the car up a few feet, which put him out of position. It was infuriating.

He needed a new plan. It had been child's play both of the other times. Linda Shelley had left her front door unlocked and he'd slipped into her bedroom closet while she was in the shower.

He'd originally planned on visiting Alexis Dole the next night, but that one-eyed freak was ready for him. She had no idea who he was, but she was ready. Visiting her would take some care and thought, he decided. He'd opted for the low-hanging fruit of the Martin family.

The Martins met him at their door when he knocked and he told them he was a newspaper reporter covering the Pennington case. He gave them a business card with a made-up name and the name of the local newspaper. It had cost him twelve dollars at the office supply store to get the cards made.

I'm working on a story about your experience, he told them. I can see it growing into a novel. There would be money in it, if you're interested. I just don't think it's right that he be let free while good people such as yourselves continue to suffer.

Mr. Martin looked at the business card and then at his wife. If we don't tell our story, someone else will, he'd said. Come in and let's talk.

In ancient times, people believed in vampires, but they also believed that a vampire could not hurt you unless you invited him into your home. There was a lesson in that, Moon thought. A lesson the Martins learned too late.

The Martins coaxed their daughter down the stairs from her bedroom. She was heavily medicated, he could tell. This man wants to talk to you, Patricia, the mother said.

Start off very slowly with her, the father said. It's going to take a while for her to open up to you.

Of course, of course, Moon told them. Do you mind if I get my bag?

They didn't mind and Moon retrieved his black schoolbag. It was extralarge and well-made. He slung it over his shoulder and carried it into the house and closed the door behind him and locked it. They didn't notice him sliding the dead bolt into position. He carried his bag to the table and laid it in front of himself. He unzipped it and reached in while they spoke.

Mrs. Martin was trying to tell him their requirements for participating in the story.

Her voice droned on and on and he sat there nodding and smiling and saying of course and meanwhile he had his hand on the knife inside his bag. When it became too much to bear, he pulled the knife out of the bag and held it up to show it to them.

What's that? Mr. Martin had asked. Some kind of writing prop?

Stupid cattle. They were still confused. They'd been coaxed into the slaughterhouse by a butcher's smile and empty promises.

He'd aimed the knife at them. We're moving into the basement.

Now listen, Mr. Martin had said, and he kept yammering until Moon stabbed him in the left shoulder. He twisted the knife's handle until the man screamed and then, after that, everyone did as they were told.

The thing Moon knew, and the thing most people don't, is that there is no discussion. When the vampire enters your house, you either fight, flee, or die. There is no talking about it. No negotiating. The vampire has come for one thing. He won't be dissuaded by conversation.

Mrs. Martin had trouble understanding that, so he helped her. He'd found a pair of pliers in his bag and wrapped them around her tongue as he cut with the knife, shucking her like a clam. After that, she didn't have so much to say.

Everything he'd done had gone smoothly, right up until he'd driven into Bill Waylon's neighborhood and found it was a fucking suburban paradise full of soccer moms who stayed home all day and walked their dogs past his fucking car a thousand times wondering what he was doing there. All of the houses were single homes of the same boring design with the same boring two-car garages sitting on the same boring plot. It was the land of middle managers. Old cheerleaders. Children who had college savings accounts opened when they were born and took tennis lessons.

A car pulled into the driveway of the house across the street from Bill Waylon's. A large SUV with sparkling black paint and cut-out cartoon figures of a man, woman, and two children on the back window. A woman came out, dressed in spandex workout clothes. The rear passenger door behind her opened and a little boy jumped out of the car, bouncing up and down on the driveway with both feet. The woman scooped him up in her arms. She snapped her fingers at someone else in the backseat and said, "Come on!" A little girl, maybe a year or two older than the boy, slid across the seat toward her. The woman held out her hand and helped the little girl down.

Moon watched them go around the car and into the house. The woman's house sat slightly higher than Bill Waylon's, giving it a clean look down at the entire front of the property.

Moon looked at himself in the car's rearview mirror. He swept back his long hair and smoothed it down. He checked his teeth. He grabbed his schoolbag from the passenger seat and swung it over both shoulders and he hurried across the street toward the driveway.

Lori O'Keefe was tired and her body ached. but it felt good. She'd gotten up at five A.M. to do hot yoga at the gym. She posted a selfie on Facebook and on Instagram when she arrived and again when she left, letting everyone know what she'd done and filling the rest of the post with as many hashtags as she could think of. *Blessed, Goals, Motivated, StayFit, ActiveMom, HotYogaBod, MyKidsRule,* and her favorite, *JustSayin.*

She came home, packed her husband's lunch, and saw him off to work. She showered and got dressed. By the time she came out, her daughter, Peyton, was already awake and sitting up in her bed, reading. Lori got her son, Kayden, up, changed his diaper, and brought both kids downstairs for breakfast.

By the afternoon, they were both driving her crazy. She got changed into workout clothes again and packed them up to go back to the gym. If you're good, we'll get a treat after the gym, she'd said. She got them situated in the daycare center and made it to spin class, just in time.

After spin class, she collected the kids. They asked if they'd been well-behaved, and she said yes. They asked for ice cream. She drove them across town to a gluten-free bakery for salty peanut butter quinoa and chia bars made with organic, fair-trade chocolate.

She stretched out in the kitchen, feeling good. She sent the kids upstairs by calling out, "Time for naps." She clapped at them to get them to move, corralling them up the steps like small calves.

She opened the refrigerator and took out the water bottle with the smoky purple crystal at the bottom of it. She popped the lid and took a long sip. Her husband had complained when he found out she spent a hundred dollars on a water bottle. She told him if he'd just try it, he'd be able to taste the difference in the softness of the water, because it had been restructured by the crystal.

Once the kids settled down upstairs, she was going to post all the selfies she hadn't had time to during the day, and meditate.

Gregory Moon went up the driveway, checking to see if anyone was watching through the front windows. When the SUV pulled in, the woman hadn't checked her mail. Moon peeked inside, seeing several bills addressed to Lori O'Keefe. He stopped at the SUV and looked inside. A yoga mat on the floor. A handful of sage in the first cup holder. A paper bag from a bakery that read *Gluten and Guilt Free! Environmentally-Friendly, Absolutely Organic, Free Trade Guaranteed. You'll Taste the Goodness.* A book on the passenger seat titled *How To Be More Woke.*

He walked up to the door and knocked.

Lori O'Keefe opened the door and said, "Hello?"

"I'm so sorry to bother you, ma'am, but I'm with Advocates for Social Change and I got separated from the rest of the group. Have you seen anyone else walking around? My cell phone's dead and I'm kind of lost."

She leaned out of the door and looked around. There were only her neighbors. "Are you guys doing fund-raising or something?"

"Oh no, ma'am," Moon said. "We're just raising awareness. Talking about different campaigns in the area that people can participate in. Right now we're sponsoring Free Yoga in the Park to help low-income women be more active and healthy."

"You're kidding! That *sounds amazing.* I do yoga."

"You do? Well, if you're interested, I'll give you the number for the coordinator. She's always looking for volunteers to help her teach. Excuse me." Moon coughed into his hand and rubbed his throat. "Sorry. Would it be okay if I bothered you for a glass of water?"

"Of course!" Lori said. "Come in and sit down. Have you tried crystal-infused water?"

"No, but it *sounds amazing*," he said.

"It so is! Come in, come in. I'll find you a phone charger."

"Are you sure?"

"Absolutely," she said, opening the door and inviting him inside.

"Thank you so much," Moon said, and closed the door behind him.

21

*C*arrie closed her eyes as the phone rang. She leaned forward against the steering wheel, resting her forehead against her right arm. "Please pick up," she whispered.

The phone rang two more times and went to voice mail.

"God damn it," she said, and hung up. "Bill's not answering. Should I call the radio room to send cars?"

"Wait," Rein said. "Can you call anyone else inside the house?"

"I think I still have Jeri's number." Carrie scrolled through her phone. She pressed the call button and waited.

"Hello?" the voice said on the other end.

"Jeri?"

"Hey. What's up? I'm making dinner."

Carrie listened before answering. She could hear the sink faucet running in the background. Metal scraped against metal, the sound of a spatula hitting a frying pan. "Is Bill there?"

"He's upstairs sleeping."

"How about Kate?"

"She's doing her homework."

"Are you sure?"

"I'm looking right at her. What's going on, Carrie?"

Carrie looked at Rein. He shook his head. She gritted her teeth and pursed her lips together. Rein waved his hands.

"Nothing," Carrie finally said. "Everything's good. I was just looking for Bill. Have him call me when he wakes up."

Carrie hung up the phone. "We have to warn them. They're sitting ducks if we don't."

"We can't risk it."

"Risk what? That maniac wants to skin Kate alive!"

"Moon is watching them," Rein said. "If you tell Bill what's going on, he'll press the panic button and have every police car in the county there in the next five minutes. Moon will see that a mile away and we'll lose him. He'll vanish. We either catch him now or no one will be safe again."

"What if we're wrong? What if he's inside Bill's house right now, ready to kill them all?"

"Then people we care about die excruciating deaths."

Carrie smacked him in the arm. "What the hell is wrong with you?"

"Well?" he said. "We'd better focus on winning, then."

Carrie took a deep breath. "Now what? I'm assuming we aren't going to Bill's house."

"No."

"So where are we going?"

"Do you know the U-Haul on Route four-two-six?"

"Next to the Home Depot?"

Rein pointed forward. "Drive."

They parked Carrie's car at the Home Depot and walked to the U-Haul. Rein told the man at the counter that they needed to rent a van for the hour. The man began to explain different pricing options and Rein waved him off and said, "Just give us the best one."

"Well, you're a big spender all of a sudden," Carrie said.

"I am now," Rein said. "Give him your county credit card."

"Typical," she said. She reached into her pocket for her wallet and pulled out the credit card and handed it over. "What do we need this van for again?"

Rein took the keys from the man's hand and made his way toward the van parked out front. He jumped in, waited for Carrie to get in, and backed the van up, only to drive it into the Home

Depot parking lot and park it next to Carrie's car. He jumped out again and hurried across the parking lot into the store. Carrie ran to catch up.

Rein flew through the aisles, checking their placards. "Washing machines and dryers," he repeated to himself as he walked. He flagged down an employee. "Washing machines and dryers?"

"Right down this aisle, sir."

He walked past the first few luxury models. He ignored the compact apartment designs with washing machines and dryers stacked on top of one another. He wanted the ones in the back. The older, larger, units. Rein stopped in front of a dryer that was half his height. He checked the size of it and said, "Go find me a salesperson."

"Rein, why are we buying a washing machine?"

A salesperson came from around the corner. He drew the pencil tucked behind his ear and pointed the eraser end at the machine, saying, "This model's from last year. I've got a few high-intensity models with vibration reduction out front that I think you'd be happier with."

"Does this model come in a box?" Rein asked.

The salesperson raised an eyebrow at him. "Sorry, sir?"

"You said it's from last year. Do you only have this floor model, or are there new ones in the back still?"

"I've got a couple in the back, or I can make you a deal on this one. But I'm telling you, the ones out front are the ones you want."

Rein looked at Carrie, assessing her, and then back at the machine. "Bring out this model, new in a box, and meet us at the register." He winked at her and hurried down the next aisle toward the wall of duct tape.

"Rein?" Carrie called out to him. "Rein! I'm starting to get a bad feeling about this."

"You have good instincts."

She watched the salesman wheel the washing machine down the aisle, toward her.

* * *

It was dark by the time Jacob Rein drove the U-Haul van back to the Bridge Motel. He stopped when he pulled into the parking lot. The parking lot was empty.

The Mexicans who'd taken the grass-cutting job from before were back. They were sitting in front of the motel room now, drinking beers. Charcoal smoke billowed out of the grill. One of them was cooking, turning over hot dogs and hamburgers.

Rein parked the U-Haul and reached into his pocket for his wallet. He had twenty dollars to his name. It was the last of his money for the month. He pulled out the bill and held it up to show the men. "I need two drivers for a local delivery. Whoever's not drunk."

Two men set down their beers and came forward. Rein looked them over. "Lean your heads back, close your eyes, and touch your noses."

The men did it.

"Walk to the van in a straight line."

The one on the right made it there no problem. The one on the left wobbled slightly.

Rein pointed the one who could walk straight and said, "You're the driver."

He let them into the van and went around the driver's side to get in. "Squeeze in on that side, you two," he said. He backed out of the motel parking lot and drove back toward Home Depot.

"What's the delivery, señor?" the driver asked.

"A washing machine," Rein said, cocking his thumb toward the back of the van. The washing machine box was strapped to the back of the van so it didn't slide around. As Rein drove, it bounced on the rough road and off the van's side walls. "It's extremely fragile so you have to be very careful with it. Don't drop it."

"Okay," the man said.

Rein handed the men a clipboard with Bill Waylon's address and specific instructions for the delivery. "Make sure you follow those if there are any problems."

The driver said, "No problem."

Rein drove to the Home Depot parking lot and got out of the van. "I'll be following you there. Take it slow."

Rein got into Carrie's car and started it. He backed out of the parking space and gave the van plenty of room to get out. He flashed his headlights at them, then waved for them to go.

The driver backed up, turned the wheel, and pulled out of the lane to make a right turn past the Home Depot to get back on the road. As he turned, the van went up and over the curb and landed with a hard jolt. Rein cringed. The driver stopped, held his hand up through the window to apologize and kept going.

Bill Waylon heard a vehicle come to a stop in front of his house and he raced up the stairs for his gun. He pulled it out of his dresser. The rubber grips of the large-frame silver revolver felt good in his hand. His hands were shaking as he unsnapped the holster and pulled the gun free.

"Dad?" Kate called out from downstairs. "What's going on?"

"You and your mother get into the den!" He hurried back down the stairs, his bare feet slick with sweat on their smooth wooden surfaces. He was only wearing sweatpants and a T-shirt that he hadn't bothered changing out of that morning when he spilled coffee and egg yolk on it during breakfast. His throat hurt. He was sucking wind and wheezing and he could feel his heart hammering in his chest. None of that mattered.

He looked through the curtains. There were two men in front of his house, going around the back of a U-Haul van. Waylon opened his front door with his gun at his side. They weren't moving fast, and they didn't look nervous. He watched them remove a hand truck from the back and set it beside the van. Together, they wiggled a large box onto the rear bumper and bent with their knees to lower it to the ground. One of them jammed the hand truck under the box and the other one tilted the box backward to get it on.

"What is it, Bill?" Jeri called out.

"It looks like a delivery," Waylon said. He tried seeing what the box was. "Did you buy a washing machine?"

"No."

"Well, one is coming up our driveway."

"Must be the wrong house," Jeri said.

Waylon hid the gun behind his back.

"Is it a good one?" Jeri asked. "Let me see it before you send it back."

"Just stay put," Waylon said. The two deliverymen were wheeling the box toward him. "You guys have the wrong address."

"We were told to bring it to this house for Mr. Waylon," the driver asked.

"Take it back. I didn't order anything."

They wheeled the box up to his door. "This is from your friend."

Waylon cocked the hammer of his pistol back, where they couldn't see. "What friend is that, amigo?"

"Some guy just paid us to bring it. That's all I know."

Waylon put his finger on the trigger. "What did he look like? What was his name?"

"Tall, crazy-looking guy. He had a beard." The driver raised the clipboard and read the instructions. "It says to tell you it's from The Burt Reynolds Foundation For Men Who Can't Grow Mustaches."

They tilted the hand truck backward to get the box over the threshold to the front door. It came down hard on the other side, and Waylon had to scurry backward to keep it from falling on his feet. The two men slid the hand truck out of the way and were back down the driveway and into the van before Waylon could slide the box out of the way and close his front door again. He decocked his pistol and laid it on the lowest step.

"Bill!" a muffled voice called out.

He flinched in surprise.

"Bill! Let me out of this goddamn thing."

Waylon tore at the tape on top of the box as his wife and daughter came into the hall. As he ripped at the cardboard flaps, someone was pushing from inside, trying to get out. He got one flap free, and Carrie Santero burst up through the box in a flutter of Styrofoam packaging. Chunks of foam and tape were caught in her hair, and she reached for Bill's shoulder to steady herself after being tossed around so much.

"What the hell is going on?" Jeri said.

"We have trouble," Carrie said. "Someone's coming for you, tonight."

22

*T*he alarm clock on the nightstand next to him went off at four A.M. He opened his eyes, sat up, and stretched. He'd lived in enough institutions to know that by four A.M., most of them were asleep. Even the guards who worked steady overnight shifts got drowsy at four A.M. He'd catch them nodding off at their desks, or tucked away in a vacant room, snoring. He'd seen the craziest inmates, ones who spent the better part of each night howling, fall quiet at four A.M.

The outside world was no different, he'd found. There was traffic on the highways almost continuously throughout the day and night. It started around five A.M. Trucks entered the roadways hauling cargo. People who worked in the big cities but lived out in the sticks entered the highways, trying to beat rush-hour traffic. It kept up, steady all the way through, until midnight when it slowed down. It got busy again around two A.M. when the bars let out. Drunks and bartenders and waitstaff and strippers all closed up for the night and made their way home. It only got truly quiet after they were gone.

At four A.M., most of the cops in the area had returned to their stations and gone inside, or found some tiny corner to park in and close their eyes for a bit.

It was human nature. It was hard for someone to fight their own biological inclinations. There were circadian rhythms wired into humans by eons of evolution that told them to wake up when the sun came up and sleep when it went away.

Gregory Moon knew that even if Bill Waylon was expecting him, no matter how vigilant the man might be, that vigilance would ebb as sleep overcame him. Especially if he'd been staying up for several nights already.

Moon got up from the O'Keefes' bed and bent down to retie his shoelaces. He'd slept with his boots on, as he always did, but he needed to make sure they were nice and tight.

He stopped in front of the mirror and tied his long black hair back, to keep it out of his face. His hair was clean and still damp. The O'Keefes had a good shower with two jets, and he'd stayed in there for almost an hour, until his skin was pickled and pink, long after all of the blood had washed off.

He picked his bag up from the floor and slung it over his shoulder. He made his way downstairs and walked into the kitchen. He opened the refrigerator, making sure not to touch the bloody handprint smeared across its pearl white door. He pulled out a bottle of water and found a plate of leftover pork chops and mashed potatoes and green beans. He walked around the puddle of coagulated blood in front of the kitchen counter and put the plate into the microwave, setting it for two minutes. He waited while it cooked. He tapped the counter with his fingers and whistled.

The microwave dinged and he pulled the plate out. It was hot to the touch. He peeled away the plastic covering and picked up the pork chop with his fingers. It came apart at the first bite. He smiled as he chewed and said, "You really did a good job with this pork chop, Lori. It's fantastic."

He found the silverware drawer and grabbed a spoon. He made short work of the mashed potatoes. Fluffy and buttery and perfect. He took a swig of cold water to wash it down. He picked the pork chop back up and gnawed the rest of the meat from the bone, then set the bone back on the plate and licked his fingers. "Delicious," he said. He passed on the green beans and scraped the plate off at the trash can then put it in the sink. He turned on the sink faucet and pumped a few squirts of All-Vegan Coco-Castilian hand soap into his palms, then scrubbed them together.

"That's it for me, folks," he said as he rinsed his hands. "Time to go. I'm sorry we couldn't have spent more time together. I'm sure you understand."

Lori O'Keefe was sitting on the couch with her back turned toward him, facing the dark screen of their large television. Both of her arms were draped over her children, who leaned against her on either side. Cute little Peyton and her younger brother, Jayden or Kayden or whatever it was.

They were sitting in the same place they had been when Lori's husband came home. The only difference was, the TV had been on then. Now, he was sitting on the couch next to them.

"All right, then." Moon waved and said, "Good night."

He let himself out through the back door and took a deep breath of the cold night air. The moon was full and bright enough that he didn't need the O'Keefes' flashlight to see. He left it in his schoolbag next to the assorted screwdrivers and rolls of duct tape and box cutter. The only weapon he kept on himself was a long hunting blade with a carbonized finish and a drop-point tip. He slid the knife into a leather sheath hanging from his belt as he came down the O'Keefes' driveway and made a right.

Bill Waylon's house was directly in front of him, but he knew better than to approach from the front. He went the wide way around, inspecting the house as he walked. All the lights were off. He checked the sides and edges of the roof for motion detectors. There weren't any.

One of the unanticipated benefits to spending so much time inside the O'Keefes' home, and to them living in such a disgustingly typical suburban neighborhood, was that all of the houses were basically built the same. By taking the time to study the interior of the O'Keefes' house, he'd been able to familiarize himself with what to expect inside the Waylons'.

There was a basement window in the back of the O'Keefes' that was big enough for him to fit through. He liked the idea of a basement entry much better than trying to come in through the front door or a side window. He crept along the side wall until he reached the back and stopped. The Waylons had a wooden deck built off the back of their house, several feet off the ground. Moon ducked under the deck into the weeds and grass that grew below it. It was too dark to see, and he didn't want to risk using the flashlight. He crawled along the ground, feeling the wall with his left hand. It was unfinished stone, and more unfinished stone, until he found the edge of a window's metal frame. Just like the one in the O'Keefes' basement, it opened sideways.

Moon retrieved his long flathead screwdriver from his school-bag and popped the window screen out. It was cheap and weak and bent easily. He laid it on the grass and wedged the screw-driver into the narrow space between the window and its frame. He was glad he'd sharpened it. The ribs attached to Linda Shel-ley's spine had been surprisingly strong. They'd chipped the screwdriver's metal tip when he pried them out.

He rocked the screwdriver back and forth, trying to create enough space between the frame and the window to unseat it. He squeezed his fingers through the gap and rotated the screwdriver until it finally popped the window out of its lower ledge. It would have fallen on the ground and crashed to pieces if he hadn't been holding it. He pinched the window with his fingertips and held it tight as he worked his other hand through the opening. He man-aged to turn the window at enough of an angle to pull it clear. He laid the window on top of the screen and sat for a second, catch-ing his breath.

Something moved behind him.

Moon spun with the knife in his hand. He sliced a wide arc, but the blade met nothing but darkness. He held his breath and searched. There was nothing but birds in the distant trees and someone's central air unit humming nearby.

He leaned back in through the basement window and turned the flashlight on to check what was inside. There was nothing but boxes and bins and a bare concrete floor. He lowered his school-bag down through the window as far as he could reach, so that when he let go, it landed quietly. He stuck his feet through and shimmied his body down past the window and clung to the frame until his feet landed.

He squatted on the basement floor and forced himself to

breathe. A deep breath in through his nose that he held. A long, slow, breath out through his lips. He needed to go slow. He needed to not get excited.

Moon went up the basement stairs and opened the door to enter the Waylons' kitchen. It was dark, but he turned right as he passed the refrigerator and found himself in the hallway leading to the front door. He crept toward the staircase and went up the first step, walking on the ledges where the wood was strongest. They creaked as he ascended but were no louder than branches scratching the house's siding, not even as loud as the wind rippling through the trees that made the branches move.

At the top of the landing on the second floor, he saw the master bedroom with a closed door on the right. There were two bedrooms and a bathroom on the left. The bathroom door was open. Moon leaned his head in and looked around. One of the bedroom doors was open as well. It was empty. The other was shut.

There was no decision as to who he needed first. If he went after Bill Waylon or his wife, the man would fight. The wife would run into her daughter's room and call the police.

But if he took the girl first, there would be no fight. There would only be the sound of the girl pleading and her mother and father promising to do whatever he wanted as long as he didn't hurt her.

Moon twisted the bedroom's doorknob and opened it.

His eyes had adjusted to the darkness well enough that he could see the white dresser to his left. It was cluttered with perfume bottles and deodorant and hair supplies. There were posters on the walls and clothing scattered on the floor around the hamper instead of in it and shoes piled in front of the closet and there, at the other end of the room, the blond-haired girl lying in bed with her back turned to him.

He raised the knife as he moved across the room toward her. His feet were silent on the bedroom's carpet. He felt himself crossing the threshold toward eternity. He was the master now. The O'Keefes had been mere prologue. What he would do now was his first full symphony.

As he drew near, the girl rolled over. He realized she was look-

ing at him. Her hands came up from beneath the blanket, holding something. She pointed it at his face. He heard a gentle electronic hum and the last thing he saw was a pulsating light that
burst into his eyes like a million suns.

Moon cried out and raised his hand to shield his face, but the
light flickered so brightly that it found its way through his fingers.
All he could do was squeeze his eyes shut and not move.

"Look at that light for more than a few seconds and you'll have
a seizure, asshole," Carrie Santero said. "Take one step forward
with that knife and trust that I will gut shoot you."

She kept the gun on him and had to wiggle out from under the
covers to get free. The strobe had worked perfectly. Shout-out to
Australia, she thought.

Moon's head was buried in the crook of his left arm. He moaned
into it, saying, "Stop! I can't see. Why are you doing this to me?"

"You're under arrest! Drop the knife and I'll shut it off."

Through the strobe's flicker, she saw Jacob Rein come into the
doorway behind Moon. She expected him to grab the knife and
put Moon on the ground. Instead, he reached for the wall and
flipped on the bedroom's overhead light. The overhead light dispersed the strobes pattern and rendered it harmless. Carrie
flicked the strobe off. "Rein, what are you doing?"

Moon lowered his arm and blinked, trying to let his eyes adjust.
He sniveled and glared at her like a rodent with red-rimmed eyes.
Snot bubbles popped from his nostrils with his every clutched
breath.

"Drop the knife!" Carrie shouted.

Rein closed the bedroom door. "Don't put it down, Gregory.
You need it."

"What the hell do you think you're doing?" Carrie shouted.

"Ending this."

"We are ending this," she agreed. "By taking him in."

"No. I don't think so."

"Goddamn it, Jacob! He's caught!"

"Listen to the girl," Moon said. He wiped his nose with his free
hand. He turned around to face Rein. "Let her arrest me."

Rein took a step sideways, moving slowly. Moon circled away from him.

"They'll take me out of jail and put me in a hospital and keep me there until the money runs out and I'm suddenly cured." Moon laughed at the idea. "It might take a while, but they'll eventually let me out."

"I know they will," Rein said.

"And then, we'll see each other again. We'll all see each other one last time, Detective. I promise."

"I believe you," Rein said. He stepped in front of Carrie, blocking her view. She yelled at him to move and Moon sprang forward with the knife, lunging for Rein's jugular. Rein turned aside just as the blade's edge sailed past his exposed neck. He spun back, coming up from below with an open palm that struck the side of Moon's jaw so hard, it made his entire body wobble.

Rein grabbed the knife away and pulled Moon in close. He held Moon close to his chest like they were embracing, while he yanked Moon's head back by his ponytail. Moon's eyes were wide open, fixed on the knife in Rein's hands.

Rein struck downward with two quick thrusts at Moon's face. Moon screeched and Rein released him.

Carrie watched in horror as Moon writhed and shrieked on the floor. He clutched his face and blood streamed through his fingers.

Rein wiped the knife's blade on the leg of his pants and stepped away, giving the man plenty of room to convulse and flop around.

"What did you do?" Carrie whispered. She could barely hear herself over Moon's high-pitched screams.

Rein set the knife on the dresser behind him. He nodded to Carrie, "I'm under arrest. I surrender."

"What?"

"You're arresting me, as soon as we get him handcuffed."

Moon howled at them and spun himself around, kicking wildly. He kicked the wall and door, screaming in agony.

There were tears in Carrie's eyes. "Why did you do that? We had him. Why, Jacob?"

"Don't be upset. Everything is okay now."

The bedroom door flew open. Bill Waylon stood in the threshold, fully dressed and holding his revolver. He looked down at Gregory Moon, writhing on the ground. Blood spilled into Moon's mouth from between his fingers. He gagged on it and coughed and spat it at them with every curse he hurled.

Waylon had been barricaded in his bedroom with Jeri and Kate. Now, those two were huddled together on the bed, and Kate had her hands clamped over her ears.

"It's over, Bill," Rein said.

"It appears so," Waylon said, glaring down at Moon. "You're about to enter a whole new world. Prison as a blind man. Can't think of anything worse. Son of a bitch, you're getting blood all over my little girl's room. Lay still." He walked over and swung his foot back and kicked Moon in the side of the head with his boot. "Lay still, I said!"

"Bill!" Carrie shouted.

Moon went limp. His hands fell away from his face and she could see only black pools of blood where his eyes had once been. "Jesus Christ, I've got enough problems already. How the hell am I going to explain this?"

"You aren't," Rein said. "When Bender gets here, I'll tell him what happened. We can let him arrest me. I'm sure he'll like that."

"Both of you sit there and shut your damn mouths," Waylon snapped. He slid his revolver into the waistband of his jeans and straightened his back. "Not another word from either of you until I say so."

An hour later, the house was flooded with police and paramedics. Jeri Waylon was downstairs in the kitchen, apologizing for not being prepared for so many people. The whole house smelled like coffee. She just kept making it, pot after pot.

EMS had strapped Gregory Moon to a gurney and pumped him with morphine until he went limp. They packed his eye sockets with gauze, piling it into the wounds until the blood stopped seeping through, then they wound a bandage around his head to keep the gauze in place. There was a bloody outline of Moon's body on the carpet. The arms and legs were splayed in a wide smear, shaped like snow angels made by children in the winter.

Harv Bender came up the stairs, followed by Sal Vigoda. Both of them were holding full mugs of coffee. Bender leaned into Kate's room where Waylon and Rein and Carrie were sitting. Waylon was massaging his throat and drinking a hot cup of tea Jeri had brought him to help soothe it so he could talk. "Evening, folks."

Bender walked in and stopped at the blood on the carpet. "Looks like the bad guy got the shit end of the stick tonight," Bender said.

"We got lucky," Carrie said.

Bender clapped Waylon on the back. "I just talked to your wife and daughter, Bill. They're doing good. Strong. You should be real proud."

"I am. Thank you."

Bender glanced sideways at Carrie. "When did you know the killer wasn't Pennington?"

"Really not that long ago. We were chasing that lead and it just wound up being a different suspect. Pretty much happened by accident."

"Bullshit," Bender said. "You left us sitting at Pennington's house like idiots while you put this whole plan into motion." He held up his hand before she could argue. "Don't. No need to say anything." He glanced sideways at Rein. "I know exactly where this came from."

Bill Waylon stepped forward. "Chief, I think the important thing here is that my family is safe and a deranged killer is off the streets. That's all anyone is going to care about."

"Fair point," Bender said. He looked at his watch. "The press is going to be here any minute, and you know who they'll want to talk to. I need to find someone to assign this to first, I guess."

"I'll take it," Sal said, raising his hand.

"You suddenly want to be a detective now?"

"Yes, I do."

"The sight of a little blood isn't going to freak you out any-more?"

"Not anymore, no."

"Fine," Bender said as he walked back into the hall. "Take state-ments and get the crime scene folks in here afterward. Keep it simple. Bad guy's in custody, no victims were injured, all's well that ends well."

"Sounds good." Sal set his coffee down on the dresser and pulled a notepad out of his pocket. "I guess I need to separate you all and get statements. Who wants to talk to me first?"

"You don't want to talk to them," Waylon said. "They were too busy dealing with the bad guy. They're probably traumatized. I saw everything. I was watching from the hall."

"What did you see?"

"The suspect had a knife when he entered the room. Detective Santero pulled her weapon and ordered him to surrender. He didn't want to surrender and went crazy."

"Bill," Rein said.

"You be quiet and let me say what I saw," Bill said. "Moon didn't want to surrender and he took the knife and he stabbed himself in the eyeballs. Boom and boom. Just like that."

"Jesus," Sal said as he wrote. "What a maniac. Who does that?"

"After that, he fell on the ground and we called you. Pretty simple."

"Anything else?" Sal asked.

Waylon winced and said, "I shouldn't tell you this, but I gave him a little kick when he was down. I admit, it was wrong. I'll take whatever punishment you feel is necessary."

"You kicked the guy who broke into your house and tried to kill your family in the most horrific way possible?" Sal said.

"I must have been overcome with emotion."

"Sounds to me like you stumbled on the carpet and your foot slipped and accidentally made contact with his head, " Sal said.

"Maybe that's what happened instead," Waylon said. He touched his throat and winced. "I think that's all you need. If you don't mind, it hurts to talk. I can stop by tomorrow and give you a written statement if you want."

Sal scribbled a few notes on his pad. "I don't think that's necessary. Like the chief said, all's well that ends well."

"So you're staying in the office, Sal?" Carrie asked.

"I figured you'd get lonely in that trailer without me."

"Well, I'm glad."

"Yeah, me too," Sal said. "I guess I better go find the crime scene people." He picked up his coffee mug and went back down the steps.

When they were alone, Waylon walked over to the bed and sat between Carrie and Rein. He put his arm around Rein's shoulders and they sat like that for a long time. Neither of them spoke. Neither of them had to.

23

"*T*he phone is ringing, Ihan," Jose said. "Aren't you going to pick it up?"

"I'm not answering the fucking phone. I'm about to win," Ihan said. He looked through the cards in his hand. He held the makings of a straight, open at either end. "I think you want me to answer the phone so you don't lose."

"I won't lose to you, my friend. I have God on my side."

They all laughed at that.

Ihan had come back late from the seminary's library, still dressed in his clerical shirt. The rest of his friends had stripped down to white T-shirts. Ihan took a swig of beer and laid his cards on the table. He glared at the telephone across the room. The damned thing was still ringing. "All day and night. these people, the Penningtons, bother me. They think because they write checks, they own me. I'm sick of it."

"Is it the man or the woman?"

"Always the woman," Ihan said.

His friends laughed. One of them elbowed him, and Ihan laughed as well. "No, it's not like that."

"You say that, but things happen. I've heard about it. Women want what they cannot have. Sometimes, it's the priest."

"What do you know about women?" Ihan asked.

"About as much as Miguel knows about altar boys," Jose said, and they all laughed again. Ihan could not help himself but laugh. He reached over and grasped Miguel by the shoulder and shook it, apologizing for laughing.

The phone was still ringing.

Ihan took another sip of beer. It was the coldest, freshest beer he'd ever had in his life, and he'd had many beers since leaving the seminary, but none that tasted so good. This beer was exactly as he'd remembered it, all those years ago.

"Go answer the phone, Ihan. You have to go."

"I don't want to. I want to stay." He raised the bottle to his lips and nothing came out. He set it down and saw that the table was empty. He threw his cards. The dream was ruined, so he opened his eyes.

He lay there in the darkness and the darkness was silent. No phone rang. Perhaps he had imagined it. Perhaps it had only been part of the dream. A reminder that he could not remain in that place.

Soon, he saw a light flickering in the distance and walked toward it. There was a campfire just ahead, surrounded by a group of men. They were seated on tree stumps and overturned logs set around the fire. All of the men had rifles. They did not look up at him when he sat.

Thad Pennington sat to his left, stirring a stick into the flames, watching it make the wood smoke. Tucker Pennington sat at his father's side, but it was a younger Tucker than the one Ihan knew. This Tucker was just a boy. His legs dangled over the sides of the overturned log without touching the ground. He kicked the log with his heels and broke off pieces of rotted bark, keeping himself content while the men sat. The rest of the men sitting around the fire had hardened faces. Stout men who had once been soldiers before they became hunters and farmers.

Seated among them was Jacob Rein. His beard was now black and full and hung down to the center of his chest, like theirs did. Ihan sat on the log next to Rein.

Thad Pennington tossed his stick into the fire and said, "Well, I guess we'd best get to it then." He looked at Ihan. "Did you get them?"

Ihan opened his left hand and saw a half-dozen pieces of straw there, all of them the same size, except one. One of the straws was shorter than the others by half. That was what he'd gone into the woods to find.

"Hold them out," Thad said. "I'll go first."

"What are you doing, Papa?" little Tucker said. The boy had stopped kicking the log.

"Drawing lots."

"Can I draw?"

The men all looked at Thad. He didn't look at the boy. "No," he said. Thad leaned forward and pulled one of the straws from Ihan's hand. It was a full-sized one. He sat back, his face red in the fire's glow. "Go on, then, you bastards. Draw."

The next man leaned forward and selected his straw, and then the next, and the next. Each of them drew, none of them getting the short one, until it came to Jacob Rein. There were only two left.

Rein reached over to take one of the straws and Thad called out, "Wait." He stood up and slung his rifle over his shoulder. "It ought to be me."

Thad turned his head away from them. In the firelight, his eyes glistened with tears. "Son. I need you to take a walk with me."

The boy slid off the log. "Where are we going, Papa?"

"Just for a walk. I need to show you something."

"In the dark?"

"It's all right. Don't be afraid."

The boy put his hand inside his father's and the two of them walked toward the darkness of the trees. Then Ihan looked at the stick Jacob Rein would have chosen. It was the last full-length one. The short stick would have been mine, Ihan thought. He tossed it into the dwindling fire and wiped his hands on his pants. It was getting cold. He could see his breath evaporating when he exhaled.

A gunshot sounded that sent birds scattering into the air. Ihan looked up at the sky as they flew past. He'd never seen their kind before. They appeared to be white doves but with bright red heads with no feathers. Just sagging skin, like someone had boiled their heads. He waited for them to fly high enough that no one else could see their deformity, then cried out, "There! Do you see the birds? They are the boy's soul, taking flight back to heaven. They will be cleansed there and then they will return."

The other men sitting around the fire seemed greatly relieved by this. They pointed at the birds in wonder, all of them except Jacob Rein. Rein picked up a large stick and maneuvered the branches inside the fire, trying to keep it lit.

"Do you see, Jacob?" Ihan whispered. "I have found a way to soothe their suffering. When the boy's father returns, I will ease his suffering too."

A great howl erupted from the woods, the roar of a frenzied beast. It rattled the woodland ground all around them. It grunted and snarled at them from the darkness. Ihan grabbed Rein's arm. "What is that?"

Something stared at them from between the trees. It had bloodred eyes and circled behind the men. Ihan was too terrified to move. "What do we do?" he whispered.

Rein blew on the red tip of his stick to make it glow hot. "Try telling it a bird story. Perhaps it likes those."

Father Ihan's eyes opened. He was in his bed in his small apartment in the church's rectory. It was dark still. The sun had not risen yet. His cell phone rang.

He got out of bed and stumbled across the room toward where it was plugged in. "Hello?" he said.

"Father! Thank God you picked up. I need your help."

"What's wrong, Mrs. Pennington?"

"Tucker. He's—something is wrong with him. I need you to come over right away."

"Should you call an ambulance?"

"No! No ambulances. The police always come when the ambulances come. We just need you."

Father Ihan squeezed his forehead with his fingers, rubbing his temples. "Let me get dressed," he said.

"Thank you. Please hurry."

He dressed in his shirt and collar and walked down the stairs into the church to see if his secretary was in the office yet. She usually came in early, and he found her sitting at her desk. "Good morning, Father. You're up early today," she said.

"Can you check the membership cards for a young woman named Santero? She told me her father is a member here."

"Let me look. What do you need?"

"A cell phone number."

She told him to wait while she looked, and he went to get a cup of coffee.

It was two hours later before Carrie saw the missed call. At the time Father Ihan had called her, the bodies of the O'Keefe family had just been discovered. Lori O'Keefe's mother heard about the big arrest and police activity at the Waylons and tried to call her daughter to ask about it. When Lori didn't pick up, the grandmother drove to Lori's house to see what was going on.

Carrie was standing outside watching the crime scene unit go in and out of Waylon's house when the grandmother arrived. Harv Bender was speaking to the press. A sea of people filled the front yard. Police and neighbors and reporters and amateurs who'd come to livestream it on their cell phones to the rest of the world. In the midst of all of that, they heard the woman scream from inside the O'Keefes' house, across the street.

The police went running. The reporters went running after them.

Carrie knew Gregory Moon was laughing, somewhere in the hospital, even with his punctured eyeballs.

"Do you want me to take this, Chief?" she asked Bender.

"Weren't you up all night trying to catch that asshole?"

"Yeah, but that's not a big deal. I can handle this."

"Go home, Santero," he said. "You did good work."

"I didn't do it alone."

Rein was standing at the edge of the crowd, looking at the O'Keefes' house. People covered their mouths in horror as the grandmother staggered through the front door, covered in the blood of her dead daughter's dead family. Two EMTs helped her from collapsing. She screamed, "Why God, why?" The EMTs stopped trying to force her to walk and let her down on the ground as she kept screaming.

Carrie came up beside Rein. "We couldn't have known Moon was in there."

"I knew he was watching Bill's house."

"But not from where. You're not a mind reader, Jacob. You'll never be able to know everything at the exact perfect moments and stop everything from happening to everyone. You did the best you could. You saved Bill and his family."

The coroner's office carried the first sealed black bag out of the house. It was small. Half the size of a regular body bag. The grandmother looked up as they walked past and began screaming again.

"Come on," Carrie said. She pulled on his arm. "We're getting out of here. We're going back to that diner and getting pancakes and coffee and forgetting about all of this for a little while. We haven't eaten since yesterday. What time is it now?" She pulled out her phone and saw there was a missed call. That wasn't unusual. She got a half-dozen missed calls per day and they were usually spam. There was a voice mail though. She unlocked her car so Jacob could get in, and she opened the driver's side door and raised the phone to her ear to play the message.

"Detective Santero, this is Father Ihan from Saint Margaret of Antioch's. I am heading over to the Penningtons' house. It sounds like there is trouble of some kind. They told me not to call, but I just wanted to let someone know, just in case. Thank you, and God bless."

She tried to call the number back. No answer. Carrie sat down and laid her forehead against the steering wheel.

"No pancakes?" Rein asked.

Carrie groaned and put the car into drive.

"I believe in God, the Father Almighty, creator of heaven and earth."

Thad Pennington gasped in shock. His entire body wracked against his restraints. The pain was bright scalding torment down the softness of his stomach. He screamed through the washrag stuffed in his mouth. It was impossible to move his jaw wide enough to scream like he needed to. He couldn't even draw the breath he needed to do it. His entire head was wrapped tight in duct tape, with tiny holes poked in the nostrils. The tape went down around his chin and up over the top of his head and over his ears, encasing him completely.

"I believe in Jesus Christ, his only son, our lord, who was conceived by the Holy Ghost."

He felt his son's fingers digging through the opening in his flesh.

"Born of the Virgin Mary and suffered under Pontius Pilate. Who was crucified, then died, and was buried."

Thad's eyes rolled back into somewhere dark and red. He was losing consciousness. There was a tug inside his gut and another tug and something snapped deep in his bowels that sprayed hot stinging liquid against his insides. He inhaled sharply, breathing in so hard, the flaps of tape over his nostrils closed.

"I believe in God, the Father Almighty, creator of heaven and earth."

Something slithered out of Thad's body. It was long and kept coming. A magician's trick where they bent their heads backward and drew a never-ending ribbon from their mouths.

"I believe in Jesus Christ, his only son, our lord, who was conceived by the Holy Ghost."

A length of wet, slime-covered coils wrapped around his bound wrists.

"Born of the Virgin Mary and suffered under Pontius Pilate."

Another loop, this time draped over Thad's fingers. He felt liquid pumping out of the coils onto his fingers. There was no strength to scream. Not enough air to scream with even if he did. He was tired of screaming. Tired of trying to breathe. He'd heard of swimmers who drowned struggling with all their might to get back to the surface until they were simply too spent to try anymore, and after a while it did not seem so important to try anyway. He understood, and Thad's body slumped forward against his restraints and went still.

"Who was crucified, then died, and was buried," Tucker said, and stood up.

He wiped his hands on one of his mother's best towels as he walked from the parlor to the dining room. The door was off its hinges. Chairs were tossed throughout the room. One of them was stuck in the far wall by its legs and hung there. Silver forks and spoons and knives were scattered on the floor, along with shards of porcelain bowls and plates. He stepped over plastic fruits to get to the round wooden table in the center of the room.

Blood streamed off the table and cascaded over the edges onto the hardwood floor below. Father Ihan was stretched out naked on the table's surface. His arms were held out wide with a nail through the center of each wrist and his legs were both nailed to the other end of the table. One nail had been driven through each of his ankles. Tucker had tried to cross the priest's legs and drive one nail through them, but none of the nails were long enough. He'd tried several times, leaving bent nails and holes in the table's surface. Finally, he settled for holding each leg down and nailing it into place, side by side.

Ihan's head raised to look at Tucker. The man was going in and out of consciousness. "Do not do this. Please," he panted. "You must not."

The doctor was standing in the doorway, watching. Her eyes were now black glass that reflected the lights in the room. She smiled hungrily at the priest, revealing her sharp fangs. Bring him to me, she said, and curled her finger.

"Where should I bring him?"

"Who are you talking to?" Ihan demanded. He turned his head frantically to see where Tucker was looking but saw nothing except an empty doorway. "Tucker, listen to me. You must release me."

The doctor turned and headed for the parlor. As she walked, Tucker saw two wings had sprouted from her back, made from shimmering white feathers.

I want him displayed for when they arrive.

"We're coming. Wait for us," Tucker said. He bent down and grabbed the edges of the table with both hands and struggled to raise it into the air.

Ihan cried out with pain as the table tilted, leaving the weight of his body suspended from the roofing nails driven through his wrists and legs. "Tucker, you are not talking to anyone. You are see-ing things," Ihan cried out. "God, you are hallucinating! There is no one there! Please, Tucker, you must resist. You are sick. Please put me down and call for help."

The table began to roll. Tucker rolled it toward the hallway, holding on as tight as he could to not drop it. If the table fell, the priest would be crushed under its weight.

"Tucker!" Ihan screamed. The pain was too much to take. "Stop! Tucker, listen to me. I will get you help, I promise. Please."

End over end, Tucker turned the table, steering it toward the wall. The priest's blood was tacky between his fingers. It made them stick together and stick to the wood when he grabbed the table. He watched the priest's bare feet come up over the top and keep rolling past, like the hands of clock. Now his head was coming around, right on time.

Ihan drew in as much breath as he could force into his lungs and threw his head back, shouting, "By the power of Christ I command you! I cast this demon out that has taken over your mind back to the pit of hell from which it came!"

Tucker stopped turning the table and held it steady. There was nothing but the sound of the priest's labored breathing.

Come to me, Tucker, the doctor called out from the parlor. This man is a false prophet. He has been condemned.

"That is why his suffering is just," Tucker said, and began turning the table again.

"There is no one there, you psychotic son of a bitch!" Ihan shouted.

"Look not to the things that are seen," Tucker said. "The unseen is eternal."

24

*T*hey drove down the Penningtons' driveway and stopped the car a hundred feet before the fountain so they could look at the house. Carrie put the car in park. There was nothing unusual from outside. She pulled out her phone and tried calling the priest again. There was no answer. "What do you think?"

Rein stroked his beard. He ran his index finger up and down his chin, moving the whiskers there. The curtains were closed on all of the windows. They could scale the walls of the entire house and still not be able to see in. "I say we go knock. See what we see."

Carrie pressed another button on her phone and held it to her ear. She cursed and put it back in her pocket. "Harv's not answering his phone either. He's probably got his hands full."

"I imagine so."

"Maybe this is nothing."

"Okay."

"Why do you have to say it like that?"

"Like what?"

"Like we're about to walk into something out of a horror movie and both get tortured to death."

"All I said was okay."

"Yeah, but it's the way you said it."

He stopped stroking his beard and said, "Okay."

Carrie put the car back in drive. "Did Bill ever tell you he hated working with you?"

"All the time."

They rolled to a stop in front of the entrance and exited the vehicle, taking up opposite sides of the front door with neither of them standing in front of it. Carrie leaned in to knock, then leaned back out of the way. They both stood, listening. No one was coming.

Rein cocked his head closer to the door. "What was that?"

"Stop messing with me."

"I'm serious. Do you hear that?"

Carrie balled up her fist and pounded it on the door. "Mr. or Mrs. Pennington?" she called out. "Father Ihan!"

Rein moved her aside and kicked the door, smashing it inward. He raced into the foyer, checking the rooms around him, and stopped at the sight of what he saw in the parlor.

Carrie ran in and cried out in disbelief even as she tried yanking her gun from her holster. She struggled with the unfamiliar plastic, her fine motor skills betrayed by the shock of the horrors sitting in front of her.

Father Ihan was positioned in the center of the room. He was crucified, naked and upside down on a round, wooden table. The table was leaning against the fireplace.

"Help—help me," Ihan moaned.

Kneeling on the floor in front of them was another naked man with his entire head wrapped in duct tape. His wrists were bound together with tape and held out in front of him in a position of prayer. He'd been eviscerated, cut open lengthwise from esophagus to the top of his pubic hair, and most of the contents of his stomach had emptied onto the floor around him. Incredibly, someone had pulled out a length of his intestines and wrapped them around his hands like rosary beads.

Carrie struggled not to vomit and raised her weapon. "Where is he?"

"Help me, I'm dying," Ihan whimpered. "Oh God, I can feel it."

"I'll get him," Rein said.

Carrie snatched Rein by the back of the collar and pulled him back. "No. Threat first."

She moved in front of Rein and blocked him with her body. "Stay behind me. If you see him, call it out."

"You have to help me!" Ihan pleaded.

"We'll be back," Carrie said.

"Do not leave me!"

"We'll be back!" She activated the gun's laser and followed the red dot down the hallway toward the dining room. "Put your hand on my shoulder and stay close. You move when I move. Go. Police department!" she shouted.

"We can't just leave him," Rein said, shuffling behind Carrie.

"We can't help him if we're dead. Job one is handle the threat, then come back for whoever you can save."

Ihan cried out for them to come back and not to leave him.

"A hundred mass shootings a year changes how you do things. Keep an eye down the hall." She stuck her head into the dining room and scanned quickly, making sure it was empty. "Clear," she said.

They kept moving down the hall toward the kitchen. Rein squeezed Carrie's shoulder to stop her. He pointed at the end of the corridor just as a shadow passed the wide archway ahead of them. Carrie nodded and they advanced toward the shadow. She clicked off her laser and led them along the right side of the hall, staying close to the wall.

Rein pointed at the pantry on the left. It looked like it had been ravaged by a wild animal. Dozens of huge bags were torn open and jars of preserves and chocolates had been swept from the shelves and smashed to pieces on the floor. Everywhere she looked, she saw piles of white powder spilled across the floor. The entire room was filled with a white dusty haze. "What is that?" she whispered.

"Flour and sugar," Rein said. "Be careful."

"Of what? Is he going to put me into a cake?"

They could hear Tucker Pennington's voice to the right. It was shrill and excited. Carrie leaned in enough to see Tucker, naked, shaking bags of flour and sugar in each hand all over the walls and cabinets and floor with white powder. Every surface was covered in it. There was so much piled on the floor, his bare feet swished through it and left trails wherever he walked. It was hard to see anything in the room through the dusty fog.

Tucker tossed the empty bags into a pile of already discarded bags and reached for two more. He ripped them open and poured them over his head. "Together, we shall enter the kingdom," he cried. "Guided by angels. Hailed by trumpets! The saints will fall at my feet and know me as their master."

Mrs. Pennington was sitting tied to a wooden chair next to the oven. Her legs and arms were duct taped at the sides, and another strip covered her mouth. She was covered in so much flour that her hair was white and black silk shirt were white. Her eyes widened when she saw Carrie, and Carrie quickly got back into the hallway.

"Who's there?" Tucker called out. "I hear you. I feel you. Who has come to bear witness to this?"

Carrie inched around the corner with the barrel of her gun. "Hey, Tucker. We making cookies in here? What's the occasion?"

Tucker spread his arms wide and flexed his hands. They were empty. His chest heaved and clumps of flour and sugar dripped from his body in plops of sweat. Tucker's eyes were peeled back wide enough that she could see white past his irises all the way around. "Today I ascend to heaven and greet my father," Tucker said.

Carrie reached for the button on the device under her gun and touched the button. "Sorry, all ascensions are cancelled today, you wacko."

The strobe activated and hit Tucker directly in the face with its brilliant, flickering light. Intermittent light bounced off trillions of white dust particles in the air between them. Tucker stared straight into the strobe and grinned. "I see the light," he said. "It's beautiful."

Tucker reached for his mother and Carrie moved her finger to the trigger, about to fire, when Rein grabbed her arm. "You'll ignite the entire room if you shoot," he said.

Tucker stroked Grace's hair, making streaks in the white powder. "Woman, behold thy son."

Rein stepped past Carrie with his hands up, showing that he was unarmed. "Tucker, it's me. Do you remember me?"

Tucker looked up at Rein and his jaw slackened. His hands tightened into fists and he began to seethe. "You. The apostate."

"What do you see, Tucker?" Rein said.

"I see your soul, defiler!"

"What else besides me?" Rein asked. He stepped into the kitchen, careful not to slip on the flour and sugar covering the tile floor. "That's the one thing I never asked you, all those years ago. I should have and I'm sorry. It's been on my mind all these years. Something talks to you, doesn't it?"

"Be gone!"

"It tells you what it wants and what to do."

"Go away!"

"You've kept it hidden from everyone for all this time, but it's not hiding anymore, is it?"

Tucker's head swung to the right with his ear cocked like he was listening to someone speak. Rein crept forward. If the ground hadn't been so slippery, he would have made the lunge already. Just a few more feet and he'd be close enough to grab Tucker and get him pinned to the ground.

Tucker glanced back at him and said, "You're trying to trick me."

"I'm not trying to trick you, I'm trying to understand," Rein said. He realized, too late, that while Tucker was talking, he'd reached back to grab the gas burner controls on the oven. Tucker flipped them both all the way to the left. The burners made a clicking sound. *Click-click-click.* A spark.

The kitchen exploded.

Carrie blinked several times, trying to open her eyes. Something loud was beeping incessantly. Everything was spinning. She closed them again. She was lying on the floor. Something was burning. It smelled like some kind of meat pie. A sweet-smelling pastry stuffed with beef or lamb that had been left in the oven too long. The beeping would not stop.

The back of her head throbbed. She reached around the back

of her head to touch it and her fingers came away slick with blood.

She couldn't move her legs. It was hard to form thoughts. Something was burning. Something was beeping. She tried to open her eyes and sit up and only made it a few inches before the world swayed the wrong way and she wanted to vomit. She fell back too quickly and struck her head on the floor again, right where it was already split open.

The pain was sharp and it cleared her mind. Something heavy was pinning her to the floor. She reached down and felt a man sprawled across her legs. It was Rein, she realized. He'd been thrown back against her in the hallway when that maniac Pennington blew up the kitchen.

She opened her eyes and saw a glowing hot ember float down through the air from the blackened ceiling. It swayed left and then right, swinging back and forth like a lazy dancer, coming down toward her until it landed on her right cheek with a hiss. Carrie cried out and swatted at her face to get the burning to stop.

The hallway was on fire. Black smoke billowed out of the kitchen and the entire house rang with wailing smoke alarms. The paint on the walls and ceiling around her crackled with flame. "Rein!" Carrie shouted. She slapped him. "Get up!"

Rein didn't move. The flames were closing in on them both. Carrie kicked herself out from under him, shoving his body off of hers with all of her strength to get herself free. "Come on, Rein! Hurry!"

It was getting harder to breathe. The flames closed in, consuming all of the oxygen in the hallway. Carrie stood up to grab Rein and realized she'd stood too high. It was thick with smoke that burned so hot, she felt the top of her scalp singe. She dropped back to the floor and grabbed Rein by the arm. "Come on, Jacob. You have to help me."

She pulled with all her might until he slid on the hardwood floor. She heaved again, unable to stand to her full height and get the leverage she needed, but the approaching flames filled her with enough terror to make another pull. Then another. Soon, she had Rein's body halfway down the hall and out of the black smoke.

Carrie dropped down beside him and pressed her ear to his mouth. She heard nothing. She looked at his chest and it did not rise or fall. She touched the edge of his throat with her fingertips and dug in but was unable to find his pulse. "Jacob!" She shouted and shook him, "Jacob! Come on."

The flames were coming.

Carrie tilted Rein's chin and squeezed his nose shut. She lowered herself to his mouth and opened her lips against his, blowing air from her lungs into his own. She blew again, watching to make sure his chest rose and fell with the breath she gave him.

She let go of his face and pressed her hand onto his chest. She interlaced her fingers and lifted herself as high as she could and locked her arms in place before she slammed down on him. She did it once, and again, and on the third time something popped in Rein's chest and he gasped for air and cried out in pain. He rolled over with his knees curled up. "What the hell did you just do?" he wheezed.

"Get up!" Carrie shouted. She grabbed him by the arm and started to pull.

Rein saw the flames and scrambled to follow her. It hurt to move and he clutched his chest. "I think you broke my ribs."

"Help me," Carrie said. She ran into the parlor to where Father Ihan was still mounted to the table, head aimed downward with his feet in the air. His body had turned a sickly pale color, as if all of the life had drained out of him through the wounds in his wrists and legs. Carrie grabbed one of the nails and wrapped her fingers around it, trying to pull, but it was sunk too deep.

Rein limped into the parlor, hunched over, to try and help. Flames had filled the hallway and were licking the entrance of the dining room across from them. He grabbed the other nail through the priest's left leg and grimaced as he tried to pull it free. "We don't have time," Rein said. He clutched his chest, wincing in pain. "He looks dead anyway."

"I'm not leaving him. I told him I'd be back."

Smoke billowed across the ceiling. Rein could feel heat scalding his back. He grabbed the underside of the table. "Come on. We'll roll him out. Help me lift."

Carrie did her best to keep the table from falling as they raised it from the wall and stood it upright. They turned the table on the carpet and rolled it toward the door. Flames bit at their arms and sides like sharp fangs.

"Turn, turn," Rein called out, trying to maneuver the table toward the front door.

"It's not going to fit!" Carrie cried.

"It better fit!"

She pulled the left door open with one hand and balanced the table with the other. In the smoke, it was impossible to tell how much space there was. Rein pushed as Carrie went onto the porch and latched onto the table with both hands, trying to pull it. There wasn't enough room.

"Tilt it," Carrie called out. She was finally able to take a deep enough breath to shout, "Come on, tilt, tilt!"

She could no longer see Rein. All she could see was the table and the naked priest's body and the flames flickering on the ceiling above. "Rein?" Carrie shouted. "Rein!"

She yanked on the table, slamming it against the door frame so hard that one of the nails holding up Ihan's left wrist loosened and his hand fell away. Carrie grabbed the nail stuck in his right wrist. Its metal was hot enough to singe her hand. Ihan's head lolled back and he muttered something incoherent. "Hang in there, Father," Carrie said. She twisted and pulled until it came loose in her hand and the priest dropped.

The weight of his body pulled the nails in his legs free. He collapsed on the porch with their sharp points sticking out an inch through his ankles. Carrie scooped him up in her arms and carried him down to the lawn. She dumped him on the grass next to the walkway and ran back up the steps. Everything was still spinning. All the running made it worse. Black smoke poured out of the front door. She took several deep breaths and filled her lungs as much as she could.

"I'm coming!" she shouted. "Hang on!"

Just as she reached the doors, a pair of hands grabbed the table by the edges and pulled it free.

Jacob Rein emerged from the smoke and staggered toward her. His face and neck and arms were black with soot. Parts of his beard had been singed away. Carrie grabbed him and led him down the steps onto the lawn, lowering him to the ground as he collapsed.

There were sirens coming. She laid down on the grass beside Rein and cradled him. She wiped soot from his face and kissed the top of his head, even as the parade of fire trucks and ambulances and police officer raced down the driveway toward them.

25

*C*arrie pulled the Band-Aid off and touched the back of her head. There was dried blood on the white part of the bandage but none on her fingers. The doctor had said she bled a little when he took out the stitches and told her to wear the Band-Aid for an hour. She figured it was close enough. She crumpled it up and tossed it on the passenger side floor of her car.

The scar itself didn't feel too bad. About an inch long and a half inch wide right on the back of her skull. It was going to be a bald spot for the rest of her life, but she wore her hair long enough that it wouldn't matter. Or, she'd get tired of having long hair and shave it all off, and not give a shit if people saw it anyway.

She stopped at the liquor store and bought two bottles of red wine. It was good just to walk and look at things without her head spinning. She felt naked without her gun. Both of her weapons were locked up in a safe in her bedroom, waiting for her to be cleared by the neurologist. They'd diagnosed her with a Grade 3 concussion. Once the headaches stopped, she'd be allowed to get reexamined and requalify with her weapon and go back to work.

There was no real rush for it. Cases came in, the same way they always had. The cases went out, the same way they always would. A temporary solution to a long-term problem. Child victims grew up too damaged to function and turned into adult predators.

Street criminals got arrested and went to jail and came back out with no prospects for a better tomorrow, but still needed money to survive. Deranged lunatics were tossed into treatment and force-fed medication until they stabilized and then they were released. After that, it was anyone's guess what would happen to them. Usually, the worst.

It was all one sick cycle.

If she stayed with the county, she'd have to work another twenty-two years. Twenty-two years of a constantly-spinning hamster wheel of incidents, victims, witnesses, suspects, and court. The wheel never stopped. You just jumped off when you'd had enough.

If she stayed, she'd be able to retire at fifty years old with a full pension. Sixty percent of her salary for the rest of her life. And then what? Buy an RV and travel the land? Settle down in a small town and get overly serious about gardening?

She'd spent most of her adult life focused on her work. Lately, that seemed like a terrible thing to focus one's life on.

When you finally jumped off the wheel, it dumped you back into the pit with everyone else. Just like Bill Waylon. Just like Jacob. Just like Harv Bender would be, when he finally said the wrong thing in public and was driven out kicking and screaming. In the end, it didn't matter what rank you attained or how many bad guys you caught. When the system was done with you, it was done for good.

Police work is just like any other job. When you retire from a factory after forty years, you get a gold watch and a plaque and are then immediately forgotten. Your place in the machine was taken up by the next person as soon as you walked away.

There were reasons to stay, she knew. For one, she was good at it. Far better than the people around her. Rein had tried to walk away and couldn't. It was the only thing he was good at, he'd told her. Maybe it was the only thing she was good at too, but also, maybe that was because she hadn't tried to be good at other things. To live a full life, she knew there had to be more. She wasn't sure what. She was sure she intended to look.

She parked her car and grabbed the bag with both wine bottles and headed up the sidewalk. She buried her chin into her coat. It was getting cold. The damp mugginess of autumn was giving way to the chill of winter. Soon, there would be snow.

She went up the steps to Penny's house and turned the doorknob. It was locked. She smiled and rang the doorbell. The door flew open and a child half her size attacked her with a hug, shouting, "Aunt Carrie!"

Carrie bent down and kissed the top of Natalie's head.

Natalie looked at the bag. "Did you bring me anything?"

"Do you like wine?"

"I don't know."

"Good answer. I didn't bring anything, but I thought after dinner we'd go to the bookstore. Is that okay?"

Natalie clapped her hands and said, "Yes, please, oh yes, please," and ran off.

There was an argument in the kitchen. Carrie stopped and listened.

"You don't do it like that," Penny said.

"That's how I always do it," she heard her father say.

"You put the sausages into the sauce to cook. It absorbs the juices."

"Listen, woman, I cook them in the oven first. You don't like it, you don't have to eat it."

"Well, you're wrong."

"You told me you want me to cook, so I cook. You want to cook and get all hot and sweaty or you want to stand there and look beautiful while I do it for you?"

"You silver-tongued devil. Stop flirting with me and get back to work."

"A chef is like a lover. He must take his time and not rush."

Penny giggled. "Stop that. Carrie's going to be here in a minute."

"I'm already here," Carrie called out. "And I just started feeling better. Stop trying to make me nauseous again."

Penny came out of the kitchen, fixing her hair. "You're here! Hi!" She grabbed the bottles of wine out of Carrie's hand. "Carrie brought wine, Rosendo," she called toward the kitchen. "Do you want a glass?"

"No, I'm good. Maybe some at dinner," he said.

"Well, I'm having a glass," Penny said. She cracked open one of the bottles and poured. "Do you want any?"

"I'm still taking meds for the headaches," Carrie said.

"Have some wine. They'll work better."

Carrie laughed. "I'm fine, thanks."

There were five chairs and place mats set at the table. Penny set down her glass. "Did you invite him?"

"I did."

"So is he coming?"

Carrie went into the kitchen to see if Rosendo needed any help.

Plates of food were shuffled around the table as each of them picked what they wanted. There were baskets of garlic bread covered in melted cheese. Trays of roasted vegetables. A bowl of handmade meatballs. Hot sausage in one pot and sweet sausage in another. In the center, was a huge dish of pasta immersed in bubbling red sauce.

"This is incredible, Rosendo," Penny said.

"I haven't seen you cook in a long time, Papi," Carrie said.

"It's Pop," Natalie said.

"Sorry?"

"You said Papi. His name is Pop."

Rosendo glanced at his daughter. "She wanted to know what to call me. What do you think?"

Carrie stroked Natalie's hair and said, "I like it."

"Okay, everyone has their food?" Rosendo said. "Let us say grace." He held out his hand to Penny on one side and Natalie on the other.

Natalie took Carrie's hand and whispered, "We say grace before we eat now."

"I noticed," Carrie whispered back. She reached past the empty table setting and took Penny's hand.

"Natalie, would you like to say it?" Penny asked.

"Sure."

They all closed their eyes and lowered their heads and some-one knocked at the door.

Carrie got up and went to check. She looked through the door's window and saw Jacob Rein standing on the porch. He'd attempted to comb his long hair back and it looked ridiculous. He'd trimmed his beard. The parts that had been singed away in the fire were starting to grow in again. Rein was dressed in a clean black shirt and jeans that looked like he'd purchased them new. Carrie opened the door. "Well, don't you look spiffy."

"Am I late?" he asked.

"No, we're just sitting down." She led him into the room and said, "Everyone, you remember Jacob."

Natalie turned in her chair and beamed at him. "Hi!"

He waved to her and said hello.

"Are you going to eat with us?" she asked.

"I am, if that's okay with you."

"I want Jacob to sit next to me," Natalie said.

Carrie scowled. "You're kicking me out of my seat?"

"No, just moving you one down."

"Well, fine. I see how it is. Out with old and in with the new." Carrie picked up her plate of food and moved it one down.

Rein took a seat beside Natalie and took the empty plate Carrie handed him. "This looks amazing. Thank you for inviting me."

"Thanks for showing up," Penny said.

"Please, enjoy. Take as much as you want," Rosendo said. "But before we eat, Natalie is about to say grace. We thank God before we eat today."

Carrie shot a look at her father. "Papi."

"Of course," Rein said.

Natalie took Rein's hand and reached for Rosendo's. Rein held his hand out for Carrie to hold. She laced her fingers through his.

"What am I supposed to say?" Natalie asked.

"What are you thankful for?" Penny asked.

"I don't know. I'm thankful for all this food."

Everyone laughed and said, "Amen."

"Perfect. Let's eat," Rosendo said. He picked up a set of tongs and bent forward to pile a serving onto Rein's plate. "Hot or sweet?"

"Both, I think," Rein said.

"A man after my own heart."

"Aunt Carrie, can Jacob come to the bookstore with us after dinner?"

"If he wants to," Carrie said. She looked at Jacob. "Do you want to?"

"Sure," he said. "Why not?"

They ate until they were full. They told stories and laughed and then had coffee to let the food settle, and everyone complained they were stuffed until Penny brought out her homemade cupcakes and everyone found room for more. After dinner, the evening was quiet, and even if only for a little while, everything was good.

ACKNOWLEDGMENTS

Of course, Brandon and Julia, who have been on this adventure with me since it began.

My mother, who raised me in used bookstores.

My father, sisters, nephew and niece, and my goddaughter. One of the themes in this book was family and I thought about each of you while I wrote it.

The Bernard Schaffer Book Review Crew on Facebook. Your energy, support, and enthusiasm are a constant source of inspiration to me.

John Gilstrap, Bruce Coffin, Lisa Scottoline, Matthew Farrell, Tanya Eby, Jack Soren, Danielle Ramsay, and Tony Healey. I am eternally grateful for your guidance and friendship.

To Steve Zacharius, Lynn Cully, Vida Engstrand, Laura Jernigan, the incredible graphics art department who have made such wonderful covers for these books, and the entire staff at Kensington Publishing. Thank you for the opportunity to be part of your organization.

Finally, and most importantly, to you. Whether you are reading this on a printed page or a digital screen or hearing it spoken to you via audiobook, you are an integral part of this journey.

Over the years, I've learned that books are created in solitude, improved by vigorous team effort, then set free to fend for themselves. Some go off to explore the world. Some only find a comfortable place on a quiet bookshelf. Wherever they go, all we can hope is that when they are found, they are loved.